COLD CRUEL WINTER

The Richard Nottingham Historical Series
by Chris Nickson

THE BROKEN TOKEN
COLD CRUEL WINTER

COLD CRUEL WINTER

A Richard Nottingham Mystery

Chris Nickson

CRÈME de la CRIME

This first world edition published 2011
in Great Britain and the USA by
Crème de la Crime, an imprint of
SEVERN HOUSE PUBLISHERS LTD of
9–15 High Street, Sutton, Surrey, England, SM1 1DF.
Trade paperback edition first published
in Great Britain and the USA 2011.

British Library Cataloguing in Publication Data

Nickson, Chris.
  Cold, cruel winter.
  1. Murder – Investigation – England – Leeds – Fiction.
  2. Constables – England – Leeds – History – 18th century –
  Fiction. 3. Merchants – Crimes against – Fiction. 4. Leeds
  (England) – History – 18th century – Fiction. 5. Detective
  and mystery stories.
  I. Title
  823.9'2–dc22

ISBN-13: 978-1-78029-005-8 (cased)
ISBN-13: 978-1-78029-505-3 (trade paper)

All Severn House titles are printed on acid-free paper.

Severn House Publishers support The Forest Stewardship Council [FSC],
the leading international forest certification organisation. All our titles that
are printed on Greenpeace-approved FSC-certified paper carry the FSC logo.

MIX
Paper from
responsible sources
FSC
www.fsc.org   FSC® C018575

Typeset by Palimpsest Book Production Ltd.,
Falkirk, Stirlingshire, Scotland.
Printed and bound in Great Britain by
MPG Books Ltd., Bodmin, Cornwall.

To Penny, With Love

The wind blawis cald, furious and bald,
This lang and mony a day;
But, Christ's mercy, we mon all die,
Or keep the cald wind away.
This wind sa keine, that I of meine,
It is the vyce of auld;
Our Faith is inclusit, and plainly abusit,
This wind he's blawin too cald

Scottish Poem of the 16th Century

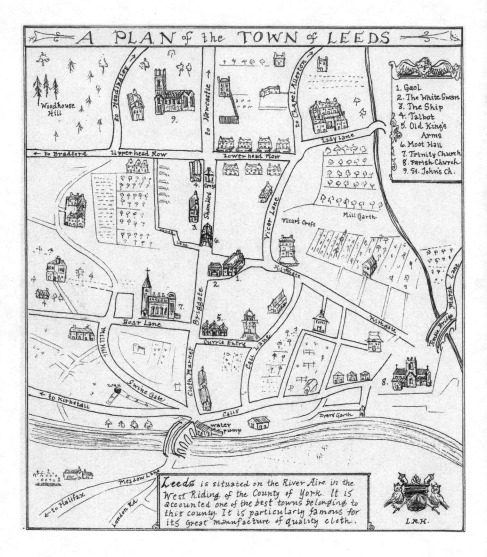

A PLAN of the TOWN of LEEDS

1. Gaol
2. The White Swan
3. The Ship
4. Talbot
5. Old King's Arms
6. Moot Hall
7. Trinity Church
8. Parish Church
9. St. John's Ch.

Woodhouse Hill

to Headingley
to Newcastle
to Chapel Allerton

to Bradford
Upper head Row
Lower head Row
Lady Lane

9.

Vicar Lane
Shambles
Cross
Vicar's Croft
Mill Garth
4.
3.
6.

1.
2.
Kirk Gate

Boar Lane
Briggate
5.
Kirkgate
7.
Currie Entry
8.

Timble Bridge
Marsh Lane

Mill Hill
Cloth Market
Call Lane
Calls

to Kirkstall
Swine Gate
well
water pump
Dyer's Garth

to Halifax
Meadow Lane
London Rd.

Leeds is situated on the River Aire in the West Riding of the County of York. It is accounted one of the best towns belonging to this county. It is particularly famous for its great manufacture of quality cloth.

L.R.H.

Prologue

Jesus, he thought, he'd believed them when they called this a road. It was no more than a track winding up the side of the valley to the rock edge above, barely wide enough for a cart, the ruts frozen and slippery as man's sin. His boots, thin enough already after the walk from Liverpool, could feel every hard, awkward step, and his breath plumed abruptly around his mouth. With a short sigh he drew the coat around himself, even though it wouldn't keep him any warmer in this raw winter cold, and hitched the pack high on his back.

In every manner it was a long way from the Indies. There the heat had prickled his skin every day and his sleeves had been sodden from wiping the sweat out of his eyes. For a moment he almost longed for that again. But then the ache from the scars on his back stopped his mind from playing him false. That was the true memory of those years, along with the screams of men in the wild delirium of yellow fever before they died. Freeborn, convict, soldier or slave, few came back from the Indies.

He paused, looking back down at Hathersage, watching the smoke from a few chimneys rising dark and skimming across the air. A mile or two further, he'd been told, and he'd find the marker for the Sheffield road. Less than a week and he'd be back in Leeds, if he didn't freeze his bollocks off on this God-forsaken moor first.

But he knew that wouldn't happen. It couldn't happen, he wouldn't allow it. He had business in the city, and he'd come too far and staked too much not to manage the last few miles. His feet trudged on, calves burning as he kept climbing the hill, sliding sometimes on the ice. Frigid slurries of wind, a few carrying flecks of snow that were as cold as a whore's heart, battered against his face. Six months before, his skin had been burned dark by the sun. Now some of that colour was gone, washed away first by the long sea journey, then another two weeks of Shanks's mare that had brought him here as winter still held the land tight into February, and drifts rose high against the dry stone walls. He'd caught a glimpse of himself in a puddle as he left the village, hair grey and lank under a cap, face pinched thin, his body hunched and spindle legs in patched breeches and torn hose. An ugly sight, he conceded wryly, but none would recognize him and his situation would improve.

At least he had a small purse in his pocket now, courtesy of a traveller over Winnats Pass who'd not be found until spring, and by then the animals would have picked him clean. No one would know who he was or that a slash across the throat had killed him. But it served the bugger right for befriending a stranger on the road.

So he'd afforded an inn in Hathersage last night, dozing on a bench at the George and letting the warm embers of the fire dry his boots and ease through to his bones. For the first time since setting out he'd felt some peace in his rest. At daybreak, with a heel of bread and a mug of small beer in his belly, he'd set out. The journey would take him close to the village where he'd been a boy, but he was damned if he'd ever go back there.

Another few days and his life could begin again. After eight years, life would begin again.

One

The road felt hard as iron, and Richard Nottingham guided the horse carefully, avoiding patches of ice that glittered softly in a weak afternoon sun. He hated riding at the best of times, but in the bleak days of winter every mile seemed gruelling. At least he was almost home; the welcoming smoke from the chimneys of Leeds rose tantalisingly just beyond the horizon. He'd be back in his house at the dying of the day, aching and exhausted.

He'd ridden to York yesterday and given his evidence at the Assizes this morning, before staying to joylessly hear the verdict of murder on a man who'd killed his wife and children rather than watch them starve. As Constable of the City of Leeds he'd made the journey many times over the years, and sat and spoken in the grand courtroom at the castle, dressed in his good periwig and best coat. Often he'd enjoyed the trips; he stayed at the Olde Starre off Stonegate, where they said the cries of men treated there for injuries during the Civil War could still be heard at night. Not that he'd ever heard them in the evenings of conversation and drinking with other travellers.

This time, though, he simply wanted to be by his own hearth, to try to shore up the world that had collapsed around him four weeks before.

It had begun early in December, when gales swept viciously from the north to batter the city, followed by the endless snow and brutal cold that stayed, day after day, week after week, until they seemed like facts of life.

At first it had been the old and the weak who died, many frozen in their unheated cellars, others, always teetering on the edge of life, fading quickly from hunger. Throughout Advent, then Christmas, the lists of the dead rose. By the middle of January 1732, with ice still thick on the streets, death was everywhere, a plague made of winter. The ground was too hard for burials, and corpses were lodged in every cool place, a village of bodies lurking in the darkness as the toll rose higher.

No one was immune. Every family, it seemed, fell prey to the unrelenting weather, although the rich, insulated by thick walls, warmth, and money, suffered less than most as they always had. And always would, he thought grimly.

Then in early February, just as the days grew longer and people began to raise their hearts and hope towards spring, Nottingham's older daughter, Rose, barely twenty and married just the autumn before, began to cough and run a fever.

Her husband spent every possible hour at her bedside. Her mother nursed her with the old medicines, and the Constable rousted the apothecary away from the homes of the wealthy to tend to her, but try as they might, there was no heat or medicine that could touch the girl's body or soul. All they could do was watch helplessly, hopelessly, and pray as the flesh slipped quickly from her bones. She vomited up the broth they fed her, and her pains grew stronger and her breathing shallower until the end almost seemed like a release. All it took was a single, shocking week to turn her from a healthy young wife into a wraith.

Nottingham used his position to have her buried when the earth thawed briefly at the end of month, the service conducted by a curate while the vicar stayed close to his roaring hearth. Just a day after he'd thrown a sod on the coffin and stayed to see the earth mounded on the girl whose childish glee still rattled in his head, the freeze returned. Since the funeral the Constable had barely slept. Even in the bare, brief hours he managed, the dreams that came pulled at his heart like a chain of beggars.

At home, he and Mary, his wife, moved as if there was a fog between them that neither could penetrate. They still talked about the everyday things, but the topic of Rose lay off to the side, pushed away behind a fence, never mentioned but always on the edge of view. They lay in bed side by side, and he knew full well that hours would pass before her breathing subsided into the uneven rhythms of a grieving sleep. Sometimes his fingers would start to reach across the sheet for her hand, but he always stopped short of touching her skin. What could either of them say that would help? In this world, simply living past childhood was an achievement. If God had robbed them of their joy, it was nothing more than He'd done to thousands of others. Every toll of the corpses he'd filled out since December bore testament to that.

Emily, their younger daughter – their only daughter now – had lost her wilful ways with her sister's death. She'd become eerily quiet and obedient, and even more withdrawn, as if Rose's passing had also killed a spark in her. Her eyes, once so bold and lively, had become dull and lost. Where she'd loved to read, losing herself for hours in a book, now she'd close a volume after a few minutes and gaze emptily. At what he could only guess.

He crested the hill. Leeds lay spread before him, the buildings worming their way up from the river. In the past he'd always loved this sight, his home, his love. Now it simply made him feel that his life had been too long.

As dusk started to fall, John Sedgwick was close to finishing his afternoon rounds, checking on the men the Constable employed. The last two days had been quiet, with little more than the usual pitiful cases of drunkenness and injury. For the first time in months, no one had died. Tall and ungainly, he loped down Briggate towards Leeds Bridge with his long stride.

He loved being the Constable's deputy, and even after three years he could barely believe a post with such responsibility was his. The hours were long, the pay poor and the job was rough and dangerous, but what in this life was any better? At least the work was steady; crime would never go away.

There'd been precious little warmth to the sun that had appeared during the day, but it had still felt good on his face after the murderous grip of winter. The worst since 1684, they called it, back when the Aire had frozen over and they'd held a winter fair on the ice. Men might have recalled the good fun of that time, but how many remembered the suffering that must have gone along with it?

Soon he'd be finished and back in his room. Lizzie would have stoked the fire, James would be playing at the table with the horse and figures Sedgwick had painstakingly carved for him. Sedgwick's wife Annie had vanished with a soldier, no word behind her, and no desire for their son. He'd have been lost without Lizzie, a prostitute he'd tumbled a few times in the past. They'd enjoyed each other's company, and the flirtation that contained something more. With Annie gone, James needed a mother, and Lizzie needed . . . truth to tell, he still didn't understand exactly what she needed, but she seemed content and loving enough, away from the trade of her past, better to him than his wife had ever been. They might have been a family sewn together from discarded scraps and shreds, but they were a family nonetheless.

He thought about the Constable, who'd looked so lost since his daughter's death, like a man walking aimlessly in a landscape he no longer recognised. His eyes were sunken, the skin under them as dark as if someone had smudged coal on his skin. Before, he'd seemed young, possessed of more energy than Sedgwick himself. Now it was as if he'd crumpled into himself, a man suddenly far older than his years.

The deputy shook his head and walked on, gazing around and taking in scenes almost without thinking. What was Bob Wright doing talking to Andrew Wakefield? They noticed his glance and turned away self-consciously. He smiled slyly to himself, and stopped at the bridge, with its worn cobbles and wide parapets. They'd held the cloth market here once, he'd been told, although it was long before his time. It must have been hell for the carters and travellers trying to enter the city from the south.

These days white cloth was sold in the White Cloth Hall and only the coloured cloth market was held outside, trestles set up on the lower part of Briggate twice a week, with business lasting just over an hour and conducted in the sedate whispers that passed for silence. It was all the lifeblood of Leeds. The city was wool, purchasing cloth from the weavers and exporting it all over Europe and to the Americas, places that existed to Sedgwick as nothing more than obscure names. Wool made the merchants and the Corporation rich. Not that men like him would ever see anything of the money; they kept that close to their purses. But he was happy enough. And his lad would do better than he had, he'd make certain of that.

There was one final area to walk: the path beside the river by the tenting fields, where cloth was pegged out to stretch, then along by New Mill to Mill Garth and through to Boar Lane, past Holy Trinity Church and back to the jail. And finally home.

He loved this short stretch of his rounds, no more than a few hundred yards from the city but as peaceful as the country. Even the occasional floating corpse in the river couldn't spoil it for him.

He'd almost reached the track at New Mill when he noticed something from the corner of his eye: a low, pale shape that didn't look quite right among the trees. Stopping, he cocked his head and squinted for a better look. It was probably nothing, but he'd better check. It was what he was paid to do.

The hard, frozen grass sawed against his threadbare stockings as he moved through the undergrowth. But it wasn't until he was three yards away that he was able to make everything out fully.

'No,' he said softly. 'No.'

It was a man, lying on his back, eyes blank and wide, staring endlessly into the face of death. One arm was thrown carelessly across his breast, the other outstretched as if reaching for something. The strangest thing was that he was bare-chested. The deep red cut across his neck showed how he'd died.

'No,' Sedgwick said again. He sighed. He wasn't going to be home any time soon.

By the time the coroner arrived, fetched by a boy clutching a coin hot in his hands, full darkness was close. A prissy, fussy man, Edward Brogden was muffled warm against the weather in a heavy new coat of good wool and a tricorn hat, a scarf gathered at his throat.

The deputy already had two men waiting to take the corpse to the jail, crouched with their backs against a tree, trying to stay warm as the temperature started to fall. The coroner gave the body a cursory look, bending to examine the sliced neck.

'He wasn't killed here,' Sedgwick said.

Brogden raised an eyebrow quizzically. He didn't really care; his only job was to pronounce death.

'No blood around the body,' the deputy explained. 'With his throat slashed he'd have lost a lot of it. And he's cold as the tomb.'

'Turn him over,' the coroner said without comment.

Sedgwick heaved the corpse on to its stomach, then stood quickly, horrified, taking an involuntary step backwards as the bile rose swiftly in his throat. He'd seen a lot in his life, much of it bad, but never anything like this. Someone had carefully, lovingly, taken all the skin off the man's back, leaving a raw, ugly pinkness that barely looked human. Unable to break his stare, he heard the coroner turn and vomit on the grass.

'Take him away,' Brogden ordered huskily, his voice shaking.

Sedgwick followed the men as they carried the body on an old door, the flesh covered by a ragged, foul-smelling blanket. In the jail near the corner of Briggate and Kirkgate, nestled next to the White Swan Inn, they laid the corpse in the cold, far cell the city used as a mortuary. Sedgwick closed the door softly and shook his head. What kind of man could think to do something like that?

When Nottingham walked into the jail an hour later, Sedgwick was sitting at the desk, gazing into the flickering fire that burned low in the grate.

The Constable was cold, he ached, he was tired, and his soul was weary. After giving the horse back to the ostler on Swinegate he'd stopped at the jail out of habit and a sense of duty.

'What are you doing still here, John?' he asked.

Sedgwick's head jerked up as if someone had pulled it by the hair. 'Sorry, boss.'

'Everything quiet?'

'No,' Sedgwick answered gravely. 'Not at all.'

'Why? What happened?' Nottingham's voice was urgent and inquiring.

The deputy rose slowly and walked back towards the cells.

'You'd better take a look at this.'

Their breath frosted the air. Sedgwick struck a flint and lit a candle, pushing the gloom far back into the corners. He lifted the edge of the blanket to show the face and neck.

'Found him in some trees down near the river late this afternoon. If it hadn't been so bad out, someone would probably have seen him earlier.'

Nottingham leaned in for a closer look as the deputy continued.

'There was hardly any blood where I found him. He was completely cold, he'd been dead a while.'

'You know who that is, John?' the Constable asked after a moment.

Sedgwick shook his head. Whenever the boss asked a question like that, it meant the person was important.

'Samuel Graves,' Nottingham told him stonily. The deputy didn't know the name. 'A merchant, or he used to be, at any rate. Retired now.' He looked knowingly at Sedgwick. 'A lot of powerful friends on the Corporation.'

'Look at his back, boss,' the deputy said in a dark tone. 'I'll warn you, it's bad.'

The Constable raised the shoulder and rolled the corpse on to its side.

'Jesus.' He spat the word out, wondering at the skinning for a moment, leaving the corpse on its side.

'Whoever did it knew exactly what he was doing,' Sedgwick pointed out. 'It's the whole of his back.'

Nottingham's mind was racing. 'Have you started searching?' he asked.

As soon as the news reached him, the Mayor would demand action on this. This was more than murder; it was a desecration of one of the city's respected citizens. He glanced at the man's back again, the skin neatly and precisely cut away. Something like this made no sense at all.

'It was too dark, boss. I'll get them organized in the morning. His pockets were empty.'

The Constable nodded. He felt exhausted, drained.

'You go on home, John. I'll look after things for now. I'll go and tell Mrs Graves.'

'What are you going to say?'

Nottingham rubbed his eyes. What could anyone say? God knew he'd seen enough murders in his time, but nothing that came close to this. Why, he wondered. Why would one man do this to another? What kind of hatred could be in him?

'I won't say too much,' he replied with a grim smile. 'I think we'd better keep very quiet about the details here, don't you?'

Two

He wrote a note to the Mayor, a brief description, knowing full well it would bring a peremptory summons in the morning. Then he gathered his greatcoat around his exhausted body, ready for the cold.

As he left the goal, Nottingham longed to keep going down Kirkgate, to cross Timble Bridge and go home. He needed to see Mary and Emily, to have the comfort of his own fire and his family close. But he couldn't, not yet. Duty had to come first. At Vicar Lane he turned, setting one foot leadenly in front of the other on the hard ground, feeling the thin whip of the weather in his flesh.

Lights were burning in the windows of the Graves house, a new, plain three-storey building standing behind a small garden at Town End, close to St John's Church, across from the Ley Lands. The path had been carefully swept clean of snow and ice, and the night had the thick feel of velvet sliding against his face as he raised the knocker to let it fall heavily against the wooden door.

A minute passed, and then two. He was about to knock once more when he heard the sharp click of a servant's shoes in the hall. The man was in his twenties, with muscled arms and a direct stare that bordered on insolence. A guttering candle cast deep shadows across his face.

'I'm the Constable of Leeds,' Nottingham announced without preamble. 'I need to see your mistress.'

The servant considered for a moment, taking in the travel dirt on Nottingham's coat and the lines cut deep on his face.

'Yes, sir. Come in,' he said grudgingly, leading the way down a hallway panelled to waist height in dark, polished wood that reflected the candle flame.

Mrs Graves was in a sitting room where coal was piled high on the fire to burn hot. A candelabrum on a side table gave her ample light to read the book in her lap. She looked to be about sixty, the Constable judged, perhaps a little older, her arms thin with mottled, wrinkled flesh, her silk gown from the time of Queen Anne, a pair of shawls gathered tightly around her shoulders to give more warmth. Nottingham ducked his head briefly and waited until the door closed softly and they were alone. She lowered the book.

'I'm Richard Nottingham,' he began. 'I'm—'

'I know who you are,' she croaked impatiently, assessing him with shrewd, sharp eyes. A few strands of grey hair stuck out awkwardly from her mop cap. A walking stick, its handle worn by frequent use, leaned against the side of the chair. 'I've lived here all my life, I know who's who. Now, what is it?'

How did he begin, he wondered. How could he give her the heartbreak?

'It's about your husband,' he started.

She waved her hand dismissively. 'If you've come to see him, he left for London on Friday. I told him he should wait until the roads were better. But he's never listened to me before, so why would he now?' She sighed, and he could hear a lifetime of closeness and affection hidden behind her words.

The Constable's face showed nothing, but he absorbed the information she gave him. Graves could well have been dead for four days already.

'I'm afraid he's dead, ma'am,' Nottingham said quietly.

She shook her head in disbelief, eyebrows furrowing. 'Don't be ridiculous, Mr Nottingham,' she scolded him brusquely. 'I just told you, he took the coach for London on Friday.'

'I'm sorry, Mrs Graves, but it seems he didn't,' he told her. 'Your husband is dead.'

For a moment he thought she hadn't heard him. Then the words hit her and he saw her face collapse in quiet anguish. Her hand scrabbled to the pocket of her dress for a handkerchief and she buried her face in the white linen. He felt powerless. He couldn't approach her, couldn't offer any comfort; all he could do was wait awkwardly.

'How?' she managed eventually, her voice suddenly a girl's small, weak sob.

He had no choice. He had to give her some of the truth; she might know something to help him, but still he hesitated.

'He was murdered,' Nottingham said finally. Her face remained hidden behind the scrap of cloth. 'Would you like me to call a servant?'

She gave a short, tight shake of her head. Her shoulders heaved, but he heard no weeping in the deep silence.

When she finally raised her eyes again, she looked as ancient as the night outside.

'Can I get you anything?' he asked.

Her eyes flickered over the room.

'A glass of that cordial,' she said, then added, 'Please.'

He walked to the sideboard, removed the stopper from the expensive glass decanter, poured some of the liquid – good French

brandy, by the smell of it – and took it to her. She drained half
the glass in a single swallow. Nottingham expected her to cough,
but she simply closed her eyes for a moment and gave a deep,
painful sigh.

'Why?' she asked him. 'Who would want to kill him?' Her
voice rustled, as thin as paper. 'Do you know?'

'No, we don't,' he admitted bluntly. 'Not yet. We only found
him a few hours ago. Do you know of anyone . . . ?'

She stared directly at the Constable, weighing the question
he'd left hanging, and slowly gathered her strength to answer.

'No, Mr Nottingham, I don't. He was a good man in thought
and in deed.' For a moment she drifted into contemplation, then
wiped at a tear leaking from the corner of her eye, the first of
many she'd shed in the coming days, he guessed. 'He was my
husband for forty years, and he loved me every one of them.
There wasn't an ounce of malice in him. He made friends, not
enemies.'

He'd heard words like this so often before, and he knew that
many times they were no more than a façade, covering compli-
cated webs of deceit, lies and anger. There were few truly good
men in this life. Graves could have been the exception, but he
doubted it.

'So he's probably been dead since Friday?' she asked. Even in
grief she was astute.

'Yes,' Nottingham admitted reluctantly. 'He might well have
been.'

'Then you'd better find whoever killed him,' she told him.

'I'll do everything I can,' he answered, offering her honesty
rather than certainty.

Her fingertips absently traced the rim of the glass, the skin of
her cheeks pale and bloodless. 'I can believe that far more than
any promise,' she told him with a short nod. 'Thank you. You
have a good reputation, Mr Nottingham.'

He raised his eyebrows for a moment, surprised not just that
she knew of him, but more that she knew what he'd done. To
most of her class he was an invisible man.

For now he could sense her holding desperately on to an inner
reserve. Tonight was no time for more questions, but there was
one he needed to ask now.

'Why was your husband going to London?'

'He had business there.'

'I thought he'd retired?'

'Retirement didn't suit Samuel well,' she explained. 'He was a man who needed to be doing things, and business was what he did best.'

He noticed that she was already using the past tense. She drained the rest of the brandy, and he could sense her slipping away from him.

'I'll get one of the servants for you,' he said, leaving softly to find a maid in the kitchen. He let himself out. The chill of the darkness was harsh and stinging after the overheated room; the wind lashed his eyes and made them tear.

By the time he reached Timble Bridge he felt frozen, even wrapped in the heavy greatcoat, as the night closed its grip on him. Just taking a breath hurt, the cold air knife-sharp in his lungs.

He turned on to Marsh Lane, his house just yards away. He glanced up, seeing a light burning behind the window, knowing it should seem welcoming. But rather than walking faster and rushing home, as part of his heart wanted, his footsteps faltered and stopped.

Inside, the fire would be banked for the night, good Middleton coals glowing red, their slackening warmth still filling the room. Mary would be sewing by the light of an acrid tallow candle, eyes squinting, her face creased and serious with concentration, square, rough fingers moving without thought to make a seam.

The place would be spotless, every surface scrubbed down to rawness, clean enough to ward off death.

He was scared for them, he realized. For Mary, for Emily, for the only two precious things left in his life, scared of losing them the way he'd lost Rose. The idea of his own existence trickling away caused him no pain – he'd been close to death too often to fear it – but the bitter, searing pain of losing someone else close halted him.

Each night when he came home, he held his breath as he opened the door, unsure if he'd find them alive and well. That was the demon perched on his shoulder, one he could only wrestle with privately and never talk about with anyone.

He began to walk again, slowly covering the distance, grasping and turning the handle, exhaling softly as the room opened before him and he saw his wife and daughter.

'You're so late, Richard,' Mary said solicitously, putting down her needle and rising immediately. 'I was wondering what'd happened to you. You must be hungry. I'll bring you something to eat.'

He wanted to hold her, to feel her warmth and life against him, but she quickly bustled off into the kitchen as if all the small normalities could patch the gaping hole in their lives. Nottingham smiled at Emily, who was lost in thought, a book closed in her lap, and then followed his wife.

'Was the road from York bad?' she asked, feeling his presence as she cut bread and cheese and poured him a mug of ale.

'No worse than you'd expect,' he answered, looking helplessly at her back, 'but there was something waiting. A murder.'

For a moment she stopped, and he knew the image of death was in her mind. Then she continued her movement, turning to hand him a plate. His hand covered hers for a second, her warm flesh brushing momentarily against his palm, before her face turned away from him.

He ate as Mary cleaned the table, wiping away the crumbs meticulously. He hadn't realized how hungry he was; his teeth tore at the food and he swallowed it so quickly he barely tasted it before drinking deep from the mug. When he finished eating, she took the plate to wash and dry fastidiously with an old cloth.

For one brief moment, as she left the room, Mary let her fingertips trail lightly on his shoulder. Nottingham drew in his breath, surprised by the first spontaneous sign of affection since Rose's death. Had she done it deliberately, he wondered, or was it just idle memory that moved her hand?

Left alone, his belly full, his mind moved back to the corpse in the jail. Why would anyone want to kill Graves? But, more importantly, why would someone take the skin off his back? That wasn't murder, it was the working of a sadistic mind, of someone with special knowledge. It wasn't a random killing, he was sure of that; it must have been planned. What could be the purpose behind it?

He reached for more ale and swirled it in his mouth. Animals were skinned for a reason, leather for boots and shoes, pelts for furs. But skinning a man . . . he couldn't even begin to imagine why someone would need to do that.

Graves would have made enemies during his life; no one could succeed as a wool merchant by being a saint. But it was business that was cutthroat, not life. How long had he been dead? When had he left home to take the coach to London?

He rubbed his cheeks. Tomorrow they'd start asking the questions and piecing together the final hours of Samuel Graves. Finding out who could have done such a thing to him, though, that would be a different matter.

In his mind he could picture the man's back quite clearly, the large wound red and livid, mottled with dirt and frozen by snow. The cuts had been straight and exact, and as far as he could judge, the skin had been peeled off smoothly and cleanly. Whoever did it had an experienced, steady hand. He wasn't someone easily revolted by a man's flesh.

But what could anyone do with that skin? It was most of Graves's back, but really that wasn't so much. A trophy, a souvenir? Whatever the reason, it terrified him to know that there was someone like that in the city. His coldness made the cruel winter seem mild.

Nottingham stood up and stretched. He could feel every moment of the day in his muscles, the ride from York, and the long hours of the evening piled atop all the compacted emotions that plagued him. He needed to sleep.

Three

Nottingham was on his way to the jail by six, boots crunching over the ice, slipping and sliding in places, shivering as he walked quickly. The first pale band of dawn lightened the horizon to the east. The city was already waking, plumes of chimney smoke rising to the sky, the sound of voices from the streets and courts, the clop of hooves and grating squeak of wheels as the first carters made their way around.

Two drunks slept in one cell, better here than freezing to death outside. He kept his greatcoat bundled tight, then lit a candle and marched through to look at the body again.

He turned Graves over and brought the light close to the skin. Part of him wanted to touch the man's back, to feel it for himself, to know it that way, viscerally, but he held back, revolted even as he was intrigued.

He'd been right; this work had definitely been done by someone who knew how to skin animals. The cuts were clear and confident, long, single strokes that met cleanly, and the skin had been peeled off evenly. Despite himself, he reached out, running a fingertip lightly down the line where the blade had gone.

This had been done after Graves had died. The lines were too sharp, the work too precise and etched for the man to have been alive. At least there was that, small comfort that it offered.

So now he knew a little more, but the knowledge didn't answer the important questions. What could anyone gain from doing such a grotesque thing? Taking a man's flesh seemed like sacrilege, leaving him less in death than he'd been before. Why would someone do this to Samuel Graves? What was the point of it? What was the meaning? Why had he kept the body for four days? Graves hadn't been just any man, either, but one of the leading citizens of Leeds, wealthy, powerful, not someone who could disappear easily.

He returned to the office at the front of the jail and stirred up the embers in the grate before adding more coal from the scuttle. Sitting, the coat still wrapped close around him, he tried to think.

But there was nothing to consider. They had a body, a respectable man mutilated after he'd been violently murdered, and only one person knew the reason.

Nottingham pushed the fringe of hair off his forehead. The room gradually warmed and he finally shrugged off the greatcoat. Soon Sedgwick and Forester would arrive and he could begin delegating tasks. The Mayor would want this murder solved quickly, and, more important, very quietly. There could be no word of the skinning to spread a creeping panic among the moneyed class.

He heard a noise outside and glanced through the window. It

was Isaac the Jew making his early rounds, calling, 'Clothes! Old clothes!' in his fractured accent. He was the only one of his faith in Leeds, a tall man with thick white hair and deep, sad eyes who'd come from somewhere across the sea. He made his living buying and selling rags and clothes, setting up his stall in the market twice a week.

They'd sold him Rose's clothes after her death, taking the memories of her from her husband and pushing coins into his hand instead. Isaac had folded the items tenderly before pushing them into his pack.

Did he miss his own people, Nottingham wondered? Isaac was a solitary figure, walking the city mornings and evenings with his hoarse, broken shouts for business. As he sometimes said wanly, the few times Nottingham had talked with him, 'Death and poverty, they have no respect.' He shook a head full of old wisdom. 'People alive, they always need the money to eat.'

The door burst open, letting in an angry breath of cold air. Sedgwick and Joshua Forester came through together, rubbing their hands and taking off coats in a quick, sharp bustle of activity.

Sedgwick had taken Forester, a young cutpurse turned Constable's man, under his wing. From living rough, the way Nottingham had once survived himself, the boy had blossomed. He'd begun to fill out, to show a sense of maturity that belied his years. He was punctual and thorough, the thief set to catch thieves who'd proved surprisingly good at his job.

'Anything more on Graves, boss?' Sedgwick asked, and all Nottingham could do was shake his head.

'According to his wife, I was wrong about him being retired. Graves was supposed to be on his way to London on business last Friday, but it looks as though he never got on the coach. That means whoever did this held on to the body for days, which makes no sense at all. Go to the King Charles, John, see if anyone saw him there, talk to the coaching people, find out if he'd booked a seat. Josh, did John tell you what had happened?'

Forester bobbed his head in acknowledgement.

'People knew Graves here,' the Constable explained. 'He was respected. A lot of them liked him. But there must have been some folk who didn't. You know what to do, ask around, open your ears. There'll be plenty of gossip in the air today.'

'What about the men?' Sedgwick wondered.

'Get them searching.' Nottingham stood and began pacing around the small room. 'He was killed and kept and skinned somewhere. We need the place, and we need to find it quickly. And not a word about his back, understood? Not even to the men. This stays with the three of us. Remind the ones who brought him in to keep quiet. Talk to the coroner, too. Can't have him prattling.'

'Yes, boss.'

Nottingham glanced at Forester.

'Yes, boss,' the boy answered soberly.

They left, and once he was alone again, a heavy wave of sadness shimmered through Nottingham. Not for Graves, but for himself, for the maw that had consumed his life. Since Rose's death it came to him often, unexpectedly, unpredictably, emptying him of everything else. All he could do was sit, wrapped in its grip as it took him, the black curtains descending around his heart, sometimes for minutes.

This episode was mercifully short, and breathing softly, he let it pass, shaking his head to clear it. He couldn't afford this. He needed to think about work, to do his duty. Study it as he might, there was little more he could learn from the corpse, but before he could release it for burial, he needed to talk to the Mayor.

They'd begun as adversaries six months before, when Edward Kenion was sworn in for his year of office. Even now there was little love lost between them, only a grudging respect.

The Moot Hall stood in the middle of Briggate, like a rock around which traffic swirled like water, with the Shambles – the butchers' shops – stinking on either side of the street. Under the ground was the dungeon for those awaiting the Quarter Sessions, and up the stairs, where the wainscoting stood polished to a high, elegant sheen, were the offices of the Corporation.

Portraits of former mayors lined the walls, faces worshipful and haughty, watching as he walked over shining boards to Kenion's office, where the windows looked up the street to the Market Cross, and thick Turkey carpets absorbed the sound of feet.

Nottingham knocked on the door and waited for the gruff command to enter. Kenion was at his desk, three heavy piles of papers in front of him. Bewigged, carefully dressed and groomed, and with his pristine stock tied just so, he was subtle about showing his riches: a suit of fine, understated cloth in a good cut, a close shave, and the aura of power that only came with ample money.

Like almost all the city's mayors, he'd made his fortune as a wool merchant. He knew the business, and he understood all too well its value to Leeds, the way it came before everything else. Leeds was built on cloth.

Nottingham sat and waited. When Kenion looked up, he showed his jowls hanging like a hound, and a mesh of fine red lines across his nose from too much good wine and too many rich dinners. His belly pushed firmly against the expensive pale grey silk of his flowing waistcoat.

'Sam Graves was good to me when I started out,' he began briskly, but Nottingham could hear the slight catch under his voice.

The Constable waited.

'I don't like anyone murdered in my city, Mr Nottingham' – he placed an emphasis on the title – 'but especially someone like him.'

'I don't like it either,' Nottingham agreed. 'But much more than that, I don't like what happened to him after.'

He described the skinning, the length of time the killer had kept the corpse, watching as the Mayor blanched before he concluded, 'We can't let word get out. You understand, I'm sure.'

Kenion nodded his agreement slowly. 'I'll talk to his widow and the undertaker. But it sounds as if we have a madman here.'

'Mad possibly, but not a madman,' Nottingham countered thoughtfully.

The Mayor looked at him quizzically.

'This wasn't a random murder. It's too deliberate, too calculated.'

'I don't care if he's rabid or as sane as me. Whatever he is, you'd better find him fast,' Kenion ordered, his face hard, as if Nottingham would do anything else. 'With some luck, we can keep this one fairly quiet. There'll be rumours, of course, but if I hear more than that . . .'

He let the words trail off. They didn't need to be spoken. Nottingham stood. He'd achieved what he wanted; the Mayor would do all he could to ensure the skinning was kept quiet. The rest, as always, was up to him and his men.

He'd never been there, but he knew where Graves had his warehouse, just as he knew where most things were in Leeds. He'd scavenged its streets so often when he was young, finding places to hide and live, little refuges and sanctuaries of hope for a few days, that he knew the city intimately, like a lover. Grown, he patrolled them, and learned the city's deeper secrets and shame.

The warehouse was one of the buildings by the river, downstream from Leeds Bridge. The stone was just beginning to wear, darkened by soot and rain, the main door painted a deep, forbidding black. He walked in, entering the office, where three clerks sat working at their high desks. They looked up together as his heels clopped on the flagstone floor.

'I'm Richard Nottingham, the Constable.'

Like brothers used to each other but not to outsiders, the men glanced between themselves before one dared clear his throat and ask, 'How can I help you, sir?'

'Have you heard about Mr Graves?' he asked.

The man stared blankly, while the others looked confused.

'He's in London, sir, he left on Friday,' the man responded with an uneasy smile. 'He'll be back next week.'

'I'm sorry, but he won't,' Nottingham told them, watching their faces as the words captured their attention. 'Mr Graves was found dead yesterday here in Leeds. Someone killed him.'

There was a low stir of voices between the men.

'I need to know about his plans, and about the business,' Nottingham interrupted them.

The man who'd answered him was somewhere in middle age, his back bent from years of writing, his fingers permanently stained with the deep blue-black of ink. He cleared his throat softly.

'This is one of the biggest warehouses in Leeds,' he said with pride, as if he owned it himself. 'We export cloth all over, to Spain, Italy, the Low Countries, sir. We're always busy. Mr Graves said he was going to London to discuss a contract there.'

His eyes were cast down slightly, not cowed, but trained by a lifetime of deference to those who'd always have more than him.

'I thought he'd retired.'

The man smiled wanly and shook his head. 'He tried, sir. He really tried. It lasted about three months. But Mr Graves wasn't a man who could take his ease too well. He'd planned on selling the business, but then he decided to keep going himself. He needed it, he said.'

'How are your order books?' Nottingham asked.

'Full, sir, they're always full.'

'And how long have you three worked here?'

'I've been here twenty-five years, sir.' He gestured at the others. 'Mr Rushworth's been a clerk with us for almost twenty years, and Mr Johnson eight years. Mr Graves trusts us to run things.' His face reddened briefly in embarrassment and sadness. 'I mean, he trusted . . .'

'Do you know who he was meeting in London?'

The man shook his head. 'He never said, but I'm sure there will be letters in his correspondence. I can look if you'd like, sir.'

'Do that, if you would. I'll need everything you can find,' the Constable told him. 'What time was his coach?'

The men looked between themselves again, shrugging.

'I'm sorry, sir, he didn't tell us that, only that he'd be gone to London for a few days. Mrs Graves might know,' he added, then paused. 'Do you know what might happen to the business now? And to . . . us?'

'I don't. I'm sorry.' He understood their fear, not knowing whether they might be cast out in a week or a month. But there was nothing more he could learn here at the moment. 'Can you bring all his correspondence about London to the jail, please?'

Outside, a weak, watery sun had started to shine, but its faint brightness did nothing to warm the air. Nottingham pulled the coat close and the tricorn hat down tight and trudged back along the river, then over the patches of ice on Lower Briggate to the jail. The drunks had woken, and he let them go with a warning. They'd be back soon enough anyway, if they didn't freeze on the streets first. All anyone could hope was that the weather would break soon, and that spring would arrive. They all needed new life, he thought grimly.

He sat, letting the heat from the fire slowly fill him. A scrawled, almost illegible note on the desk told him that the undertaker had collected Graves's body. Tomorrow there would be men hacking at the frozen earth for his burial and the day after a sombre crowd in thick woollen coats in the churchyard to hear his eulogy.

Pinching the bridge of his nose, then sweeping the fringe off his forehead, he gathered together what he knew about the killing. It was precious little, a spider's web made up of mystery and questions.

To the best of his knowledge, Graves had never been one to frequent the inns and taverns. On a few occasions Nottingham had seen him at Garroway's coffee house, and the merchant had seemed uncomfortable enough there, surrounded by brittle noise and the prittle-prattle of chatter.

He was at the Parish Church every Sunday, in his own pew with his wife and some of the servants, parading down Kirkgate and back, the soul of rectitude. And that was what he might have been, a man who lived for his work and his family. But now, no more.

That wasn't the question that gnawed at him. What he couldn't understand was why one man would take the flesh of another. Why had he held on to the body? What could he do with the skin? There seemed to be no reason behind any of it. His imagination could conjure up nothing, and that left him at a disadvantage.

The more he considered it, the more certain he was that there could be nothing spontaneous about the killing. Everything had been planned with the greatest care. It had taken place somewhere the skin could be removed, and the murderer had held on to the corpse somewhere before leaving it, quite deliberately, to be found.

That meant someone had a deep reason to kill Graves. So someone, somewhere, had a motive, some history, some explanation for it all.

That much he could accept. But the skinning still made absolutely no sense.

For now all he could do was wait until Sedgwick and Joshua returned, and hope they'd discovered something. In the meantime there were lists to complete, reports to be written, the terrible minutiae of his job.

Writing never came easily to him. For his daughter Emily,

who maybe still harboured the secret, ridiculous notion of becoming a writer, words flowed easily, like water in a brook. For Rose, like him in so many ways, they never had. She'd been a kindly girl, with few pretensions, one who greeted each little twist of life with a smile.

He sighed loudly, aware once more of the large void in his life. In his head he knew others had suffered more, much more, but that was no comfort while his heart still broke at each memory.

Nottingham picked up the quill and dipped it in ink, hoping to lose himself in the effort of work. He'd learned to read and write as a young boy, before his father had convinced himself that his wife had been unfaithful and the lad was not his. He'd thrown the pair of them from his merchant's house, and a life of luxury became a daily fight where books and words held no place.

He'd come back to his letters reluctantly when he took the job as a Constable's man, but still found no pleasure in them. Now he was teaching Sedgwick to read and write, watching as the deputy eagerly embraced this new world of learning like a child, his writing shaky at first, then quickly becoming firmer, his eyes striving to make sense of words on the page, forming them slowly, then with more confidence. He worked hard at it. Nottingham knew Sedgwick had ambitions to succeed him as Constable, and he'd need these skills for the job. In time, he thought, it might happen. Maybe even sooner than anyone had imagined, he thought, if his weariness with the world didn't end.

He was still scribbling when the door opened, forcing in a hard rush of bitter air, and Sedgwick entered, shaking a few flakes of snow from his hair.

'It's started again,' he complained, taking off his coat and standing close to the fire, holding out his hands as if to grasp its warmth.

'What did you manage to find at the inn?' Nottingham asked.

'Graves was booked for Friday's coach, but he never got on it. Paid for his seat, too, so they were surprised when he never took it.' He rubbed his palms together. 'He used to take the coach every two months, they said, and he'd always been punctual.'

'What time did the coach leave on Friday?'

'It was a little late – supposed to go at ten, but it was almost eleven when it finally got off. There'd been a problem with one of the wheels, and they had to repair it before they could leave.'

Nottingham looked at the deputy. 'Did anyone see Graves on Friday morning?'

'Maybe, they're not sure.' He shrugged helplessly. 'You know what it's like there when there's a coach, boss. It's always madness for a few minutes. Then they had to take care of the wheel and the passengers. A couple of the men say they might have seen him, but they're not sure; no one's going to swear to it, they were all too busy.'

'What about strangers?'

Sedgwick gave a hopeless smile. 'I tried that one, too. Between the travellers and the gawkers, they're all strangers. No faces anyone remembered.'

The Constable sighed. He hadn't truly expected much, but he'd hoped for something. He thought for a moment, then said, 'John, go down to Graves's warehouse. I was there earlier. They don't seem to know much, but try asking them about anyone who's been sacked.'

Sedgwick nodded and gathered up his wet coat, which was just beginning to steam in the heat, then left.

Nottingham needed to speak to the widow Graves again. It was never easy, cajoling the bereaved into the past, the last place they wanted to visit, picking and probing at wounds that were still fresh. But he knew it had to be done. Give them a day, that was the way he'd been taught, just long enough to dull the first shock but while things were still clear.

Once again the widow received him in the sitting room, the fire a bright, roaring blaze. She looked as if she hadn't slept, eyes rimmed red, her skin pale and waxy. She glanced up as he entered, staring not so much at him as through him, as if he were a ghost, without substance, and she was straining to see the reality.

'I'm sorry to have to come again,' he began, not even sure she'd heard him. Her old hand was curled tight around an embroidered linen handkerchief as if it was a rope that could save her.

'I know this is a difficult time,' he continued gently, watching the blankness of her face. 'I need to ask you some more questions, so I can try and find the man who killed your husband.'

At the last two words she looked up sharply.

'He's dead, though, isn't he? You told me that yourself. Nothing

I say is going to bring him back.' Her voice was distant, speaking through the haze of a thousand memories.

'No,' he admitted, 'but it might bring him justice.'

She returned to her lost silence. He tried again, kneeling by her chair so his face was level with hers.

'You said he didn't have any enemies, Mrs Graves. But someone killed him, something happened to cause that. Is there anything you can think of, anything at all? It doesn't matter how long ago.' He realized he sounded as if he was pleading, but it didn't matter. He needed information, the tiny scraps from the table of Graves's life.

'I know he was a good man, but I'm sure my husband wasn't always a saint in his work.' She spoke slowly, sadly. 'He never really talked about his business at home, but I know there were times he must have cheated and stolen a little. He didn't tell me, of course, but it was obvious. That was years ago, though.' She glanced at him, her eyes suddenly focused, her voice sharper as the words began to rush from her mouth.

'I know he had some sort of feud with George Williamson for a while. Do you remember him, Tom Williamson's father? He died a couple of years ago. And I'm sure that from time to time Samuel had to dismiss men who worked for him, but he never talked about that with me, and it wasn't my place to know. He didn't play cards often, he rarely gambled, as far as I know he didn't have any debts, and he wasn't interested enough in women to keep a mistress.'

'I see,' was the only way he could respond to her candour.

'What I mean, Mr Nottingham, is that I really don't know of any reason someone would kill my husband.' She paused, letting her thoughts collect. 'If he'd been worried about anything, I'd have known it; after so many years, you can tell without words. He seemed hopeful. He'd been going to London regularly for a few months. All I know is that he was negotiating for a contract of some sort.' Her eyes opened wider. 'I suppose if we'd had a son, he'd have followed Samuel into his business, but we only had girls. He'd talked about taking on an apprentice or a partner for years, but he'd never done it.'

The Constable nodded. Girls, he thought. Just like himself. *Girl* now.

'Is there anything else?' she asked, her mood suddenly imperious.

'No,' he told her. 'No, there's nothing.'

She didn't attempt a courteous smile. 'Then, please, leave me now. I really don't think there's anything more I can do to help you.'

Four

He'd trimmed the paper to the right size, carefully tearing the sheets. He'd prepared his words, a rough draft written on fragments that he'd gathered in a pile and were now ready for a fair copy.

The rough table was uneven and he steadied it with a shim of wood under one leg. As he sat he tested it, nodding approvingly when it barely moved. He inspected the quill, pleased with its sharpness, then dipped it into the pot of ink. He breathed deeply before making the first mark on the paper.

Every man has a tale to tell, or so they always say. This is mine, the story of one who has been wronged by life. It is a tale that needs to be told, for people to hear, a tale I have kept in for far too long. Now, though, in this cruel winter, it is time for me to sit and write this. I have been maligned, but I have stood tall always, and now these are the days of my revenge.

I am not a Leeds man by birth. I came here later, seeking work and finding it. I was a clerk, I knew my letters and my sums, and I had a fair hand. I still do, as you can see. Leeds held opportunity for someone like me.

I was born in Dronfield. It is a place few people know, little more than a piece of dust on a map of the kingdom. The village itself is in Derbyshire, six miles from Chesterfield, a city famed only for its market and the crooked spire of its church, and not so far from Sheffield. Dronfield was a mean place during my childhood, the stone houses cold and damp, the inhabitants poor and low-spirited. My father was a labourer, my mother a laundress to the vicar and his family.

I suppose I should be grateful for that connection, as it helped me gain an education. I was intelligent, precocious and eager. If I had been otherwise no doubt I would still be there, passing a scythe over a field or wasted away to my death.

But the vicar saw my talents, and in his good, Christian way, wanted to encourage them. It was through him that I was able to go to the Fanshawe School, founded by no less a man than one of Good Queen Bess's courtiers. A haughty man by all accounts, his name in all the beneficence in the area.

I was the ragged one in a class full of those from good homes, with their refined manners and good clothes. They disliked me for that, cruel as all children are. But once it was evident that I outshone them in the classroom, they shunned me. When they did deign to speak, they taunted me, pinched me, hurt me. My lot was to be cleverer than they, and they didn't like that in such an urchin.

They were the first to make me feel inferior.

He sat back, looking at his work. The copperplate script was beautiful, a delight to the eye. But after so many years of clerking, it should have been. He put down the quill, flexing his fingers.

In Christ's name, it was bitter here. Even with a fire, there was a chill deep in his soul, one that felt as if it would never leave. He'd spent too many years away from English winters, down in the heat and the sweat, and it had lightened his blood.

Still, the cold weather had brought something good. It had been easier to keep Graves's corpse without the smell of rot filling the air. And then, when he was ready to let it be discovered, there were so few people on the streets that moving it to the riverbank had been a simple task.

Yes, there was luck involved, but also planning and preparation. He'd spent years readying himself for this, filling his days and dreams with the triumphs. Now it was becoming real, the first stage almost complete.

But it wouldn't be finished until he'd celebrated it, written it all down, and sent it on to be read. His only regret was that he wouldn't see the looks when he revealed his secret, and allowed them to understand what had mystified them.

Still, a man couldn't have everything in this life. But he'd get much of what he wanted. Enough, certainly enough.

Five

Leaving Graves's house, Nottingham turned back towards the jail, then changed his mind and walked briskly up Briggate before turning at the Head Row towards the fuggy warmth of Garroway's Coffee House.

As always, the exotic smells of coffee, tea and tobacco overwhelmed him. Steam plumed from a kettle, and low, murmured conversation filled the air, a mix of business and gossip from the merchants who frequented the place, smoking their pipes as they talked and drank.

It was one of them he was seeking. Tom Williamson was sitting by himself, grimacing as he read the *Mercury*, an empty cup pushed away on the table. Standing over him, the Constable said quietly, 'Tom.'

Williamson raised his eyes and began to grin until he remembered.

'Richard. I heard about your daughter. I'm so sorry . . .'

Nottingham set his mouth in a grim line and nodded. There was so much he could say to this man, as close as he had to a friend among the merchants, but it was better to keep his peace. If he began to talk about the things on his mind he might never stop.

'Sit down. Do you want something to drink?'

Before Nottingham could reply, he was signalling for two dishes of tea to be brought. In his thirties, Williamson had taken over the family business on his father's death. He'd been groomed for it all his life, apprenticed to a merchant in his teens, then spending time abroad to understand the markets before coming back to

Leeds. In the two years he'd been running Williamsons, so Nottingham understood, business had boomed. He was a symbol of the success of Leeds, the rise of the city, the dominance of the wool trade.

'How are you, Tom?'

Williamson crumpled the newspaper, letting it drop to the floor. His open, honest face could hide nothing – something Nottingham had always imagined a disadvantage in a merchant, although it never seemed to hamper his trade.

'Fair, apart from the weather, of course. Business is down, but that's to be expected in the winter, of course.' He shrugged and paused. 'But you want to talk about Sam Graves, don't you?'

The Constable nodded. 'A good guess,' he said with a faint smile.

'Hardly,' Williamson responded. 'The murder's on everyone's lips, and you're not the type to just pass the time of day.'

'I gather he and your father didn't get along.'

Williamson laughed, shook his head and rolled his eyes. 'That's an understatement, Richard. They hated each other. Sam beat my father on a big contract – this was years ago, you have to understand that. You didn't know what my father was like, but he held his grudges close, especially when he believed Graves had bribed people to get the contract. I don't think they ever spoke again.'

A man brought the dishes of tea and the Constable waited until he'd gone.

'What was Graves like?'

Williamson considered his answer as Nottingham raised the cup, blowing across the surface of the dark liquid before sipping. As always, it tasted bitter to him, not worth the money people paid for it.

'I liked Sam, although I'd never have dared tell my father that. He was good at what he did and he made money. He knew wool and he knew the market. He cut corners at times, but most people do, that's how business works.'

'How about other people? Did they like him?'

'He was as popular as anyone,' Williamson replied guardedly.

Nottingham raised his eyebrows and Williamson grinned, suddenly looking ten years younger. 'Show me a merchant

everyone likes and I'll show you a bankrupt.' He cupped his hands
on the table and leaned forward. 'The thing you have to realize,
Richard, is that business is competition. It's all well and good
being liked, but being respected is better. We're looking for profits,
and those don't come with pleasantries. But Sam was respected,
there's no doubt about that. He'd been in business a long time,
he'd served on the Corporation. About the only thing he hadn't
done was be mayor.' He paused. 'Do you have any idea who
killed him?'

'None,' the Constable answered briefly.

'That's not going to stand too well with Mr Kenion,' Williamson
suggested wryly. 'Sam helped him a lot back in the old days.'

'It doesn't stand well with me, either,' Nottingham said bitterly.
'Do you know anything about a new contract he was discussing
in London?'

The merchant furrowed his brow. 'I'd heard something about
it – well, rumours of it, nothing more than that. I know Sam
kept going down there, but that's all. He was tight-lipped about
the whole affair, but that's the way he was about most things in
business. That was his generation, never let a word slip or someone
will be there before you; my father was the same.'

'Nothing more than that?'

Williamson shook his head. 'Sorry, no. Some people thought
it was the government, some people thought it might be with
the Spaniards. Sam was the only one who really knew. He'd smile
about it, but that was all.'

Nottingham took another small sip of the tea, swallowing it
quickly to avoid the harsh taste. He leaned forward, confiding
quickly and softly. 'I'm baffled, Tom. I don't have any idea who
might have wanted to kill him, where he was killed, and certainly
not why. That worries me. I feel like a blind man in a crowd. I
don't know where to turn.'

Williamson sat back in his chair, considering.

'What do you know about him beyond business?' Nottingham
wondered.

'Not a great deal,' the merchant answered eventually. 'If he did
anything bad, he hid it well. Truth to tell, Richard, he probably
really was all probity and rectitude, just as he seemed. I know he
went to church every Sunday, he seemed to love his wife, and

his daughters married well, if I recall. There was never a word of mistresses, but he might just have been very discreet. And if he was ever seen with a whore, well, no one would ever hold that against him.'

Nottingham sighed.

'I'm sorry,' Williamson said again. 'Sam wasn't a man for scandal. I know it makes your job harder.'

'It makes it bloody impossible,' Nottingham replied with a sour laugh.

'You'll find him, Richard. You always have.' Williamson stood up. 'I need to go.' He tried to lighten the tone. 'If I'm not there, the business will surely fall apart by noon. I'll try asking a few questions for you, but I honestly don't think there's much to learn.'

'Thank you.'

Joshua Forester was doing what he did well, what he'd come to love. He was listening. In the inns and stableyards, all people were talking about was the murder. It was all speculation – not one of them had known Samuel Graves – but that didn't matter.

They all had plenty to say; gossip was the common currency of everyday life, a relief from numbing work. At times Josh felt as if they couldn't see him, that he wasn't really there, as they carried on around him as if he didn't quite exist.

But his whole life had been like that. It had saved him, allowed him to steal food and cut purses to survive, and helped him become a good Constable's man. He pushed his hands deeper into the pockets of the coat that was four sizes too big for him and belted with a piece of rope.

At least he had good boots. He'd taken them from the corpse of a merchant's son the month before; his old ones were worn through at the sole and leaked. But why would the rich need boots after death, anyway? For them it was just a short walk to heaven.

The boss had noticed, of course, giving him a short, hard look, but saying nothing. He protected his men. Josh had been astonished to learn that Richard Nottingham had once lived like him, out on the streets, scrabbling, fighting, hungry. Even now, with the pain of grieving written on his face, he seemed in control of everything.

Nottingham could move among the wealthy, converse with the powerful men of the city, and also those who had nothing. But his life had covered both sides of the coin. At times Josh had to wonder if that was why he'd been appointed Constable: because the Corporation were embarrassed to see a merchant's son, even one that had been cast out, among the poor.

But he knew the truth was much more than that: that Nottingham was good at his job. He kept order in the city, and he was a strong leader. He knew how to get the best from his men. He'd encouraged Mr Sedgwick to learn how to read and write, grooming him for the future. He saw things in people that others didn't.

Josh didn't know his letters or numbers, and he didn't care. He was happy as he was. Thirteen or maybe fourteen now, he relished the steadiness of his work, and the sense that for the first time in his life he had a future that went beyond the night. The companions he'd had when he was a thief had mostly drifted off. He saw a few in the city, and the rest, well, the winter would have taken its toll on those who'd stayed in Leeds. He shared his room with Frances, a girl he'd known for four years. She was, he supposed, around his own age; he'd never asked and she'd never volunteered the information, if she even knew. In the old days he'd protected her, fed her, and she'd clung to him. When the others slowly melted away, she'd stayed; by then it seemed perfectly natural for them to be together without even discussing it. Not that they ever talked about much, words weren't their way. She had food ready for him when he returned from working, and held him close in the cold nights. She'd said she thought she might be having a bairn, but her belly was still flat, so he wasn't sure what to make of that. Time would tell, he imagined.

He liked his job, knowing there would be work tomorrow, the day after and next week, and the regular pay. It was more than he'd ever known before. So Richard Nottingham had his loyalty. And Frances, in an odd way, had his love.

Today, though, he was going to disappoint the boss. People were out, in spite of the cold – they were always out, it seemed, no matter the weather – but they had nothing worthwhile to say, just rumours and idle thoughts. Throughout the day he shifted from place to place, from stable to draper, but there was nothing useful. The only consolation was that they didn't know about the skinning. They would, sooner or later. Someone would talk.

He made his way back to the jail, face numb from the bitter weather, hungry for some warmth. Nottingham raised his eyebrow as Josh walked in. When he simply shook his head, the Constable murmured, 'Damn.'

Sedgwick had gathered a list of the employees sacked by Graves. He'd been thorough, insisting the clerk go back ten years. There were only twelve names, so either the merchant had picked his men well or he was a soft-hearted employer, which the deputy found impossible to believe in the wool trade.

One man had been sent to prison, another transported, both for theft. As to the others, their offences had been quite trivial – smoking in the warehouse, late to work too often, minor infractions but enough to warrant dismissal. He knew enough to follow up, to find the men if he could and talk to them. One of them might well be the murderer. Anyone could do anything in the right circumstances, he'd learnt that much in his time on the job.

By late afternoon, after trudging from address to address and feeling as if he was chasing shadows, he'd managed to find three of the men. One was so wracked with consumption that he seemed to shimmer between life and death on his mattress in a foetid room. Another had hands turned into crippled, shiny claws by a lifetime of work; he couldn't have held a knife.

The third was more interesting. Adam Carter was in his late thirties, tall, broad, still strong, still without work, his manner curt and furtive, scabs on his face and knuckles as prizes from the fights he'd been in over the last fortnight. He'd lost his job in the Graves warehouse five years earlier. Sitting in the dram shop, spinning out one glass of gin as his eyes craved another, he remembered Graves.

'A right bastard, he were,' he said, the froth of bitterness full on his words. 'I were late five times in a month, that's all. I told him I was willing to work later to make up for it. My daughter were ill, see, and I'd to look after her since my wife weren't well.

They both died a month back from the cold.' He swallowed a little more, grimacing at the taste while Sedgwick sat, listening. 'Anyway, I tried to tell him, but the self-righteous bugger didn't want to know. Sent me packing.'

'You still hate him?' Sedgwick asked.

Carter looked up, blue eyes lifeless. 'I've lost my family,' he answered flatly. 'Of course I hate him. I fucking hate everyone now.'

'You know someone killed him.'

'Aye, it's all over for him, and about bloody time, too.'

Sedgwick stared at him, an accusation in his eyes.

'No, it weren't me.'

'And can you prove that?'

'Course I can't.' Carter hawked and spat on the stone floor. 'You can't prove it were me, neither. If you could, we wouldn't be here now, you'd have me in the jail.'

It was true, and Sedgwick acknowledged it. Carter didn't have the cunning of the killer, and probably not the skill. This man had given up on living. Whoever killed Graves had a force within him, a deep desire that drove him.

'I might want to talk to you again,' Sedgwick warned.

Carter shrugged carelessly.

'Tha's found me once. I'm not going anywhere.'

When he reached the jail, Nottingham and Josh were sharing a jug of ale from the White Swan next door. Sedgwick poured himself a mug and gave his report.

'So there are seven we still need to talk to,' the Constable mused. 'You two can work on that tomorrow, you know what to do. I'll find out about the ones who were convicted.'

He rubbed his chin thoughtfully. 'Go home, the pair of you. There's nothing more we can do tonight.'

Alone, he drained the cup. The evening outside was loud with the sound of voices, carts, and horses. He wanted the peace of silence. He wanted to be somewhere the thoughts didn't crowd him, where all this vanished and he could feel free.

Terrible as it was, he knew this murder was what he needed. It was forcing him out of himself, pushing him away from the darkness that had consumed him since Rose died.

Nottingham looked at the names of the two convicted men

scrawled in his notebook. Had he given evidence at both their trials? He couldn't recall. But he'd testified so many times, against so many men, that it was impossible to bring many details to mind.

Elias Wainwright had been found guilty of stealing cloth from the factory. It was just scraps and offcuts that would have been thrown away anyway. But he'd taken them without permission, and that was a crime. He'd almost certainly have been released long ago.

Abraham Wyatt had been more calculating, he remembered that much. A clerk, he'd been clever enough to embezzle from Graves, and it was sheer accident that he'd been caught. Everyone expected him to hang, but he'd pleaded benefit of clergy and instead he'd been transported, given seven years in the Indies, something many considered worse than the noose. Death out there came slow, he'd heard, from heat and sickness. Few ever came back. Not many lasted a single year, let alone seven.

He banked the fire and blew out the candle, locking the heavy door behind him as he left. A thin wind funnelled down the street and he pushed the collar of his greatcoat close around his neck. Kirkgate was quieter now, the people gone to their houses, trying to keep the winter at bay for another night and praying for the advent of spring.

Six

A long week passed and they found nothing. Whoever had killed Samuel Graves had left no clues, no hints. For all the hours of questions and long searches, he might as well have been invisible.

Deep down, Nottingham knew full well that the man was still in the city. There was more to come, he could feel it. There had to be; no one did that then just vanished. All he could do was keep looking and wait.

Graves's papers arrived. He'd pored over them for hours, reading through every piece of correspondence. He'd been going to

London to try to secure a contract to provide blankets for the army. It would have made him a very wealthy man if it had happened, but the Constable was certain that it wasn't the cause behind a murder like this.

Every day the Mayor ranted at him to solve the murder. Every night, when he lay in bed, it preyed on him, until the thoughts of Rose replaced it with something even deeper and darker.

What baffled him still was the skinning. It was easy enough to make sense of a killing, however warped it might be. But so carefully, so delicately, to remove the skin from someone's back? There had to be a reason, but for all his thoughts he couldn't find it.

He'd managed to learn that Wainwright had died, another victim of the killing winter. He'd dispatched a letter to London to learn if Abraham Wyatt had died in Jamaica or been released, but it could well be weeks before he received a reply.

Seven frustrating days had passed since Sedgwick had found the body, days of half-hopes that proved as substantial as October mist. The only consolation was that the weather had hesitatingly begun to warm, melting much of the ice and turning packed snow into grey, creaking slush.

He'd been sitting in the jail since seven. Sedgwick and Forrester had gone out to ask more questions, although he already knew the answers would be of no help. On Briggate the sounds of the Tuesday market echoed loudly, cheerful and competitive as the traders vied with each other.

The door opened and a boy entered hesitantly, his eyes wide at being in such a place. Nottingham looked down at him and smiled gently.

'Please sir . . .' the boy began in a small voice. He was tiny but already careworn, and from his rags he was obviously one of the urchins whose life on the streets of Leeds would be pitifully short.

'What do you need?' he asked.

'Someone told me to give this to the Constable.' He brought a small parcel from behind his back, wrapped in an old sheet from the *Leeds Mercury*.

'I'm the Constable,' Nottingham told him kindly. 'Who told you to do this?'

'I don't know, sir,' the boy answered. 'But he gave me a penny for it.'

'I see.' He was alert now, staring at the package the boy had put on the desk. 'And when did he do this?'

'Just a few minutes ago, sir. Over near Lands Lane.'

'What did he look like? Do you remember?' He tried to make the questions sound casual; he didn't want to terrify the boy into silence.

The lad shook his head. 'I couldn't really see him, sir. He had a hat pulled down, and a heavy coat.'

'Was he big? Small?'

'Not so big,' the boy said with confidence. 'But he said he'd watch me and if I didn't do the job he'd take the money back and hurt me.'

'Well, you've done it, so everything is fine.' Nottingham smiled at him. 'What's your name?

'Mark, sir. My mother said it's for one of the followers of Jesus.'

'She was right. Where is she now?'

'Dead, sir.'

'I'm sorry about that, Mark. You can go now, you've done your job well.'

As the door closed, he sat down and unwrapped the package.

Seven

They were the first to make me feel inferior.

Nottingham realized he'd been holding his breath and forced himself to exhale slowly. He was sitting at his desk, holding the slim, bound volume. The binding was pale brown leather, thin and crinkled, and dry to the touch.

He ran his thumb across it, feeling the rough texture. On the front, in exact, immaculate copperplate, was the title: *The Journal of a Wronged Man*, and underneath, in smaller letters, *In Four Volumes* written in ink the dark, rich red of fresh blood.

Revenge, he thought. Abraham Wyatt. He didn't know why but it had to be; he could feel it, the way some pieces fell into place so perfectly that it was impossible to be any other way. Wyatt must have survived the Indies somehow, to be carried home by hate. He'd had eight years to plan all this.

He picked up the small book and began to read again, his face set in a frown, concentrating intently on the even, copperplate script.

And then there was Samuel Graves. That should be a name to capture a reader's attention in this place and this time. He was another to think less of me because of my beginnings. He looked down on me, and offered no respect for my talents. But more of him later.

At school I revenged myself on my fellows in minor ways. Small things went missing, belongings of theirs, or items from the school that appeared among their possessions and brought them harsh punishments. I was sly and careful. Suspicion was on me, but I made certain that they could never prove a thing.

My education was too brief. I could have done great things, I know this, but the opportunity and the time were not there for one like me. Poor circumstances make their own needs. There were mouths to be fed in my family; they required me to bring in a wage. So I was torn from my school and each day I walked into Chesterfield and back to do my work as a clerk for a grain merchant. Six miles each way for the privilege of being little better than a slave.

The pay was miserly, and he worked me long and hard. He made money, and plenty of it, far too much for such a stupid man. Once I understood his system, it was not difficult to take some of his profits. He never even realized.

My intention was to amass enough money to enter business myself. Having seen the dubious qualities of those who managed to do well in life, I knew I could be successful. I left my position before anything might be discovered and moved to another. Slowly I accrued some small savings.

Then I was trapped by a ruthless girl. She was friendly enough, and soon free with her favours. But then she came to me, saying she was having our baby, and wanting marriage. There was I, barely sixteen, with my plans, my ambitions.

I had tupped the girl with pleasure, but intended nothing more, certainly not wedlock and a life of misery and poverty. I had seen enough of that. Instead, I gave my small fortune to the whore who had tried to trap me, and took to the road.

That was a meagre time, with jobs in Sheffield, Barnsley, Doncaster. There was a little money to be made from my skills as a clerk, and a little more, over and above, from my native intelligence. Finally I arrived in Leeds.

However, more of that will come in the future. That is a tease, I know, but there is something more immediate to be told. It is full of sensation and horror, all those things people love but claim to hate.

Samuel Graves. He did me the gravest wrong, and so he paid the greatest price. I have found that a man can learn a great deal by listening. People talk to listen to their own pompous voices with no thought of who else might hear them. If a man is quiet and still, he can often go unnoticed; it is a skill I have learnt over the years, and put to good use here.

Following Graves – I cannot feel enough respect to offer him the honorific of Mr – I was able to discover a great deal. Initially, it was a pleasure to find him still alive, still hale and hearty and involved in his work. If he had died before our paths crossed again, I would have been sorely disappointed, and this volume would never have been written.

It only took a few days to hear about his plans to take the London coach, and when he would be leaving. I knew that would be my chance. After all, Graves lived a remarkably ordered life between his warehouse, home and church. If I had not known him somewhat better, I might have been tempted to call him a good man.

In the clamour surrounding the arrival of a coach, it is quite remarkable what a man can do if he is quick and thinks on his feet – another skill I acquired in my travels.

Some damage to a wheel ensured a delay and loud frustration among the passengers. In that time it was very easy to be Graves's shadow, and once he was alone, to take advantage of the situation. A little something in his drink, and suddenly he was no longer feeling too well.

What should happen but a caring friend appears to help him away to a quiet place? One man helping a drunk, hardly an uncommon sight in any city in the kingdom at any time of day, as I am sure you will agree. A different hat, some dirt on the coat and the wig gone and no one would recognize Graves or even give the pair a second look. Nor would he really be missed as the coach rushed away late.

By now I am sure you must have realized I have a place somewhere, and I took him there. When he woke, of course, he was firmly bound and gagged – after all, I did not want him shouting for help, did I? Not that it would have helped him. There was plenty of time to apprise him of all the things he had done to me, for him to be aware of his responsibilities, and how he would pay for all the ills he had caused me. You might even say he was a lucky man, really, for how many of us come to learn of the time and manner of our death before it happens?

Nottingham felt a shiver of fear in his spine. His palms were clammy, although the fire was low in the grate. He set the book down on the desk and paced around the room for a minute, trying to take in what he'd just read. Wyatt was insane, there seemed little doubt of that, but at the same time the man's mind was filled with a clarity whose focus scared him.

And he was positive, beyond any shadow of doubt, that it was Abraham Wyatt. The clues were there, clear to anyone who could read them. Finding Graves alive, the mentions of the things Graves had supposedly done, the grievances of the murderer, they gave so much away.

The book was a taunt, a piece in a game he was playing, a tournament of catch-me-if-you-can, a direct challenge to the Constable. The way he relished putting it all on paper, the sheer pleasure Wyatt was taking in every step of this, disturbed and chilled him. He brushed the fringe off his forehead and forced himself to sit again, taking a deep breath before he picked up the book.

For whatever it's worth, I killed him on the Saturday morning, with one slice of the blade across his throat. He knew it was coming, I had told him, and, to offer him a little credit, he neither fought nor flinched. He understood his time had arrived at my hands and accepted it with equanimity.

There was a great deal of blood, of course. But a chilly room is a fine place to keep a corpse so it does not stink, and a workroom and the lengthy winter have been good to me in that. When I was ready, disposing of the body was an easy task. I was only surprised that it took so long for anyone to notice him lying there.

But there is something more you want to know, is there not? There is something you cannot understand, something that makes you believe I am inhuman. Why, you wonder, did I remove the skin from his back?

I had not told Graves about that, it would have been far too cruel, even to a man like him. The knowledge of his death was punishment enough, not the use to which he would be put, and after death what would it matter to him, anyway?

Some of the skills a man learns in rural areas are very strange. But in a place where self-sufficiency is vital, it is important to be able to turn a hand to everything. So, among many other duties, I was taught how to skin a beast and to cure the hide. The technique is not especially hard, and even the act of skinning is not particularly complex, once one learns how to do it properly. For what it is worth, the real art is in peeling the flesh away evenly, and I had an old, excellent teacher with some long-held tricks and a very sharp knife.

The difficulty here was in curing the skin. Ideally it should have had at least a week longer, but I confess I was eager to share my triumph.

But no doubt you are mystified as to exactly what I mean. Why would I cure the flesh as if Graves was no better than a common beast?

The answer is, quite literally, in your hands.

Take a look at the cover of this small volume, Constable.

If it seems like good quality leather, that's a testament to my meagre skill. It seems very apt, somehow, to have the description of the death of Samuel Graves wrapped in his own skin.

Nottingham stood up quickly and the book fell to the floor. His mouth filled with bile, and for a few short moments he struggled for breath, certain that he'd vomit, the room swimming in front of him.

Jesus. He held on to the desk, eyes closed, the sweat cooling rapidly, chilling on his skin, as he tried to steady his lurching stomach. The relish which the murderer – Wyatt, it had to be Wyatt – took in all this went beyond any belief. In his job he'd dealt with madmen before but none who came close to this. This was evil. He'd read the words, but he couldn't begin to understand the mind behind them.

He glanced down, seeing the book on the flagstones. To know he'd touched it, laid his hands on a dead man's flesh, made him shudder, and once again he tasted the sickness in his throat and forced it back down. He'd have to pick it up, to read what remained, and then comb through it all again and again for any hints it might offer.

Those would be precious few, he was certain. Wyatt might be moonmad, but he was cunning as Reynard, one who'd hide his tracks well. He'd planned carefully, and he had luck on his side. And that, Nottingham knew from experience, could be a dangerous combination.

Gingerly he sat again, reaching for the volume but loath to touch it and feel death on his fingertips. Very cautiously, hands pressing on the paper, not the binding, he read on:

Have I horrified you? Have I revolted you? I trust I have. After all, what I have done is inhuman, is it not?

You will recall that I wrote that this book will extend to four volumes. When they are all done, my revenge will be complete. If you are a clever man, and I trust you are to have your position, you may already have deduced who I am. That is of no import. Think of me merely as an instrument of retribution. Three more volumes will mean three more victims. What should concern you are their identities. Who are they, and how can you keep them safe? Even if you know who they might be, how do you dare to tell them the truth without causing a panic?

And now I've presented you with a challenge, Constable. When my mission is complete I shall leave Leeds, and if that happens, you will never be able to catch me. So now you have it. You need to find me, to stop me. I don't believe you can. I have had a long, long time to plan this, what felt like lifetimes, and all you can do is try to keep up with me. Forgive me if I do not say that I wish you well.

He sat back, staring at the book, lost in thought. Time passed, he had no idea how long. The door banged open and Sedgwick ambled in, frowning, snapping the Constable back to the present.

'John,' Nottingham said quietly, 'let's go next door to the Swan. I need a drink, and believe me, you're going to, as well.' He slid the book into the desk drawer, picked up his coat and walked out into the cloudy, suddenly unreal day.

Eight

'Christ Almighty.' Eyes wide, Sedgwick shook his head in disbelief as Nottingham told him about the book. 'He's not a man, he's a devil.'

'Oh, he's a man, no doubt about that. But he's evil – that's absolutely certain.' He took a long swig of strong ale to clear his mouth. A low buzz of conversation filled the inn, but he'd been talking quietly, anxious not to be overheard.

The book had shaken him. It had terrified him. His hands felt unclean, tainted; he could still feel the brittle dryness of the binding against his fingers. That was horror enough. What was far worse was what he saw when he looked beyond that.

Wyatt was a man who planned meticulously, whose revenge had been simmering for years. He'd thrown down his gauntlet, and Nottingham had no choice but to respond. More than that, he had to win, to catch Wyatt before he could complete his mission. Three more deaths. He couldn't allow that to happen.

'There can't be any word about the book, John,' he warned, taking another mouthful of beer. 'You and I and the Mayor will be the only ones to know. The same with his plans. He's told us what he intends to do. We're going to stop him.'

Sedgwick pushed his mug around the table. 'So how do we do that, boss?'

Nottingham sighed deeply. 'I don't know yet. He wants to murder three more people. We have to start by identifying the people he wants to kill and protecting them. And we have to keep hunting for him.'

He knew that it sounded little enough, and it was. He'd need to review the trial transcript and see who'd given evidence, who would be in danger. But how could anyone reach inside a mind as twisted as Wyatt's and see things through his eyes?

'I'd better go and tell the Mayor,' he said finally. 'Get the men out, John.'

'They're already out, boss.'

The Constable's face tightened. He breathed deeply.

'Then double their efforts. We're not just fighting a man here, we have to fight against the clock, too.'

Sedgwick returned to the jail. He had a little time. Rummaging in the drawer, he looked at the book. Lying there, it seemed so ordinary, so harmless. The cover looked like any other leather, and he reached out to touch it. He knew he shouldn't, he knew what it was, but he couldn't help himself. It was macabre, of course it was, yet his fingers still irresistibly stroked the binding, then riffled through the pages. His reading was improving, and with a little effort he could slowly make out the sentences, even if he couldn't follow every single word.

The boss was right. Word about this could never leak out. The city would panic, and there would be no chance of containing it. He closed the drawer again. He'd never imagined that writing could be too powerful and too dangerous.

Nottingham had to wait at the Moot Hall, although he'd insisted to the clerk that his business with the Mayor was urgent. Sitting, he tried to empty his racing mind. The luxury of the city building, with its dark, highly polished wainscoting and heavy carpet, seemed a whole world away from what he saw every day. The courts and yards, the ragged men and women, the children scavenging at the market or on the river bank, the lives and deaths that took place every day just outside these walls, that was what he really knew. He never felt comfortable in the homes of the merchants, surrounded by wealth, the muted chime of a long clock announcing the passing of hours, or the luxurious, moneyed sheen of fabric of a suit or gown.

The Mayor looked harassed. He was halfway through his one-year term, and all the deaths of winter, which he could do nothing to halt, had weighed on him; it still showed although the thaw had begun.

He looked up from his papers as Nottingham sat.

'You'd better have news on Graves's killer,' he said brusquely.

The Constable could hear the weariness in his voice. 'I do,' he replied carefully. 'But it's not good.'

He described the book, watching Kenion carefully as the colour fell from his face and he retched silently, hands gripping tight on the desk. When the Constable finished, the Mayor was silent for a long time before asking, 'Where's this book now?'

'It's at the jail,' Nottingham replied.

'And who else knows about it?'

'Only my deputy.'

Kenion raised an eyebrow.

'You trust him?'

'Completely,' the Constable replied.

'You'd better be right. No one else can know about this. If words spreads, I'll know who to blame.'

Nottingham nodded. He understood the importance of silence.

'We need to find this bugger fast,' Kenion said. He stared directly at the Constable. 'We can't afford another killing like Sam's. What are you doing about it?'

There was nothing to be gained now by hedging, Nottingham decided.

'My men are looking, but there's been nothing so far. But now I know who's responsible, I can do a lot more. If I can identify his other targets from the trial transcript, I can guard them.'

The Mayor rubbed his fleshy chin and nodded.

'And we'll keep looking, of course. We'll find him.'

'Just make sure you find him in time.' It was half-command, half-wish.

Before he left the Moot Hall, Nottingham visited the clerk in the archives and collected the transcript of Wyatt's trial. It was thin, a saddeningly short hearing. In itself, that was no surprise. Justice was dispensed swiftly and harshly in the city. But he needed clues, names. With a deep, heartfelt sigh, he walked back to the jail.

Nottingham read through the trial transcript four times. The first time his eyes slipped hurriedly over the words, familiarizing himself with the events in court; he hadn't attended the trial himself. Afterwards he studied it in more detail, pausing to think and examine statements, trying to imagine himself in Wyatt's position.

The guilt had never been in question; the evidence was obvious and overwhelming, and presented clearly and concisely. Wyatt hadn't spoken in his own defence, although it wouldn't have made any difference. Both Graves and one of his clerks had been able to show how he'd embezzled a total of twelve pounds over two years. It wasn't a fortune, by any means, but enough to make a real difference. Wyatt had thought he was being clever, of course, but once examined his methods seemed obvious, banal.

He recalled arriving at Wyatt's lodging to arrest him. Nottingham was still the deputy then, accompanying the old Constable, David Arkwright, in case of trouble. He'd seen how Wyatt lived. There was nothing expensive or fancy in the room he and his woman shared with another couple. A small, battered chest to hold their clothes stood at the foot of the bed. The walls were bare, stained by ragged brown patches of damp, but the floorboards were swept scrupulously clean, a blanket folded neatly across the pallet.

Wyatt himself was a small man, dressed in clean clothes, the coat worn but carefully brushed and mended, the waistcoat plain, home-cut but well stitched. His fingers were heavily coloured by the ink he used every day, but the nails were short and free of dirt. The wig on his head fitted well.

His woman wore a simple grey gown, a shawl gathered close

around her shoulders, hair loose, brushed to a shine and falling long down her back. Her eyes were large, a deep, dreamy brown, and her skin was the colour of summer dust. There was an exotic tinge to her that he couldn't place. She held his gaze evenly as she moved next to Wyatt and took his hand.

'You know who I am?' Arkwright asked, and Wyatt had nodded.

'Then you'll know why I'm here, Mr Wyatt.'

'If Graves had paid a fair wage, I'd never have had to steal.' Wyatt's voice was husky, on the edge of emotion.

It was as good an admission as anyone needed, Nottingham thought.

'I'm going to take you with me to the jail,' Arkwright said. 'You'll get a fair trial, I can guarantee you that.'

'And what about her?' The man inclined his head towards the woman. 'How's she supposed to survive if there's no money coming in? What's she going to do?'

Arkwright shook his head briefly. It wasn't his concern, Nottingham understood that. The city employed them to stop crime and arrest criminals. They couldn't affect anything beyond that; if they tried, they'd go mad. Lives fell apart; it was the way of the world. Crime had its consequences, even for the innocent. The woman stayed silent, head held proud and high.

'You're going to have to come with me,' Arkwright told him. 'It'll be a lot easier if we just walk out of here together, but I'll put irons on you if I must.'

Wyatt turned to the woman, lacing his arms around her and kissing her deeply. He knows he'll never see her again, Nottingham thought, and braced himself. He gripped his cudgel. This was often where it became dangerous, where they tried to run and the violence started. But Wyatt broke away, lowered his head, and shuffled slowly towards the Constable.

Wyatt said nothing as they trudged out of the miserable court. The Constable and Nottingham stayed close, braced for the man to bolt, but he just trudged on, submissive and cowed. At the jail Arkwright put him in a cell, locking the door with a heavy clunk. Through the grille Nottingham watched as the man looked around then sat on the bed, legs together, hands gathered in his lap. Then he filled out the ledger, giving the date, the prisoner's name, and his crime.

For embezzlement, he'd go to the Quarter Sessions, which wouldn't sit for another month. They'd move him to the prison in the cellar of the Moot Hall. It was a dismal place with little light, but still better than most. The prisoners were fed fairly, their families could visit without bribing the jailers, and they weren't kept chained and shackled like animals.

There was no doubt that Wyatt was guilty. Graves had gone over the accounts himself and presented the discrepancies. No one on the judge's bench would dispute the word of one of the city's most distinguished merchants. The best Wyatt could hope for would be seven years' transportation, possibly even fourteen. Since he was an educated man Wyatt would plead benefit of clergy, speak a sentence from the Bible and escape the hangman's noose. The severity of the sentence would depend on how gracious the judge was feeling that day.

The transcript told Nottingham little. The trial was reported in flat, straightforward terms, a catalogue of statements, verdict and sentence. He sat back and wondered. Wyatt's journal was going to be in four volumes. It didn't take a great leap of the imagination to see he'd target the judge and the clerk who'd given evidence against him. But with the old Constable dead Nottingham couldn't see who the fourth person might be.

Joshua Forester was sitting on his pallet, watching Frances in her fitful sleep. She took small breaths, her long hair a tangle on the rough pillow. There was a sheet on the bed, and he'd piled two heavy coats on top for warmth, but even in the thaw the room was still bitter.

She looked so vulnerable, and he worried about the tiny life in her belly. He could look after the two of them, but how would they manage with a baby? Frances had no idea how far along she was, and was too scared to ask anyone for advice. Soon she'd begin to show, he imagined, the way he saw all the time.

He could talk to Mr Sedgwick, but he wasn't even sure where to begin. No one had ever really asked about his life, they didn't even know where he lived. He simply arrived at the jail each day and did as he was told. Josh knew he was lucky to have a regular wage, to be one of the Constable's trusted men.

Frances stirred, and he stroked her cheek.

'What time is it?' she asked, her small voice not really awake.

'Still dark,' he told her. 'You go back to sleep. You need your rest now.'

She closed her eyes and he was struck again by her velvetlike beauty, so meek and fragile.

'Why are you so good to me?' Frances wondered.

He gazed at her and kissed her eyelids softly. He didn't even really know why himself. Habit, perhaps, or the feeling that someone cared about him, someone he could care about in return.

She reached out and held his hand in her thin fingers.

'I love you,' she told him gently, and drifted away from him. He watched until she settled again, a small smile on her lips. What was she dreaming about? He picked and worried at a loose thread on his shirt. They'd survived the winter, managed to keep food and a fire and fashioned a life together. And a new life, he thought.

After working he needed sleep, but it wouldn't come. The night seemed to stretch forever, and dawn was a faint hope. Dark wakefulness gave rise to too many thoughts, a time when the imagination ran all over the mind. They left him uncomfortable; he preferred doing things to thinking. But he knew he had to make decisions, find things out. What would it be like to be a father? What would he do?

Josh leaned back against the wall and closed his eyes. He could tell that this murderer scared the boss. Nothing had been said, but he knew anyway. He'd seen Graves's back, the skin stripped off. He'd seen Nottingham take the slim book from the drawer, look at it, and handle it with distaste. He'd heard as John and the Constable talked quietly, about things they didn't want him to know. He understood all the same. His mind had made the leap and connected the two things. He'd stayed quiet, not wanting to believe what his eyes told him yet accepting it was the horrific truth.

Anyone who'd do something like that was more devil than man, Josh decided. Someone who'd stop at nothing to exact his revenge. He'd been out looking and listening, but there'd been no sighting, no whisper about Abraham Wyatt. How could that happen? How could a man carry out a crime like that and disappear? There were plenty of people in the city, that was true, but it wasn't endless, the way he'd heard London was. Only a devil could vanish . . .

Frances stirred again, and he reached out to gently take her hand, letting the sound of her breathing lull him to his rest.

Josh came in, ready to work. He'd looked preoccupied recently, the Constable thought. But he'd been so lost in his own problems that he'd taken no account of the men. As long as they did their work, he'd let them be.

'I've got a job for you,' he told the boy. 'Do you know Judge Dobbs?'

Forrester shook his head.

'Owns a big house at Town End, the other side of the Head Row. It's the first one beyond the Free School. Use a couple of the men. I want you to follow him everywhere. Don't let him know you're there.'

'I can do that,' Josh agreed easily. 'Why do you want him watched, boss?'

'I think the man who killed Sam Graves will be going after him. Keep your eyes open for anyone else who seems to be around, anyone at all. If they seem suspicious, bring them here and I'll question them. This might be our best chance to find Wyatt.'

'Yes, boss.'

He gathered up his old greatcoat, so large that it seemed to engulf him.

'Is everything all right, Josh?' Nottingham asked gently.

The boy looked at the Constable, eyes guileless, startled by the question. 'Fine, boss. Why?'

'I just wondered. You've been quiet these last few weeks.'

Forrester shrugged, then slid out through the door. Concern hadn't worked, Nottingham thought. He wrote a note for Sedgwick, telling him to organize men to follow Ralph Rushworth, the clerk from Graves's warehouse who'd given damning evidence at Wyatt's trial.

He smiled. Things were changing. They were taking action.

Nine

Walking home at dusk, Nottingham's steps faltered as he reached the Parish Church. He slipped quietly through the lych gate and crossed the ground to Rose's grave. A little slush remained, but most of the snow had melted into the earth leaving it boggy and clinging, sucking softly at his boots. He hadn't been here for a week; his time had been taken up with the murder. He felt ashamed for ignoring his daughter.

In time, once the earth had fully settled, he'd pay for a headstone. For now, there was only a sinking mound and memories to show that she'd ever lived. He stood, head bowed, scenes from the past twenty years slipping through his mind. Rose as a baby, as an infant toddling on unsteady legs, as a girl with the sun on her hair, playing by the river. Rose on her wedding day, eyes turned in adoration to her husband . . . Rose in her final illness, face wan, eyes lost to the world in her fever.

He hadn't been able to save her, and that guilt bit painfully into his soul. He could catch murderers, but he couldn't keep death from his own daughter, his little girl. He'd failed her, and he'd failed Mary and Emily, too. It was a pact, unspoken, unwritten, but always understood – he was the man, he'd keep them all safe. But he hadn't managed in his duty.

He wanted to believe in God and the life eternal, that Rose was in heaven. But belief was near impossible when you were empty. He silently mouthed prayers for her that came from years of church services . . . *shelter her soul in the shadow of Thy wings, make known to her the path of life*. He hoped they'd bring him a little peace, a communion with her. Instead all he could feel was a thin tear burning down his cheek. Slowly he wiped it away, then stood for a few more minutes until the damp chill roused him.

At the gate he turned right, heading for Timble Bridge and home. He wasn't sure he felt comforted by his visit, but it was something he'd needed to do. Not for Rose, but for himself.

After a few yards he paused.

'Are you going to show yourself?' he asked loudly before turning.

'I was wondering how long it would take you, laddie.' A bulky man detached himself from the shadows to stand beside the Constable.

'So what brings you here, Amos?'

Nottingham had an uneasy relationship with Amos Worthy. The older man was a procurer and pimp, the most successful in Leeds, though he didn't display it in dressy finery. For years the Constable had loathed him and tried to prosecute him, always without success, for Worthy had powerful friends on the Corporation.

Then, the previous year, in the wake of a murder, Nottingham had learned that Worthy had once been his mother's lover. It had come as a disturbing revelation, one that left him even more wary of the man.

'I was sorry to hear about your lass.'

The Constable gave a small grunt, unsure how to reply. He knew the man hadn't followed him just to give his condolences. He said nothing, waiting for more.

'There's a lot of talk going round about old Sam Graves,' Worthy continued. Even speaking softly, his voice filled the street.

'There's always talk,' Nottingham replied blandly.

'You've not caught the killer.'

'No,' he admitted. 'But that's common knowledge.'

'Someone told me summat interesting,' Worthy said slowly. 'He said there was a patch of skin missing from Graves's back.'

Nottingham kept his face impassive. He'd known that much would leak out sooner or later; the only surprise was that it had taken so long.

'You always listen to idle gossip, Amos?'

He could sense Worthy smiling.

'I paid good money for that, so it'd better be true.'

Men didn't cross the pimp, or lie to him, at least never more than once. Anyone who tried ended up beaten or dead, an example to others.

'Why did you want to know?' Nottingham asked. He knew Worthy liked to stay abreast of the happenings in the city, but usually the dead only concerned him if the corpse was one of his whores.

'Knowledge is power, laddie. You should know that by now,' Worthy snorted.

The Constable gave a short, harsh laugh. 'If that was true, Amos, I'd be running Leeds by now.'

'You've too much honour, laddie. The folk who run things here would never be scared of you. You wouldn't use what you knew.'

'Unlike you.'

'Aye,' the pimp agreed. 'Unlike me. So was I told the truth?'

'Yes, you were.' He could admit that much, he decided. If Worthy knew, others would too. They'd reached Timble Bridge, and Worthy stopped, hand on the parapet, staring down into Sheepscar Beck running fast below. The night was drawing in deeply around them, the air filled with the kind of damp chill that penetrated right through to the bones.

'An odd thing to do to a man,' the pimp speculated. 'He must have had a reason.'

Nottingham shrugged.

'Maybe. Maybe it was just madness. We'll know when we catch him.'

'You haven't managed that yet, laddie. No one in mind?'

Nottingham turned to stare at Worthy, who was still gazing at the water. 'This isn't like you, Amos. You've a lot of questions tonight.'

Worthy turned to face the Constable. He must have been in his late sixties, but he was still a large, solid man, sturdy as the forest, face weathered and battered by violence and time.

'I knew Sam Graves long, long ago, back when I had another life. He was a good friend to me then, and he stayed one. He'd still talk to me if we met on Briggate, not like all the others. And before you ask, he never used my girls. Or any others, as far as I know.'

Nottingham nodded. Years before, Worthy had owned a shop. After discovering that his own wife and Worthy were lovers, Nottingham's father had thrown out his wife and son then done all he could to destroy Worthy.

'I don't like the idea of someone killing him then doing that,' the procurer continued.

'Neither do I.'

'Aye, laddie, I know that. I'm offering you help if you want it.'

Nottingham raised an eyebrow in surprise. 'And what's the price?'

With Worthy there was always a payment. Not money, but a debt to be paid sometime.

The pimp shook his head. 'No price, *Mr* Nottingham.' He emphasized the word and spat.

The Constable sighed. 'I don't believe you, Amos. I've known you too long.'

'I'm offering you my men to help you. Simple as that. And I'll pass on anything my whores hear.' He exhaled loudly. 'I respected Sam Graves, and I'll not say that about many, in this city or elsewhere.'

The Constable weighed the options. He could use more help, it was true, no matter where it came from. That was especially true if his men had to follow and protect two people. No one on the Corporation would condone him bringing in Worthy and his men, but the Mayor was pressing for a quick arrest. Finally he smiled.

'I'm not going to say no, Amos. I'll sleep on it tonight. I'll come and see you tomorrow, unless you want to visit me at the jail.'

Worthy grinned.

'You already know the answer to that, laddie. And keeping things as quiet as possible is best – for both of us.'

He doffed his hat, half in friendship, half in insolence, turned and began walking back into the city, his silver-topped stick pushing into the mud. Nottingham watched him go. He was unsure what to make of Worthy's offer. It was generous, but that was the problem: Worthy wasn't a man known for his generosity.

Slowly, deep in thought, the Constable walked up Marsh Lane to his house. It was a small place, provided by the city as part of his job, but even though it needed repairs it was so much better than the rooms and garrets where he and Mary had lived before. It felt warm. Even now, in these days of loss and heartbreak, it felt like home.

The fire was burning bright, coal crackling in the hearth. Emily was seated, staring lost into the blaze with a book closed on her

Twelve

The drizzle had edged into heavy, cold sleet by the time Sedgwick made his way home, and a chill wind stirred up around him. The old scar by his mouth itched and he scratched it without thinking. Along with Josh he'd spent the evening questioning the inhabitants of the courts that snaked off the ginnel where Rushworth had vanished.

There'd been nothing, of course. No one had seen anything or heard of a man with skin burnt by the sun. The empty rooms were accounted for. They'd forced their way into three of them, but there was no sign of evil or murder. Rushworth had vanished, and he knew what that meant.

He shook his head, throwing off raindrops, as he entered the house where he had a room. Lizzie would be waiting, and James would be asleep on his pallet. A fire was burning in the hearth. That cost them in tax, but it was worthwhile for the heat, the thing that had helped keep them alive in the depth of the winter, when morning cold had iced deep over the inside of the windows.

He unlocked the door, smiling as Lizzie held a finger to her lips, her eyes turning to James under his blanket.

'Hello, love,' he whispered as he held her, her face warm against his damp cheek. Some said he'd been mad to take on a girl who'd been a prostitute, but he had no regrets. It was love of a fashion, and she'd already proved herself to be a better mother to James than Annie had ever been.

She busied herself, cutting cheese and bread, pouring ale, and putting it on the table ready for him.

'Another late night,' she said, but without any touch of the criticism that had always sharpened Annie's tone.

He took a deep drink, feeling his body begin to relax.

'Aye,' he agreed. 'A lot of people to talk to. Looks like the murderer has snatched his next victim.'

Lizzie shuddered and gathered her shawl more tightly around her shoulders.

'Knowledge is power, laddie. You should know that by now,' Worthy snorted.

The Constable gave a short, harsh laugh. 'If that was true, Amos, I'd be running Leeds by now.'

'You've too much honour, laddie. The folk who run things here would never be scared of you. You wouldn't use what you knew.'

'Unlike you.'

'Aye,' the pimp agreed. 'Unlike me. So was I told the truth?'

'Yes, you were.' He could admit that much, he decided. If Worthy knew, others would too. They'd reached Timble Bridge, and Worthy stopped, hand on the parapet, staring down into Sheepscar Beck running fast below. The night was drawing in deeply around them, the air filled with the kind of damp chill that penetrated right through to the bones.

'An odd thing to do to a man,' the pimp speculated. 'He must have had a reason.'

Nottingham shrugged.

'Maybe. Maybe it was just madness. We'll know when we catch him.'

'You haven't managed that yet, laddie. No one in mind?'

Nottingham turned to stare at Worthy, who was still gazing at the water. 'This isn't like you, Amos. You've a lot of questions tonight.'

Worthy turned to face the Constable. He must have been in his late sixties, but he was still a large, solid man, sturdy as the forest, face weathered and battered by violence and time.

'I knew Sam Graves long, long ago, back when I had another life. He was a good friend to me then, and he stayed one. He'd still talk to me if we met on Briggate, not like all the others. And before you ask, he never used my girls. Or any others, as far as I know.'

Nottingham nodded. Years before, Worthy had owned a shop. After discovering that his own wife and Worthy were lovers, Nottingham's father had thrown out his wife and son then done all he could to destroy Worthy.

'I don't like the idea of someone killing him then doing that,' the procurer continued.

'Neither do I.'

'Aye, laddie, I know that. I'm offering you help if you want it.'

Nottingham raised an eyebrow in surprise. 'And what's the price?'

With Worthy there was always a payment. Not money, but a debt to be paid sometime.

The pimp shook his head. 'No price, *Mr* Nottingham.' He emphasized the word and spat.

The Constable sighed. 'I don't believe you, Amos. I've known you too long.'

'I'm offering you my men to help you. Simple as that. And I'll pass on anything my whores hear.' He exhaled loudly. 'I respected Sam Graves, and I'll not say that about many, in this city or elsewhere.'

The Constable weighed the options. He could use more help, it was true, no matter where it came from. That was especially true if his men had to follow and protect two people. No one on the Corporation would condone him bringing in Worthy and his men, but the Mayor was pressing for a quick arrest. Finally he smiled.

'I'm not going to say no, Amos. I'll sleep on it tonight. I'll come and see you tomorrow, unless you want to visit me at the jail.'

Worthy grinned.

'You already know the answer to that, laddie. And keeping things as quiet as possible is best – for both of us.'

He doffed his hat, half in friendship, half in insolence, turned and began walking back into the city, his silver-topped stick pushing into the mud. Nottingham watched him go. He was unsure what to make of Worthy's offer. It was generous, but that was the problem: Worthy wasn't a man known for his generosity.

Slowly, deep in thought, the Constable walked up Marsh Lane to his house. It was a small place, provided by the city as part of his job, but even though it needed repairs it was so much better than the rooms and garrets where he and Mary had lived before. It felt warm. Even now, in these days of loss and heartbreak, it felt like home.

The fire was burning bright, coal crackling in the hearth. Emily was seated, staring lost into the blaze with a book closed on her

lap, scarcely noticing as he entered and said hello. As she did so often these days, she'd withdrawn into her own safe little world where life couldn't touch her.

Nottingham took off the damp greatcoat, hung it from a sturdy nail in the wall, and walked through to the kitchen. Mary was kneading the dough for tomorrow's bread, hands pushed deep into the mass. She glanced up and smiled at him, the gesture more comforting to him than any fire.

'I hadn't expected you yet, Richard. I've made a pie, but it won't be ready for a little while.'

'It doesn't matter,' he answered, reaching out and stroking her cheek with his fingertips to brush off a small smudge of flour. She didn't pull away, didn't flinch at his touch, and he felt his heart lighten. Could the scars have begun to harden, could they begin to move out of the morass?

Her hands continued to work the bread, her eyes focused on her labours. Slowly his hand dropped from her skin.

'You should go and sit with Emily,' Mary suggested.

'Is she still quiet?'

Mary sighed and nodded, turning her gaze to her husband. 'She barely says a word these days. She does everything I tell her without question or demur. You know what she was like . . .'

Relations had soured between father and daughter in the autumn. Emily had been full of ideas, wanting to become a writer, wayward, secretly seeing a man who'd turned out to be a killer, and she'd been so faithful to him that Nottingham had been forced to hurt her to find his name and stop more death.

After that, the house had become a place of brooding, simmering silences. Until Rose's death; then life itself had become fringed with black. Emily's quietness had turned inward; the girl had barely wanted to leave the house.

'She liked to think for herself,' he answered.

'She thought she knew everything,' Mary corrected him. 'Now she's so meek, it's as if she's a different person. She needs to get some heart back in herself.'

'Maybe she's not the only one,' he said.

She looked questioningly into his face.

'All of us,' he explained.

After long moments, she nodded sharply, gathered her breath

and began to speak. 'Most of the time I feel like my heart's going to break. I see something and it makes me think of Rose. It's everything. You, Emily, this house. And I don't know what I can do about it. I don't even have the words to tell you about the things I've been feeling.'

'You think I don't feel all that too?' His voice was soft, a little stung by what she'd said.

'I don't know.' She wiped her hands on her apron, pausing, pulling together her words. 'I mean it, Richard, I really don't know. You go on to work each day. You come home. You exist, and all we do is talk about all the little things as if nothing had changed, as if Rose hadn't died.'

'I . . .' he began, but couldn't go further. She was right.

'As long as I've known you, you've rarely discussed your work.' The emotions started to rush out of her, as if she'd kept them in a bottle and now she was uncorking it. Mary placed her hands firmly on the table, trying to anchor herself in place. 'I know you've done it to protect us. I've always loved that about you. But now, when you don't talk about work, and we daren't talk about family, what do we have left to discuss safely?'

He reached out, covering her hand with his own, rubbing it slowly, feeling her rough skin under his. 'I stopped at Rose's grave on my way home,' he told her. 'I go there when I can. Sometimes I pray for her, sometimes I just speak to her in my head.'

'Does it help?' Mary asked.

'I think so,' he answered after a moment. 'Sometimes I feel closer to her.'

'I've been there, too,' she said. 'I've stood for hours. I've tried to pray. But all I've seen is some earth and no God around it. Rose isn't there. Not to me.'

'Where is she, then?'

Mary tapped her head, leaving a smudge of flour on her cap.

'I talk to her, too,' she said. 'I tell her things, the little things I'm thinking or doing. And she talks to me. She answers me.'

Nottingham listened.

'She should still be here. A child shouldn't die before her parents.'

'It happens all the time,' he said softly.

'I know that, Richard.' Her voice flared with bitterness and injustice. 'That doesn't make it any better.'

'No,' he agreed.

'I cry a lot. I'll be doing something, anything, and I'll start crying. Sometimes it feels like I'll never stop. Sometimes I don't want to.'

'We both miss her, you know that.'

'I've watched you,' she continued, her gaze fixed on him. 'After Rose died, you seemed lost, but it was as if you wanted to be that way. You wanted it to hurt. You didn't want anyone too close to you, you wouldn't have let me near if I'd tried.' She paused. 'Now you have this murder the city's talking about, and suddenly you're you again. You're Richard Nottingham, the Constable. You have a purpose.' Her eyes were large and moist. 'You have all that. And I'm Mary Nottingham, I'm still here. I'm still surrounded by the same things, the same memories, every single day.'

Slowly, with tenderness born from years together, from happiness and grief, he gathered her to him. She cried softly as he held her close. Silently, he thanked God. She felt so familiar in his arms, so much a part of him, a part he'd missed in these last weeks.

She pulled back suddenly, not hiding the tears, and wiping them away with the back of her hands.

'Let me finish here.'

He smiled then unfolded her from his arms. They'd begun again. Together.

He'd barely taken three bites of the pie before there was a hurried pounding on the door. Glancing apologetically at Mary and Emily, he rose from the table to answer it. Josh was there, his legs muddy, breath coming fast and steaming on the air so he was hardly able to push the words out.

'Mr Sedgwick asked if you'd come, boss. Right now.'

'What's wrong?' Nottingham asked.

'It's that man from Graves's warehouse.'

'Rushworth?' The Constable felt the pit of his stomach fall.

'Yes. He's vanished.'

Ten

'Damn it.' Nottingham paused to think. He thought he'd covered everything, that he was in control again. 'Go back,' he ordered quickly. 'Tell John I'm on my way. Get men out. Look where he lives. Look in the taverns in case he went there. Look everywhere. And I want whoever was supposed to follow him at the jail in an hour.'

Forrester took off again, running as fast as his legs would move. Nottingham knew the reality. They'd search. If they were very, very lucky, they'd find Rushworth. But even as he hoped, he knew the truth would almost certainly be different. Wyatt had snatched him. The next time they'd see the man would be as a corpse with the flesh stripped from his back.

He turned back to look pleadingly at Mary. Emily gazed at him curiously.

'I'm sorry,' he said. 'I have to go.'

Mary nodded in understanding. She'd heard the words so often before in their life together. He put on his old, plain buff coat, gathered up his greatcoat and swept out of the door, buttoning the garment as he walked quickly over the bridge and up Kirkgate, ploughing through the dense mud of the road.

At the jail Sedgwick was sitting behind the desk, frowning anxiously.

'How did it happen, John?' Nottingham asked angrily before the deputy could say anything. 'There were supposed to be men on him.'

'I had Morris following him. He's not the best, but he's usually reliable. He said Rushworth went down a ginnel. By the time Morris got there, Rushworth had vanished. He says he looked all over then came back here. Josh was on and he came and got me.'

'Has someone tried his home in case Morris just lost him?'

'I went over myself. Lives alone, his neighbours said. His wife died during the winter. Don't worry, boss, I didn't tell them anything.'

The Constable rubbed his chin, feeling the stiff rasp of stubble. 'Have you talked to Morris?'

'Aye, just for a minute, then I sent him out again.'

'And what do you think. Is he telling the truth?'

He watched the deputy carefully framing his answer.

'I believe him. He's not a liar. He's always been a solid man, boss, he does the work as best he can. It's just . . .'

'What?'

'He's not too sharp. He's fine for little jobs, but this might have been too much for him.'

Nottingham stared hard at Sedgwick. 'So why did you pick him? You know how important this is.'

The deputy look back evenly. 'You said you wanted men on it right away. He was there, the better ones weren't.'

Nottingham grimaced in frustration.

'I'm sorry, John, you were just doing what I'd ordered. I told Josh I wanted Morris back here. I'll find out what happened. How many men do you have out looking?'

'Every single one of them, except those keeping an eye on the judge, and he's tucked up at home.'

Nottingham let out a long, slow sigh. 'We'll need men on the judge. We can't afford any problems there. And scour the bloody city for Rushworth. We need to find him sharpish.'

'Yes, boss.'

Nottingham was trying to sort through some papers, fretting and hoping for news, when the man walked into the jail. He knew Morris's face, although they'd not spoken often. Morris was a stooped, scrawny man with a heavy, dark beard that grew to his chest. His hair was lank and matted, face and hands dirty; he looked like a beggar in his layers of ancient clothes.

'Tha' wanted to see me, sir,' he said.

'You were following Rushworth.'

Morris considered the statement. 'Aye, that's what Mr Sedgwick told me to do.'

'I want to know everything that happened. Everything. Take your time. It doesn't matter how small.' Nottingham perched on the edge of the desk

'I went down to that warehouse. Tha' know the one?'

The Constable nodded.

'I waited till they all come out for the day.'

'Did you see anyone else waiting around?'

Morris shook his head.

'No, sir.'

'How did you know Rushworth?'

'Mr Sedgwick had told me what he looked like.'

'Where did he go after they all came out?'

He could see the man trying to slowly marshal his memories.

'He went along the Calls. There were some people about, so I didn't let myself get too far behind him.'

'How far away were you?'

Morris tried to estimate the distance in his head. 'Mebbe forty yards. Little bit more, perhaps. Fifty yards at most.'

'Did he look around? Did he talk to anyone?'

'Nay, he had his head down and he was striding out. Like people do when they're going home from work. Glad to be free.'

'And when he was in the Calls?'

'He ducked into this ginnel. I know it, it's just a short one, leads through to Kirkgate not far from t' Parish church.'

'What did you do?'

'I walked faster so I wouldn't lose him, sir.'

'But you did lose him.'

Morris hung his head.

'I know.' He paused. 'I'm sorry.'

'And by the time you'd reached the ginnel he'd gone?'

'Aye. It was like he'd just vanished.' He opened his eyes wide. 'I ran to the end and looked up and down the street, but he wasn't there. He'd just disappeared.'

'Could he have gone into any of the courts off the ginnel?'

'He could.' Morris admitted slowly. 'But I didn't hear a door or owt. I've got good ears,' he said with pride.

'What did you do after that?'

'I were starting to get worried. I looked around a bit, but I couldn't find him, so I came back here quick as I could.'

'You did the right thing, then,' Nottingham told him with a small smile. 'You go and get some rest. Report to Mr Sedgwick or Josh in the morning.'

'Yes, sir.' Morris looked up hopefully. 'I still have a job? Only I need the money . . .'

'You still have a job,' the Constable confirmed.

Once Morris had gone, a grateful grin lighting up his dirty face, Nottingham put on his greatcoat and left the jail. He needed to see the scene for himself, to try to understand how Rushworth could simply have gone.

He was certain Wyatt had him now, and barring a miracle, no one would see him alive again. Anger burned in his gut, fury at the killer. But there was also a tinge of admiration. The man was daring – and clever.

On Lower Briggate there was plenty of noise from the inns and beer shops as people drank the evening away. Whores plied their trade in isolation or gossiped in small groups as they waited for business, walking on tall wooden pattens to keep their cheap dresses from the mud. With the thaw had come the return of the city smells, the rich stew of shit, piss and rubbish all hidden by the cold.

He turned into the Calls, trying to keep his mind open to all the possibilities. By now the street was almost empty, and his footsteps resounded off the cobbles. Nottingham knew the ginnel Morris meant: a small lane close to the Parish Church that ran alongside the large property owned by Berkenhold, the merchant.

There was enough moonlight to see the high brick wall that kept people out of the orchard behind the big house. The other side was the frontage of old houses, the gaps between them leading to a warren of courts, the homes of the poor and desperate who could afford no better. How many people would be living back there, he wondered? Hundreds, most likely.

Snatch a man and take him into one of those and it would be almost impossible to find him. The entries were barely wider than a man's shoulders, dark, foreboding, and menacing in the night.

He walked through the ginnel and back. It was barely thirty yards long, a lost little place. There were three courts. He didn't even try to walk into them. He'd get the men down here and have them scour the places. It was always possible that the murderer had his rooms here. Someone might have seen something. He'd

have Sedgwick talk to the tenants here; with his easy manner they seemed to open up to him.

He'd been angry at Morris, but he understood the man wasn't to blame. He'd done exactly what was expected, and he'd never stood a chance against this murderer. In truth, he'd done the right thing to return to the jail and raise the alarm.

The ginnel came out on Kirkgate and Nottingham ambled slowly back to the jail. Could he have put all the pieces together earlier and identified Wyatt? No, he didn't have the information. And as soon as he'd found out, he'd taken steps to protect Rushworth and the judge. But Wyatt had the whip hand. He knew who he wanted, he'd had the time to spy on them and make his plans.

Finally Sedgwick returned, and Nottingham explained that he wanted all the courts off the ginnel searched, and everyone questioned.

'I don't know if Wyatt's there, John, so be careful. He's dangerous. If you even get a sniff of him I want to know about it.'

'I'll lay odds he won't be anywhere close to the place,' Sedgwick said.

Nottingham shrugged. 'You're probably right. But he wouldn't know we were following Rushworth. That must give us something.'

'But not the poor bugger he's got.'

'No,' the Constable acknowledged bleakly. In frustration he slapped the desk. 'Wyatt's spent seven years in the Indies. He must still be brown from the sun. That means he should be easy to spot in Leeds. He can't stay inside all the time. Why hasn't anyone seen him?'

'He's a smart bastard. You said so yourself, boss. He's worked this all out.'

'I know.' There was a sense of resignation in his tone.

Clouds had blown in from the West and a thin drizzle had started by the time Nottingham walked down Kirkgate. It would take away the last of the slush and leave many of the roads no better than quagmires. Carters would be stuck, tempers would fray. More problems for the morning.

He let himself into the dark house, removed his boots and climbed the stairs quietly. Stripping to his shirt, he washed at the ewer then pulled the blanket over himself, Mary's warmth radiating close by. In her sleep she turned to him, curling by his side. Smiling, he put his arm around her and pulled her closer.

Eleven

He left the cellar, closing the door firmly behind him, and stretched. Downstairs Rushworth was tied to a chair, his eyes covered and an old cloth stuffed into his mouth to keep him quiet.

He was already weary of the man's voice, his sorrowful whine no better than an infant's, grating in the ears and on the brain.

Wyatt took a tired apple, its flesh withered with time, from the table and used his knife to cut it in two. The autumnal smell rose and made him smile.

So far everything had been so easy. He'd expected some problems, but there had been nothing. He'd prepared carefully, calculating everything, his plans immaculate.

It would be harder the next time, he knew that. That was the challenge and he relished it. Gain something too simply and there was no triumph in it, no sweetness. He thought of Rushworth downstairs, talking inanely, grovelling to stave off the inevitable.

He knew the man was hoping for mercy, but there'd be none of that. He'd waited too long for this, endured too much to be magnanimous. This was his time and he'd relish every moment of it.

Wyatt finished the apple and drank deep from a mug of ale. He felt alive, he felt happy. There was still so much of Rushworth to enjoy, as long as he could keep the man quiet. And then there was much more work to do after he was dead.

He pulled down on the waistcoat. He'd worn it when he slashed Graves's throat and the spurting blood had turned the front of the garment an ugly red-black. It had terrified Rushworth when he put it on. Wyatt smiled grimly and opened the cellar door.

'No trace?' she asked.

'Nothing. He's just vanished. This murderer's a clever bastard.' Sedgwick shook his head in a mix of sadness and admiration before changing the subject. 'How's James been?'

'Good as gold.' Lizzie beamed. 'I took him down by the river earlier, over the bridge. I held him up so he could look down at the water.' She paused. 'You know what?'

'What?'

'He called me mam,' she announced proudly.

He took her hand, stroking the skin lightly.

'Does he ask for Annie any more?'

'Not in a fortnight now, John. He seems happy.'

And why wouldn't he be? Sedgwick wondered. Lizzie treated the boy like her own. She talked to him, played games with him, took him out.

She leaned across the table and kissed him as he ate. The gesture took him by surprise, but she was forever doing daft things like that, holding him, kissing him. At first the affection had astonished him; now he liked it.

'I love you, John Sedgwick,' she said softly.

Who cared what she'd been, he thought. She was a good lass even then, friendly and always ready to laugh. The six months they'd been living together had been joy. They'd made him realize how ground down he'd become with Annie, how their marriage had been ultimately as fragile as gossamer. She'd hated his job and vanished for something she believed was better, a life as a soldier's woman. He wished the man luck with her; he'd need it.

As soon as she'd heard the news, Lizzie had knocked at his door. He was amazed that she knew where he lived.

'She's gone, then?' she'd asked bluntly.

'Aye,' he admitted. The truth was that he was relieved when Annie left; he had his son, but he was uncertain and fearful for the future.

'Who's going to look after the little lad?'

With that she'd become part of his life, spending her days with James, her nights with Sedgwick. Within a week she'd brought over her possessions, two worn, faded dresses and a few small things. A month later, they'd moved to this new room, warmer and airier, just before winter began to exert its grip. A new start, he said, fresh surroundings and no memories.

'Tired?' she asked, jarring him out of his thoughts.

Sedgwick rubbed his eyes with the heels of his hands. 'Long past tired.'

'You get to bed. I'll blow out the candles,' she ordered tenderly.

In the dark he stared at the ceiling. The bed was cosy, and his arm slid around her.

'Do you ever think of going back?' he asked her.

'To what?' she answered sleepily.

'To what you used to do.'

That was his fear, that she'd grow tired of this domesticity and leave him. Leave James. Leave a hole in their lives.

She laughed gently, a sound that moved him more than any words.

'You're a daft beggar, you are. I've wanted you ever since I saw you. I'd have taken you away from her if I could. Does that tell you owt?'

'Aye.' He drifted away, a smile on his lips.

Nottingham was at the jail well before light. He'd heard the dawn chorus as he walked down Marsh Lane and over Timble Bridge, but it had brought him no pleasure. Holding Mary had soothed his soul a little, but once she was asleep his thoughts had begun to whirl uncontrollably.

All his life he had been a fighter. There had been times when that fight – finding enough food or a safe place to sleep – had meant the difference between life and death, and that had given him the desire never to lose. It was one of the qualities that made him perfect for this job.

Knowing that Wyatt had snatched a victim from under the nose of one of his men made him burn. He would not be outthought and outwitted by a killer, by a madman who saw death and defilement as apt revenge for the crime he'd been the one to commit.

He paused at the head of the ginnel, where the shadows slipped away from Kirkgate and the darkness seemed briefly absolute. Leeds wasn't that large, maybe seven thousand people. Wyatt was in it somewhere. Someone had seen him, someone sold him food, someone had rented him . . . what could he have rented?

Not a room, that much was certain. He couldn't have tortured, killed and skinned there. He needed somewhere larger, somewhere private. That narrowed it down a little. A house perhaps, or a workshop. He unlocked the door of the jail, glancing in the cells for anyone brought in by the night men. Just a pair of beggars, by the look of them, glad of a rest indoors for once, burrowed under their blankets and quiet to the world.

He put coal on the fire that had been banked for the night, and stirred the embers, watching the flames dazzle and heat seep into the room before taking off his heavy coat and pushing back his fringe.

For the first time since Rose's death he had hope in his heart. Inch by inch he and Mary were drawing closer again, beginning to emerge from the fog. It was painful and there was still so far to go, but they'd made their start.

He wouldn't allow Wyatt to crush that. He'd find him and mete out justice. That was his job. There would be no trial where details of the killing could emerge, nothing to tarnish the reputation of Leeds, so carefully tended and burnished, nothing that could affect the heartbeat of trade. He'd had to do this before, always reluctantly, and he had no doubt he'd have to do it again. The instances had been rare, but in every case he'd had no regrets.

He sat at his desk, a jumble of papers stacked before him. He knew he needed to take up Worthy's offer. It meant more manpower, more information. But what, he wondered, really lay behind it? He'd known the procurer far too long to take what he said at face value. Worthy was a man with his own reasons for things, his own brand of evil.

The door opened and Sedgwick ambled in, his eyes morning bright, his hair a tangle.

'Anything last night?' Nottingham asked him.

'No.' The deputy gave him the short answer. 'We searched almost everything, but there was bugger all to offer a clue. No one saw anything, no one heard anything.' He shrugged. 'Of course.'

'We need to find him before he kills Rushworth.' He didn't need to mention what would happen after Rushworth was dead. That knowledge hung between them like a dark promise.

'How?'

'Wyatt has to have space for what he does. And privacy.' He paused to allow the idea to sink in, waiting until Sedgwick began to nod his understanding.

'Makes sense,' he agreed. 'Somewhere with some isolation.'

'Start looking around today,' Nottingham ordered. 'He needs to eat and drink, too. He's buying things somewhere. Get Josh out asking around the shops and the traders.'

'I will.'

The Constable looked up at Sedgwick. 'Someone was talking to me about Graves's murder last night. He knew what had happened after.'

The deputy raised his eyebrows. 'It wasn't from me,' he said defensively.

Nottingham waved the idea away with his hand. 'I didn't think it was. Or from Josh. It was Amos Worthy who stopped me.'

'Oh aye? What's all this to do with him, then? I was hoping the winter might have claimed him.'

'He says Graves was good to him long ago.' He'd never explained to the deputy that his mother and Worthy had been lovers once; it was a history he needed to keep private.

'And?'

'And he wants to help us catch the murderer.'

Sedgwick glanced out of the barred window at people moving along Kirkgate, the sounds of the morning rising.

'I'd be wondering what's in it for him.'

'That was my first thought, too,' Nottingham agreed quietly.

'I've never seen him do owt that didn't benefit him or his purse.'

'Hard to believe, but I think he might be sincere this time. I can't see any way he can use this to his advantage. And the more people we have looking, the sooner we'll catch Wyatt. Agreed?'

'Maybe,' Sedgwick conceded cautiously.

'People will say things to Worthy's men they wouldn't say to us.'

'Rather than face a beating, you mean?'

'Not always, John.'

He waited as Sedgwick considered.

'You're going to use him, aren't you?'

'If Rushworth hadn't gone, I wouldn't have,' Nottingham replied reasonably. 'It's urgent now. And we've got sod all so far. You know that.'

The deputy let out a loud, slow breath.

'Aye, that's true.'

'So we've got nothing to lose.'

He wasn't sure if he was trying to justify the decision to himself or to the deputy.

'If we can save Rushworth,' Sedgwick warned. 'It might already be too late. And what about the Mayor? Or the Corporation?'

'We don't tell them.' His eyes flashed for a moment. 'They only ask that I do my job, not how I do it.'

'It's dangerous, boss.'

The Constable nodded slowly. He knew that well enough. He just had to make sure he kept control of everything.

'I'll be back in a while.'

His coat warm around him, Nottingham walked through the drizzle down Briggate. His mind was a jumble of thoughts, of Rushworth, of Worthy, of Graves, of Mary, of Rose.

Just before the bridge he turned on to Swinegate. With the thaw there was plenty of life on the street, the squall of families, shopkeepers setting out their wares, the powerful smell of horseshit from an ostler's yard, the heady scent of malt from an innkeeper's brewing.

He pushed open a nondescript door. It was never locked; there was no man in the city mad enough to try to steal from this place. An ageless crone sat in a room off the corridor, a mug of gin balanced on her lap, her eyes a thousand miles away.

He walked through to the kitchen. The windows were dirty, probably never cleaned, and a scattering of crusted dishes stood in the corners. Worthy was there, in his usual spot, standing by the table in the same coat and breeches as the day before, an empty plate on the table before him with a jug of small beer and cups. Two of his men, both young, large and imposing, idled in the corner, hands going for daggers as soon as they saw the Constable. The pimp raised his hand to stop them.

'It's all right, lads. You can go. I was expecting Mr Nottingham.'

The men sidled out, giving the Constable wary, suspicious looks.

'Were you?'

'Was I what, laddie?' Worthy sat back in his chair, exploring his teeth with a sliver of wood.

'Expecting me?'

The pimp gave an easy grin. 'Aye, I was. You're not a fool. You know you need help but you've wondered why I offered my services.' He tossed the wood aside and wiped his hands on his old, greasy waistcoat. He might well be one of the richest men in the city, Nottingham thought, but he never spent a penny he didn't have to on himself or his surroundings.

'You've turned it around in your head and you can find no hidden reason. So you've come here. Reluctant as ever.'

The Constable reached across and poured himself a cup of beer. 'And you're as astute as ever, Amos. I need your help.'

'Then you'd better tell me all about it, laddie, so we can work together properly.'

'Did you ever hear of a man called Abraham Wyatt?'

Worthy shook his head. 'Means nowt to me.'

'He was one of Graves's clerks. Stole some money, ended up transported to the Indies for seven years.'

'And he came back with revenge in his head?'

'In his heart,' Nottingham corrected him.

'So you think he's the one who murdered Sam?'

'I'm sure of it,' Nottingham said flatly. 'It's the first of four murders.'

Worthy's head snapped up, his eyes sharp and inquisitive.

'How do you know that?'

'That's what he implied in the first volume of his book with its special binding.'

'Special binding?'

'Now you know what happened to the skin,' the Constable told him.

Worthy remained silent for several breaths then shook his head. 'That's not the work of anyone human,' he declared finally. 'Four murders, he said. All like this? With the same ending?'

'Yes.'

'You believe him?'

'I do.' Nottingham paused. 'He's already snatched the second victim. That's why I'm here.'

'Who is it?'

'A man named Rushworth. He clerks for Graves, and he gave evidence at Wyatt's trial.'

Worthy nodded.

'And who are the other two?'

'Judge Dobbs. He handed down the sentence.'

'And?'

'I don't know.'

Worthy sighed lightly. 'Who arrested him?'

'The old Constable.'

'Who was there with him?'

'I was.'

'I know your mother didn't raise you to be both blind and a fool, laddie,' the pimp said in exasperation. 'Old Arkwright's dead.'

Suddenly, Nottingham understood. *He* was the fourth victim. For the love of God, he must have turned stupid. How had he missed something so obvious?

'Not nice to know someone wants to kill you, is it?'

'You'd know if anyone would,' the Constable responded, the anger at himself brimming over into his voice.

'Aye, I would,' Worthy replied mildly. 'Enough of them have tried. And failed.' He poured himself more of the beer and drank it down in a single swallow. 'You'd have done it yourself if you could.'

'I'd have put you in jail, Amos.'

'It'll never happen, laddie, and you know it.' He tapped the side of his nose. Worthy had too many important protectors in the city to end up convicted of anything: the merchants and aldermen who used his whores or borrowed his money.

Silence filled the air. Nottingham rubbed his chin, feeling the harsh bristle, a reminder that he needed a shave. He needed to be better armed, he thought. All he usually carried was a small dagger, little better than a penknife. Another knife, perhaps a primed pistol in his coat pocket. It wasn't something he wanted to do, but he was forewarned now. Wyatt was clever. He needed to be constantly aware and alert.

But unless they had the devil's own luck and found Rushworth soon, it would likely be several days until Wyatt tried to strike again. He'd need time with his victim, and longer still to cure the skin and write his book.

Doing that was as important to the man as the act of killing, Nottingham understood that. He needed it all to be known, put it all on paper, to indulge his evil and play out his part.

'Penny for them, laddie?'

Nottingham shook his head. 'Just thinking.'

'So how are we going to stop him?' Worthy asked.

'We need to find him.'

'And when we do?'

The Constable paused for a moment. 'Kill him quietly.'

Worthy nodded and drained his cup. 'Aye, that's what I thought. They won't want folk to know too much about all this.'

'But that doesn't happen until I've talked to him.'

The pimp gazed at him quizzically.

'Why? You think you can make sense of something like this?'

Nottingham shrugged. 'I doubt if I'll be able to do that,' he admitted. 'I just want to know.'

'Don't waste your time,' Worthy advised. 'There are some things that are beyond understanding.'

The Constable stood up.

'You'll get your men out?'

'Aye. Do you know anything about him that might help?'

'He's spent seven years in the Indies. His skin will still be dark, he'll stand out. I don't know what he's doing for money. He's probably taken a place that's quiet. Not a room. Bigger.'

'It's a start. I'll tell my lads.'

'And he stays alive until I talk to him.'

Worthy held up his palms in submission. 'If that's what you really want, laddie.'

'It is. And I don't need one of your men watching me.'

The pimp's eyes twinkled. 'The thought never occurred to me.'

Thirteen

Wyatt would need to buy food. The Constable had said that, but Josh had already worked it out for himself. A man couldn't live on air. But a man could be sly. Josh knew the tricks, the places to find food without spending money and without being seen by those who cared.

For the last few days he'd kept his eyes open, talking quietly to the folk who lived that way themselves, out on the edges of society. They were what he'd been himself just a few short months before. The dispossessed, the invisible, the hopeful and the hopeless. Most of the time they stayed out of sight, taking only what they needed, so that the good citizens were hardly aware of their existence. But there were those who saw things the others missed. These were the ones who'd notice someone like Wyatt. They were the ones to talk to.

His hair was wet from the light rain, lank against his face. Frances had cut it with an old pair of scissors a few days before. The blades were dull and she'd ended up hacking off hunks. Still, at least he didn't look like a beggar lad now, she'd told him. He'd caught his reflection in a shop window a few times, taken aback by the change, his hair short, almost neat. The boss had said nothing, but he'd noticed and exchanged a short glance with Mr Sedgwick.

Josh drifted up the road that extended beyond the Head Row into Woodhouse. Beyond lay Headingley, then Otley, Ilkley, and a whole country past that. All places he'd never been and didn't care about.

After a mile he turned on to a small track of bare, muddy earth and made his way up to a copse on the peak of the hill. Hidden away within the trees was a small community of people surrounded by their painted wooden caravans, with all the horses, their real wealth, hobbled beyond that. Old canvas had been pitched from the branches for shelters.

They'd arrived before winter's grip turned cruel, and made the raw place their own. They'd been coming for years now, arriving with the season and departing in spring. Josh had first gone to see them when he was still a child, oddly drawn to these exotic folk. They'd treated him kindly, and he'd come to know a few of them, to like and trust them. He'd often brought Frances with him. She been entranced by the bright colours of their clothes and caravans, by the simple pleasure they took in their hard lives, and even by their strange tongue. Once they'd discovered he'd become a Constable's lad they'd been wary, but their suspicions had quickly vanished.

Josh nodded at some familiar faces. A stewpot hung over a fire, and the tempting smell of rabbit meat filled the encampment. Water sat nearby in a pair of ewers, both cracked and ancient.

Women young and old tended babies and small children ran wild, their faces and hands rimed with dirt, feet bare in the mud. They laughed and danced, and Josh envied them the carefree times he'd never known. He walked on to where five men gathered together around a small fire by a cluster of the painted vehicles. Two were still youthful, their beards wispy, the other three older. The eldest sat in the centre, a man of indeterminate age, his skin darker, a sharp contrast to his heavy white moustache. They knew Josh, they'd welcome him, but they still kept their reserve. He was an outsider here; he was the law.

He bowed his head for a moment and drew a loaf of bread from under his heavy coat, putting it down near the flames.

'Thank you,' the oldest man said, his eyes smiling, speaking slowly in strongly-accented English. 'You are well?'

'Yes, I am,' Josh responded, and added, 'thank you.'

'And your girl?'

'She's going to have a baby.'

The man beamed and translated. Everyone smiled widely.

'New life is a good thing,' the old man told him. 'But I think you come for other reasons today.'

'I'm looking for someone. I thought you might have seen him.'

One of the young men, who wore a permanently angry expression, raised his voice.

'And why would we tell you if we had, boy?'

'Because he kills people,' Josh answered.

The elder raised his hand to bring calm. 'Why you think we see him?'

'You and your people see things most folk miss. You go to the places a lot of people don't go.'

The man nodded slowly. 'And this man, who is he? How we know him?'

'He has dark skin. He was in the Indies for a long time.' Josh hesitated. 'That's all I know.'

The men looked from one to another, communicating with small facial inflections.

'It is possible,' the old man admitted cautiously. 'We maybe see man like that.'

'I need to know where he lives,' Josh told them. 'Before he kills more people.'

The old man talked with the others once more, words flying in their incomprehensible language. Josh half-watched the men while he listened to the lively sounds of the camp and the whinnying of the horses tethered in the distance. The Gypsies made their money from horse trading, they'd told him, and from the small things they could sell.

'We see him again, we find out where he live,' the man agreed finally. 'Some of my family, they feel is wrong to help the law. The law is often unkind to us.' He frowned momentarily as memories slipped through his mind. 'But you are our friend.'

'Will he pay to know?' the young man burst out.

'The Constable will pay for information,' Josh said. 'And you'll have his gratitude.'

'That can be a good thing to have,' the old man decided.

'If you find him, you can send one of the children to tell me.'

The old man nodded. The deal had been done. Josh walked back through the camp and down the track, finally resting against a dry stone wall.

He knew they were men of their word. They'd keep any eye out for Wyatt, and if they found him, he'd hear. There'd be a small tug on his sleeve, a few whispered words.

Slowly he stood and began to walk back into Leeds. He gazed down at the city from the hill, smoke rising from the chimneys, the low grey haze of cloud. Wyatt was there. Rushworth was there. Frances was there. But he had a day's work to do before he saw her again.

Nottingham felt the grit churning in his soul. Many people had threatened him in his time as Constable, but few had ever done anything about it, and never as cold-bloodedly as this.

He'd been given his warning. But if Wyatt wanted him dead, he'd have a fight on his hands. At the jail he took a pair of knives from the cupboard and sharpened their blades carefully on a whetstone before sliding them into their sheaths and then into his coat pockets. For a brief moment he considered a pistol, then dismissed the idea. He'd never enjoyed the idea of guns; they only offered a single chance, and he preferred better odds than that when playing for his life.

Armed, he gathered his coat tight about him and locked the jail. Outside, the wind was beginning to whip up from the north. The temperature was falling again and the rain was turning to light snow that rushed angrily around his face.

No more winter, he prayed. There had been enough of that already, too much of it, too many dead, too many hopeless. As he walked up Briggate, past the Ship Inn and the Moot Hall, he saw the faces of the people, the happiness drained from them, walking with heads bowed like penitents.

He ducked into a court between two houses, the opening barely wider than his shoulders, and the wind ceased. He stopped, breathing slowly. Beyond the short passage the ground opened out, muddy and cloying, surrounded by ramshackle houses of stone and wood where the gardens had once stood a century or more before.

Nottingham picked his way across the mire and hammered on a faded blue door. There was no latch or lock he could see, but he knew the man inside would have taken care to make it secure.

He waited, standing back slightly so he could be seen. Finally, as he was about to give up and turn away, the door opened soundlessly. He walked into a dark hallway, following a moving shadow, then into a room where sober grey light fell through dirty glass. Finally he stopped and said, 'Peter.'

The other man turned. He had to be in his fifties now, the Constable thought, wizened, the wrinkles carved deep into his face, grey hair a thinning tangle on his head, like so many other men who'd been ground down by life. He wore a dusty, dark coat with rips in the shoulders and pockets and dirty, buff-coloured breeches. In a crowd no one would notice him, which was exactly what he wanted. Peter Hawthorn was a peacher, a man who heard about crimes and made his money by informing on the criminals.

'Mr Nottingham.' He had a rough, low voice, scarcely more than a growl. As long as the Constable had known him he'd never used more words than absolutely necessary, hoarding them close like bullion.

'You know who I'm looking for.'

Hawthorn nodded.

'There's very good money in it for whoever finds him for me.'

Hawthorn nodded again.

'But it has to be soon.'

He didn't know how the peacher had managed such a long life, and he'd never asked. Over all the years some must have known he'd given them up. But he was still here, still making a bare living from his trade in souls.

'He's been in the Indies, so his skin will be burned dark. He's staying out of the way, but he's in Leeds somewhere.'

He waited for an acknowledgement, but Hawthorn said nothing. Finally Nottingham turned on his heel and left.

On Briggate snowflakes still lashed his face and hands, and it felt even colder than before. If this grew any worse, he thought, the slush would freeze and the streets would be treacherous. The snow was already starting to settle on his shoulders and in his hair as he walked, and back at the jail he had to shake his great-coat clean.

He stoked up the fire in the grate and settled into his seat to compose his latest report for the Mayor. It would be brief; there was precious little new to tell. As he wrote, he wondered about Rushworth. Was he still alive, or had Wyatt already killed him? He realized in his heart that they'd never find him in time. The next they'd see would be the body and then the book that would inevitably follow.

Worthy's help could make the difference. He hated to admit it, but he knew it was true. With more men looking, it had to only be a matter of time until they took Wyatt. But how much time did he have? Not enough, that was certain. And there'd be a price to pay in the future for the pimp coming to his aid. There'd be some kind of favour to be done, an eye to be turned away at a crucial moment. Nothing in this life came free.

He set the pen down. He couldn't settle; the world was buzzing in his head. Someone wanted to kill him. Someone he loved more than his own life was dead. He'd have given himself up for Rose to live, and so would Mary. But God never made his bargains so easily. Instead you had to learn to live in the long shadow of sorrow and face whatever else He put before you.

There was nothing more he could do here. Putting on the coat, still wool-damp and heavy, he set out for home. The temperature had dropped further, the mud freezing rapidly and crunching under his boots, the snow still coming down, small patches lying deceptively white and pure atop the hardening dirt. It would be bitter tonight, and for the next few days as winter gave a harsh reminder it wasn't done with them yet.

Emily was sweeping the floor. She held the broom awkwardly, pushing it in short stabs that gathered no dust. Without thinking he came up behind her, put his hands over hers and said,

'Try it this way, love. It'll be easier.'

He guided her so she made long strokes across the wood. This had been Rose's job when she lived here, and she'd always tackled it briskly and efficiently.

'That's the way,' he told her. 'You've got it now.'

She turned and smiled gently at him. He was aware of how small and dry her hands were, and uncomfortable with the way her hips swayed as she moved. He returned her smile, for a moment feeling the weight of all the dying lifting from him.

She was the future now, with her dark eyes and long, smooth hair. His only little girl, a young woman now, moving further away from him with each day. Pray God she'd survive, even if his name didn't.

'I didn't know you could do housework, papa,' she teased. They were the first joyful words he'd heard from her in weeks.

'You know me, I can do anything.' He winked and walked into the kitchen. Mary was trimming the fat off a piece of pork.

'I just wanted to be with you for a little while,' he explained before she could say anything. He needed this woman, he needed her love, her trust, the way she accepted his devils and his truths.

'I don't think you've ever come home in the daytime before, Richard.' Her voice tried to be light, but he could hear the undertone in it.

'I just wanted a few minutes of peace.'

She put down the knife and wiped her hands on an old cloth before holding him close.

'Well, there's precious little of that around here today. Emily's decided she wants to be helpful, and I've spent half the morning having to go over what she's done.'

'She'll learn. At least she's trying. We should be grateful for that.'

'Oh, I know. But it would be quicker if I did it all myself.'

'She needs to know. Before we know it she'll be a wife herself.'

He could feel the ghost of Rose rise briefly, then vanish again.

'All in good time,' Mary said.

'Yes,' he agreed. 'No hurry.'

But time might not be something they possessed. He dared not tell her that his name was on Wyatt's list. She felt warm in his arms, a part of himself, the best part.

'I'll get you some food,' she said, breaking away to bustle, cutting bread and cheese and pouring a mug of ale. He sat at the table, watching her work, fingers nimble and assured in her kingdom, until she put a plate before him.

'I'll go back after this,' he told her. 'There's plenty to do.'

'When isn't there?' she wondered.

'More than ever at the moment.'

'It won't ever end, and you know it.'

'True.'

'And that's why you love it, Richard.'

He nodded, knowing that was true as well. Some men had drink as their weakness. For him it had always been his work. From the moment he'd become a Constable's man, all those years ago, he'd known this was for him. It meant too many hours away from his family, but even now it was a price he'd gladly pay to do the job.

He chewed slowly, washing the food down with the ale, and watched Mary as she worked, carefully cleaning the knives and scouring dishes. She glanced out of the window and sighed.

'Do you think this winter will ever leave?' she asked bleakly.

'Eventually,' he answered. He knew exactly what she meant. As long as the cold gripped them, Rose was still close. Once the sun finally arrived and the season changed, there would be fresh, true hope for the future, a warmth they could feel inside as well as out. He stood, held her tight and kissed her brow softly.

'I need to get back to the jail.'

She nodded and drew back to hold him at arm's length.

'Why did you really come home, Richard?'

'Because I wanted to be with the people I love most in the

world.' He squeezed her arm lightly. It was an honest answer, even if it wasn't a complete one. He couldn't tell her how scared of life he felt sometimes. He couldn't tell anyone. He just needed the quiet reassurance of his home. Softly, he stroked her sleeve with his fingertips.

'I'll be back tonight. I'll try not to be too late.' It was a promise he'd made and broken so often that the words were more ritual than promise.

Emily was on the stairs, awkwardly pushing the broom into the crevices and corners. He paused for a moment to watch her until she felt his glance and turned to face him.

'You're seeing how it's done now.'

'I'm slow.' She smiled. 'Rose was much better.'

'We all have to start somewhere, you know.'

'I think mama will see I have plenty of practice.' She pushed the hair away from her forehead in a gesture that was so like his own it disarmed him.

'Well, they say practice makes perfect.' He gave her a wink and pulled on his coat.

The besom stopped its swish across the stair.

'Papa?' Emily asked.

'What is it?'

'They say that God gathers those close whom he loves, don't they?'

'Some people do,' he agreed, wondering at her question.

'If that's true,' she said with real concern in her voice, 'does that mean He hates the rest of us? He leaves us here to miss them and mourn them.'

'I don't know, love' he told her finally. 'All we can do is hope He loves us all.'

Outside, the sky had lowered further, and the snow was still coming down. Endless clouds the colour of dull pewter rolled into the city. Even before he reached Timble Bridge the greatcoat was covered in white. Underfoot the mud had hardened into a treacherous, slippery mass.

For all that, his heart felt lighter. For the first time in months Emily had sounded a little like the girl she'd once been. Quieter and more thoughtful, definitely, and less challenging, but none the worse for that, given how wilful she'd been.

Children dead in body, children dead in spirit, he thought. He shivered. This winter, tossing up its dead and throwing them into the earth, was going to make atheists of them all.

At the jail he tried to settle back into his report. The words came slowly and awkwardly, vainly attempting to catalogue progress where there was none. He laboured to the end, scratching and sawing on the paper, then threw his quill down on the desk. The afternoon had slipped away into twilight while he'd worked. He lit a candle and sat back in the chair.

Sedgwick and Josh came in together, their voices loud in the small room as they complained about the weather. Nottingham waited as they shook out the snow from their coats.

'You'd better sit down,' he said. 'I've got something to tell you.'

'What's that, boss?' Sedgwick asked.

'It seems our friend Wyatt wants to kill me.'

Fourteen

He could count his heartbeats — two, three, four — whilst they digested what he'd told them. It was Josh who spoke first.

'How do you know?' he asked.

'Wyatt said his book will be in four volumes. That's four victims.'

'I know,' Josh replied. 'I heard you two talking.'

'You weren't supposed to,' Nottingham chided him, then softened. 'But I'd have been disappointed in you if you didn't.' He held up one finger. 'He's already killed Graves, the man he stole from.' A second finger joined the first. 'He has Rushworth, unless we're lucky enough to drag him back alive.' The third finger. 'Judge Dobbs, who sentenced him to transportation.' Then the last finger, pointing at himself. 'Richard Nottingham. I was with the old Constable who arrested him, and the old Constable is dead.'

'So what are we going to do, boss?' Sedgwick wondered seriously.

Nottingham reached into his greatcoat where it hung on the hook and produced the knives.

'We're going to be prepared,' he announced. 'He's set us the challenge, and I'm damned if I'll let him win it. I want you two armed. If you find him, let him find the mercy of God, not of justice.'

He looked at them calmly, watching them both. 'I don't want any of the men shadowing me. Wyatt already proved how good he was when he snatched Rushworth. I can look after myself. I want to tempt him to come for me.'

'But boss—' Sedgwick started to protest, but the Constable held up his hand.

'No buts, John. I need you out there looking for him. It's bad enough he's beaten us and got Rushworth, but can you imagine what'll happen if he gets the judge? The whole story will come out then, we won't be able to stop it.'

'What about me?' Josh asked.

'You're my ears and eyes out there.' He smiled. 'You hear things and you see things no one else sees. You know what I mean.' He watched the boy's skin flush with pride, then saw Sedgwick's frown. 'I mean it, John,' he warned.

'Boss—'

'No.' It was a short, simple word, and this time it conveyed everything. 'I needed you to know what was happening. Wyatt's not going to get me, and he's not going to get the judge.'

Inside, he'd already given up on Rushworth, sacrificed him. Failed him. Another victim of the winter. Wyatt had him, and they weren't going to find him alive. Who would be left to mourn him and try to understand what had happened?

'What else can we do to find Wyatt?' he asked aloud.

'We've been scraping the barrel for days, boss,' Sedgwick said. 'The man's vanished.'

'Only the dead vanish. And this bastard's not going to die on us yet. Not until we have him.' Nottingham's eyes were as hard as the weather outside. 'Get the night men looking everywhere.'

The deputy glanced at him quizzically. The Constable leaned forward, rubbing his fingers across his mouth.

'The fact is that he's almost certainly killed Rushworth by now. That means he has to get rid of the body.'

The others nodded.

'His best chance to do that without being seen is at night.'

'He did it in the day last time, boss.'

'And we weren't looking for him then. Have the men check everyone where one man is propping up another or seems dead drunk.'

'Some nights, that could be half the population of Leeds.'

Nottingham waved away the objection.

'Let them earn their money for once. It's as good a chance to find him as we've got.'

If he isn't too clever for them, he thought. So far Wyatt had shown more tricks than a conjuror.

'Get them on it, John.'

'Yes, boss.'

Outside, Sedgwick quickly dragged Josh into the White Swan and found a bench in the corner, away from the fire and the loud voices of people railing at winter's return. He held his hand up for ale, and once the pot boy had served them, he began to talk quickly in a low voice.

'So what are we going to do about the boss?'

'What can we do?' the boy asked.

'We're not going to leave him to go up against Wyatt himself, that's for certain.'

'But he told us not to follow him.'

The deputy took a drink and shook his head. 'There's a time to ignore orders,' he said firmly. 'You're the one to do it. I'm too tall, he'd spot me in a second. You're the one no one sees, he said so himself.'

Josh nodded slowly. He couldn't deny it. It was a skill that had kept him alive for years before he'd become a Constable's man. He'd grown in the last months, but he was still small, able to slide in and out of places, to avoid the eye. And he desperately wanted the boss alive.

'So what do you want me to do?'

'Your job now is to follow the boss and make sure he never knows you're there. I'm ordering you, I'll take responsibility.'

'What do I do if I see Wyatt?' Josh asked. He knew his limits. He'd never best a grown man in a fight.

'If anyone looks threatening, you yell and kill them. Simple as

that.' He said the words flatly and with finality. He raised his
eyebrows. 'Understand?'

Josh nodded.

'Right. Finish your ale and get to it.'

Nottingham was deep in his sleep when the noise woke him,
loud and persistent. Slowly he groped his way to wakefulness and
realized someone was knocking on the door. He pushed the
fringe off his face, picked up the cudgel he kept at the bedside
and walked quietly downstairs. In a swift single movement he
opened the door, ready to strike. The bitter air was a shock
against his flesh, pushing him immediately, fully awake.

Josh was there, his hair wild from running, his breath clouding
as he panted. The Constable could see his footprints in the snow
that now lay on the road.

'What is it?'

'There's been a riot,' the boy gasped. 'The apprentices. Mr
Sedgwick said you'd better come.'

Nottingham nodded, trying not to shiver in the cold. 'Tell him
I'll be there as soon as I can.'

'He told me to wait for you.'

The Constable dragged on his clothes, feeling every year of
his age.

'What is it?' Mary asked, sounding sleep-dazed, her mouth
hidden by the blanket, the words curious more than concerned.

'Just the apprentices.' It was the only explanation needed. From
time to time they'd go out drinking, against the terms of their
contracts, and it would bubble over into fighting and destruction.
They'd arrest a few of them, break a few heads, and that would
be the end of it for a while. It was the way it had always been,
further back than anyone remembered.

Josh was standing outside the door, trying to burrow himself
into his greatcoat, his hands ploughed into his pockets. The
Constable knew why Sedgwick had ordered him to stay. Security.
Just in case Wyatt was lying in wait, the wolf hiding in the places
where there was no light.

'Is it bad?' Nottingham asked as they started to walk.

'No worse than usual, Mr Sedgwick says.'

'That's a small comfort, I suppose.'

He strode out hard, feeling his eyes beginning to tear from the cold. The snow had ended, but there was about two inches of it atop mud that had frozen hard into awkward waves and gullies. The clouds remained, low and thick, a feather bolster over the city, leaving the night moonless.

'Boss?' Josh asked in a tentative voice as they crossed the bridge.

'What is it?'

'How old were you when you became a father?'

What a strange question, he thought, and had to ransack his memory for the age.

'Twenty-one. Why? Is that girl of yours in the family way?'

The silence gave him his answer. Jesus, he thought, they begin so young. Or maybe they simply didn't know any better.

'She says she is. But she doesn't look big.'

Despite himself, Nottingham grinned. 'You give her time. If she's carrying, she'll grow. How long have you known her?' he asked, trying to sound as if the question had no weight.

'A long time. She was one of those I looked after back when . . .' Josh's words trailed away. 'You know.'

Back when you were a cutpurse, the Constable thought. She'd probably be dead now if you hadn't taken responsibility for her.

'Do you love her?'

The boy took his time about answering. 'I don't know,' he decided. 'What is love, anyway?'

'Now that's a question men have been asking for centuries.' They were heading up Kirkgate, past the Parish Church and close to the jail. 'We'll talk more about this later. Meanwhile we have work to do.'

A pair of candles lit the office and the fire roared in the grate, as welcoming as a kiss. Noise came from the cells, the overloud voices of young men filled with anger and drink. Sedgwick was leaning against the desk, blood clotted around a gash on his forehead, a heavy cudgel sticking out of his pocket.

'They got you?' Nottingham asked.

'One did, but he's hurting a lot worse now.'

'Is everything all under control?'

'Pretty much, boss. We've got the worst of them here, the men are returning some to their masters. A few ran off.'

'How many were there?' Nottingham wearily took off his coat

and sat at the desk. There would be all the documents to fill out, some prisoners to commit to the Petty Sessions, a few to release with no more than hard threats, all of them requiring words written on paper.

'About forty, near as I could tell. They'd been at the Talbot.'

Nottingham rolled his eyes. More bad things happened there than at any tavern in Leeds. 'Did they do much damage?'

Sedgwick shrugged.

'We've had worse. Some windows broken on Briggate. They started a few scraps but nothing major until they ran into us.'

Nottingham nodded. His men knew how to deal with the apprentices when they turned rowdy.

'What time is it?'

'Three, maybe?' Sedgwick shrugged. 'Four? I've no idea.'

'You go on home, John. You've done a good job. Tell the men that, too. I'll take a look for damage when it's light. You can leave, too, Josh.'

It wasn't worthwhile walking home to his own bed, his own wife. His mind was working now, there'd be no more sleep. He noted the silent glance between the other two as he wished them good night.

The dawn came in stages of grey that slowly swept night off into corners and crevices. He heard the bell of the Parish Church strike seven and glanced through the window. Smoke was rising from the chimneys, Leeds was alive but staying behind closed doors where possible. Stragglers hurried down the streets, their heads bowed in protection.

He put on the coat, grateful it had had a few hours to warm. He'd deal with the apprentices later, once he'd tallied their damages.

It was more than he'd hoped but less than he'd feared. A total of twelve windows broken and four signs torn down. The shop-keepers were out, attempting to clear up the mess, seeking glass in the snow and boarding up the holes. He made note of their complaints and tried to mollify their anger, softly reminding a few of them that they'd once been apprentices themselves and wild as the night.

At least they'd had the sense not to do anything to the Moot

Hall. That would have seen the Corporation come down on them hard. But they hadn't even managed the wit to throw things at the statue of old Queen Anne above the doorway.

He was up at the Head Row, about to cross over and see if there had been any problems on New Street when someone called his name. He turned, one hand sliding into his pocket for the knife, only to see Kearney the butcher.

'Thank God I've found you,' he said, his voice urgent and afraid, his eyes wide. 'I think you'd better take a look. There's a body at the top of Lands Lane.'

Fifteen

Rushworth, he thought anxiously. It had to be Rushworth.

He dispatched a boy to find some of his men and rouse Brogden the coroner, then he walked up Lands Lane, following it from Briggate, around the corner, up to where it met the orchards of the old manor house.

He could see the body from a hundred yards away, its shape dark and rounded against the glittering white of the snow. Nottingham slowed his pace, eyes on the ground, seeing how many had left footfalls.

Ten yards from the corpse he stopped completely. This wasn't Rushworth. He recognized the small cap pinned to the hair and the tumble of rags that served as clothing. It was Isaac the Jew.

He edged closer, eyes examining everything. A runnel of blood under Isaac's head had left a wide stain. He reached down and dipped his finger in it. It was cold now, but it had been warm enough to melt the snow a little.

The corpse lay on its side, head tilted back, old empty eyes gazing to heaven, hands clenched into small, gnarled fists.

Isaac had told him once where he was born, but he'd forgotten the name of the country. It had sounded like poetry in the man's faltering English.

'Here you hunt animals,' he'd said, his accent guttural and heavy.

'There they killed us for their sport.' And the mist of tears would cover his eyes as the memories came, to stay unspoken.

He'd tried to explain, too, about the skullcap and what it meant, but Nottingham had never understood its significance. Now it was just a circle, another scrap of old cloth.

The Constable walked very slowly around the body, kneeling, examining. Someone had hit Isaac hard on the back of his thin old man's skull. Nottingham gradually widened the circle of his search, looking for Isaac's pack, for a bloodied branch, for anything that might help.

By the time Brodgen arrived, heavily bundled, face flushed by the cold air, he'd found the murder weapon. A dead branch ripped from one of the apple trees in the orchard, just yards away. It was heavy enough to need two hands, but easy to swing hard, and deadly. Fragments of bone clotted with hair and brains were stuck to one end.

There was no sign of the man's pack.

'Constable,' was all Brodgen offered as a greeting. Nottingham dipped his head in reply. The coroner seemed determined to make everything as simple as possible and return to the warmth of his hearth.

'Murder?' he asked.

'No question,' the Constable said.

Brodgen nodded, not even pausing to look closely at the body. It was just another poor man of no interest, someone beyond his horizon and past his concern.

'Murder it is, then,' he agreed and walked away. The judgement had been given; the corpse could be moved. He waited until the men arrived with the old door and the winding sheet stained with the blood of so many. They'd take Isaac to the jail where he could lie until he filled a pauper's grave.

He had no idea what the Jews did for their dead, how they shrived them. He didn't even know what had brought Isaac to Leeds, why he'd stayed or how lonely he'd been for his own kind.

Josh arrived as the Constable was writing his daily report detailing the riot. The apprentices were already at the Petty Sessions to wait on their fines and their masters' wrath. The boy's eyes were red-rimmed, his face tight.

'Couldn't sleep?' Nottingham asked, and Josh shook his head.

'It's like my head won't empty. The thoughts won't go away.'

'That's what happens,' the Constable sympathized. He'd experi-enced so many nights like that since Rose's death. 'They build up and gnaw at you.' He paused. 'Someone killed Isaac the Jew last night.'

He watched as Josh's face sharpened and his mind focused. 'Where?'

'Lands Lane, by the orchard. Hit him on the head with a branch and cracked his skull open.'

'He gave me and Frances clothes.'

Nottingham waited.

'Back when I started working for you. He told me I was doing a good thing, so he was going to do a good thing. He had some strange word for it.'

'Do you know where he lived?' Nottingham ran a hand through his hair.

'The last I knew he had a room in that old court off Vicar Lane, you know, the one everyone says is haunted.'

Nottingham knew it well. The story had circulated for years, probably even generations. A woman who'd starved to death in the days of Queen Bess was supposed to appear screaming out for God's mercy on herself and her child. It was a good tale, and there were plenty of those who'd sworn they'd seen her. When he was young he'd waited there for her himself, still and silent through a pair of long autumn nights. But cold bones were all he'd received for his pains.

'I'll go and see what he had.'

'I can come with you,' Josh offered quickly.

'If you like.'

So that was the plan, he thought. Keep the lad close to him to help hold Wyatt at bay. Josh was willing enough, but he was too young, too slight. Wyatt was ruthless; the boy wouldn't stand a chance.

On Vicar Lane the ample richness of the Vicar's Croft gave way to smaller dwellings, the entrances to the courts like knife openings between houses. He let Josh lead the way, sliding down a small passage with snow hard underfoot, the walls of the build-ings rough and dark against his shoulders.

'Over there,' Josh pointed. 'Top floor.'

'Are you coming in with me?'

'I'll wait out here.'

Nottingham nodded. The boy was taking his duty seriously, and he was glad about that. Josh was dedicated; he'd proved to be a good find.

Half the stairs were missing, making the ascent dangerous. The only light came through a single broken window on a landing, shards of glass on the wood covered with years of cobwebs and grime.

At the top a door had been forced off its hinges, hanging forlorn, awkward and broken. Nottingham gripped the knife in his pocket and eased his way through the gap.

Perhaps the room had been neat yesterday. Now, though, it was chaos. A chest had been broken open, the jaws of its lock gaping, the contents cast wide on the floor. The bedsheet had been cut, and the old straw of the mattress scattered.

Other than destruction and violence, there was little to see. A six-pointed star, beautifully carved from wood and polished, was nailed to the wall. The glass inside the tiny window was clean and clear.

So someone killed Isaac then came here looking for something, he thought. He walked the room, five paces by four, inspecting the floorboards to see if any were loose, looking for any hiding place. There was nothing.

No papers, no memories. Isaac was dead and there were no anchors of his life here. A few clothes, worn but carefully cleaned, a spare pair of shoes. But what did any poor man have to leave behind besides debt and despair?

He turned, ready to leave, and was shocked to see an old woman standing in the doorway. For a moment he thought the stories were true after all, that the ghost did walk. She was so frail as to be insubstantial, and he wondered if he blinked whether she'd be gone. Then he saw her eyes, blue, sightless, and knew she was very real.

Her back was as straight as a girl's, her wrists as thin as wire, her clothes fashionable three decades earlier but cared for, the apron and cap starched crisp and white.

'So you thought you'd rob him, too.' Her voice was firm, unwavering. 'I'm not afraid of you.'

No, he thought with admiration, you're afraid of nothing.

'Mistress, I'm the Constable of Leeds,' Nottingham introduced himself.

'He's dead, isn't he?' she asked, and he saw her hand tremble before she clutched her dress. 'I thought he must be when he didn't come home. He always came home. And I knew it when the others came.'

'The others?'

She answered his question with one of her own. 'Did they kill him?'

'I suspect they did,' he told her.

'There were two of them. I live under here. I heard their footsteps and their voices during the night. They woke me. By the time I could dress and get up here, they'd gone. Was he murdered?'

'Yes,' Nottingham told her. 'I'm sorry.' That was why he'd never heard her. She was intimate with this place and moved silently, knowing each inch.

'They were looking for his gold. Not that there was any to find. Isaac was as poor as me. Look around, you can see that, can't you?'

'I can,' he agreed.

'But people think, he's a Jew, he must have a fortune hidden away.' He could hear her bitterness. 'We ate together. He cooked for me, he gave me clothes.'

'He was a good man,' was all Nottingham could say. 'Did you hear anything these men said?'

She stayed perfectly still. Only fury and sorrow were stopping her vanishing before his eyes, he thought.

'Not the words.'

'But?' He could sense there was more.

'The tone. They were young. There was money in their voices.'

'I see.' He walked across the room, careful to avoid what was left of the things here, the detritus of Isaac's life. Gently he took her hand, her skin like aged vellum under his fingertips. The texture reminded him of Wyatt's book and he let go quickly.

'What was he like?' Nottingham asked.

'Like?' She turned into his words, and he was disconcerted to see blind eyes looking up at him. 'He was a good man, just as you said.' She let out a long sigh. 'He kept his faith when most would have given up. Do you know, ten years ago he walked to London and back because they have a synagogue there – that's where the Jews pray. When he returned he seemed to sparkle for a while.'

'How old was he?' Nottingham asked her. She shrugged briefly.

'He thought he might be seventy, but he didn't really know. He always said he was a man who walked across the world. He was a boy when he saw his family killed. He never even knew why it had happened. After that he just began walking.'

'And ended up here.'

'Eventually.' She smiled wanly. 'It took him many years. He had plenty of stories to pass the evenings.'

'How long did you know him?'

'Longer than I've known anyone.' Her hand clutched his, her fingers surprisingly strong. 'It wasn't long enough. He should have lived for a long time yet.'

'Yes,' Nottingham agreed soberly, 'he should. What's your name? In case I need to talk to you again.'

'Hannah. Hannah MacIntosh. My family came down from Scotland when I was small.' She allowed herself a small, quavering smile. 'So I know about wandering, too. I was born blind, just in case you were wondering. But I've learned to see in other ways.'

'Can I do anything to help you?'

She shook her head. 'No need for that. I'll manage. But thank you, Constable.'

He left her standing at the entrance to the room and made his way gingerly down the stairs, not daring to look back lest he'd imagined her.

Josh waited in the court, idling against the wall.

'His room's been ransacked. I saw the woman who lives in the room below. She heard two young men.' He decided not to mention the idea of a wealthy family. 'I couldn't find his pack there or near the body, so someone has that. They'll probably try to sell the clothes.'

Josh nodded his understanding.

'Get out there, start looking, talk to people. They'll help. Isaac was well-liked.'

The boy hesitated and Nottingham took him by the arm.

'I know John told you to look after me, but we have work to do.' His face softened. 'Don't worry, I can look after myself if Wyatt comes for me. Now go on, let's find whoever killed Isaac.'

Josh took off at a run, with all the energy of youth. Nottingham pulled up his coat collar against the cold and made his way through the ice and snow.

At the jail, Sedgwick was sitting behind the desk, his face dark and sober. As the Constable entered, he stood, the chair scraping back loudly on the flagstones.

'Boss—'

'You saw Isaac's body?'

'Boss.' There was foreboding, warning, in his voice. 'Rushworth,' he said.

Nottingham closed his eyes and felt the world explode. He'd become distracted; for a few hours he'd forgotten about the clerk.

'Is he here yet?'

'In the cold cell with Isaac.'

He walked through slowly, knowing what he'd find but hoping to put off the moment, to make it wait forever. The deputy followed, a lit candle in his hand.

'Where was he?'

'Down by the river. Close to where I found Graves.'

So this was Ralph Rushworth, he thought. He made a small corpse, with a bare, concave chest. His white breeches were dusty and dirty, stained with piss at the crotch. Nottingham stared down into the face. The features were tight, compact, the mouth drawn back over yellowed teeth, the nose long and bulbous at the tip. He lifted the right hand, light, almost weightless in death. The fingers were deep-stained with ink, calloused from years of holding a quill, nails bitten down roughly and rimmed with dirt. Just another clerk, with nothing to distinguish him from hundreds of others besides a few words spoken years ago in court.

He pushed the corpse on to its side. The skin had been neatly taken off the back, removed in a single sheet. What remained was livid and bloody, the body within no longer contained. Like Samuel Graves. This is the way they'll find me in time, Nottingham thought, if Wyatt has his way. He lowered Rushworth again.

'Anything by the body?'

'There was a set of scuffed footprints down from the bridge,' Sedgwick answered with a shrug. 'For what that's worth. No blood, nothing else.'

'Just one set? No sign he'd dragged Rushworth?'

'Only one,' the deputy confirmed. 'I'd just left home when a lad came and grabbed me. They'd gone down there for a snowball fight and seen him.'

'None of the night men saw anything?'

'Nothing out of the ordinary. Sorry, boss.'

Nottingham turned to look at the deputy.

'Two corpses in one night,' he said sardonically. 'Spring must be here.'

'Isaac . . . any idea who killed him yet?' Sedgwick asked.

'Two of them, by the sound of it. He was up on Lands Lane, by the orchard. They ransacked his room, too.'

'So they'd been watching him.'

'Seems like it.'

And we failed him. We failed both of them, he thought. We can't keep people alive. If the weather doesn't claim them, sickness does. If not that, then it's a knife or a blow. They all die, and we can't stop it. He felt as if the cold was seeping through his flesh and deep into his heart.

'We can't do anything more here. Let's go into the warmth.'

He put more coal on the fire, thinking as the blaze began to take hold.

'Get the men out and question people as they cross the bridge later. Someone will remember one man carrying another in this weather.'

'I've already got two of them asking around,' Sedgwick told him.

Nottingham smiled. 'I'm sorry. You know what to do. But get down there yourself. You're smarter than they are. You know what to ask, and how to listen. Even a good description of Wyatt would be something.' The Constable continued, 'Josh is looking into Isaac's murder.'

'We'll get Wyatt, boss.'

'Will we get him in time, though?' He sat down and ran a hand through his hair. 'You'd better put a closer watch on the judge, too.'

'And what about you? Who's going to watch you?'

Nottingham smiled slightly.

'You tried that with Josh. We don't have the men for it. I'm ready for Wyatt if he comes.' He paused and corrected himself. 'When he comes.'

'Boss.'

He looked up and saw the anguish on Sedgwick's face. The deputy began to pace.

'I've never gone against you, have I?'

'No, John, you haven't,' the Constable said mildly.

'Do you want to get yourself killed?'

'No.' Even as he answered, he considered the question. A month ago, even a week ago, he might not have cared. Now that he'd felt Mary's touch again, seen Emily smile, life had the possibility of becoming liveable again. 'No, believe me, I want to stay alive.'

'Then why won't you let me put a couple of the men on you? It could make all the difference.'

'Because . . .' Nottingham began. If he was going to be abruptly honest, there was little reason beyond his pride. He needed to show he was better than a murderer, however wily the killer might be. 'Who do we have who wouldn't be spotted in a minute by Wyatt? Apart from Josh.'

'No one,' the deputy admitted reluctantly.

'We've got men on the judge, we have men looking for Wyatt, Josh is out hunting for Isaac's killer. We just don't have enough people. Certainly not enough good people.'

'I know.'

'Go back to the bridge. See if the men have heard anything, and start asking some questions. If we can learn something, if we can take Wyatt soon, none of this will matter.'

Sedgwick nodded briefly, an agreement and an admission of defeat.

Alone, Nottingham penned a brief new report about the two murders. He knew that the Mayor would only be concerned with one of them, and then only for the murderer, not the victim.

He gathered up the paper and went out into the thin, angry cold to deliver it. As he passed the White Swan a figure emerged from the shadow of the door. His coat collar was turned up high, the hat pulled down to protect him from the weather.

As he passed the Constable he stumbled and slid on the ice, arms flailing for support, then grabbing Nottingham's coat. The Constable felt panic soar through his body. He'd let his guard fall. He couldn't react, couldn't reach his knives. Christ, this was Wyatt.

Sixteen

The man hissed two words — 'For Isaac' — righted himself and strode on quickly. For all the world it was an incident of the weather.

Nottingham turned back to the jail, bile rising in his throat. His hands were shaking, his back coated with a clammy sheen of sweat. He steadied himself against the wall for a moment, glad of the crude, real feel of the stone against his palm.

Inside, away from eyes that might see too much, he reached into his pocket and removed the scrap of paper that Hawthorn the Peacher had put there.

'The Henderson brothers' were the only words.

He breathed slowly, feeling his heartbeat slowly calm as he paced the floor. God save me, he thought. How could he have been so stupid? A moment was all it ever took. Any stranger, any man, could be Wyatt. He drank some ale from the mug on the desk, gulping at it greedily, waiting until the fear had all drained out of him. Then he looked at the paper again.

The Henderson brothers. Peter and Paul. It made sense, he thought, terrible, awful sense. For the last three years they'd felt themselves above the law of ordinary men. They'd swaggered around the city as if they felt it owed them everything, that it was theirs to claim.

He'd had them in the jail at least a dozen times, accused of theft, beatings, even rape on two occasions. But their longest stay had been overnight. The accusations had always been withdrawn. It was all a mistake, he'd be told; the wrong men identified, no crime really committed. Then he'd been forced to release them, impotent as he watched them leave the jail with the smirks wide on their privileged faces.

Their father was Alderman Henderson, a wool merchant who'd been on the Corporation for more years than Nottingham could recall. A man of influence, a man with money, who'd spend it to keep legal stains from the family name.

Nottingham was sure the man knew the truth about his sons. But to admit it would mean admitting his failure with them. So each time they were arrested the family lawyer came scurrying. He jingled money in his purse, the walls of power were quickly thrown up, and the law was turned away empty-handed. It was the cobweb justice that prevailed throughout the land. The small were caught fast, helpless. Those who were bigger simply broke their way through.

Murder, though, was something else. If he could find the proof, Peter and Paul might yet dance on the gibbet. And he'd make an enemy for life on the Corporation.

It wasn't what he'd expected from Peacher Hawthorn, but he was glad to have the names. Now Nottingham had to do his job and find evidence strong enough to convict. At least there'd be plenty willing to talk against them; Isaac had been well-respected in Leeds. The Hendersons' ways might have bought them syco-phants, fearful of their arrogance, but they had precious few friends.

To start, he'd bring them down here, a duty he'd relish. Let them see he knew the truth and was going to prove it. He locked the jail behind him, eyes taking in the faces on Kirkgate, straining at the shadows. His right hand was in his pocket, fist close around the knife hilt. He'd been given a warning, and he knew better than to trust to luck to keep him alive.

The return of the bitter weather kept the streets quieter than usual. Carters were reluctant to risk their valuable horses on the slick ice of the roads. Men trod carefully, their heads down. At least the city smelt clean in the cold, all the usual stinks of shit, piss and life buried away under snow and ice.

As he made his way down to the bridge he stayed aware of others, where they walked, how close they came. But if he wasn't going to accept one of the men following him, this was how it would have to be. Constantly aware, constantly ready.

Nottingham only let himself relax when he saw Sedgwick. He was questioning a man with a heavy pack on his back, pointing down at the riverbank. The man rested the weight on the stone parapet of the bridge for a moment, his eyes looking up at the deputy intently, then shaking his head. He stood slowly, shifting his body forward to settle the large bundle, then trudged on into the city.

'Anything, John?'

'Bugger all so far.' Sedgwick rubbed his hands together to warm them, then spat in disgust. 'You'd think Wyatt was invisible.'

'I can give you a little joy, at least.'

'Oh?' He raised his eyebrows.

'The Henderson brothers for Isaac. The Peacher passed me the word.'

The deputy started to smile, then looked suddenly dubious. 'You think we can make it stick?'

'If we can find the evidence, yes. Then even the alderman won't be able to buy them off the scaffold. Want to come up and help me bring them to the jail?'

Sedgwick grinned.'I think you've just made me a happy man, boss.'

The alderman's house stood close to the top of Briggate, above the market cross, near to the Head Row. It was an old place, he knew that, but Nottingham had no idea how long it had stood there. The wood of the frame was dark with age, the limewash still bright and fresh after being renewed the year before. Inside, he knew, the rooms were filled with dark wood and hardly any light. It might be ancient, but there was precious little beauty about it.

He banged on the heavy door, the thick oak worn and scarred by so many hands, then glanced at the deputy. The servant who opened looked warily at them. He knew who they were and what this visit meant.

'Is the alderman in?' Nottingham asked, knowing full well he'd have been at his warehouse for hours.

'No, sir.'

'And the brothers?'

'They're still sleeping.'

'Go and wake them. Tell them they have visitors.'

The man nodded. It wasn't the first time they'd played this

scene together. He showed them through to the parlour, where the fire was laid but not lit, and scurried off. Above his head Nottingham could hear angry, muffled voices. Good, he'd catch them groggy, not rested and still climbing from the depths of drink.

It was a full half-hour before the brothers burst into the room. Peter was the older, the taller, the leader. Paul trailed just behind, his pale eyes not yet fully awake. Peter Henderson drew himself up, his face haughty and lazy.

He was as tall as Nottingham and broad, in his early twenties but already running to fat, the buttons straining on an expensively stitched brocade waistcoat. Thick thighs filled a pair of well-cut breeches. His eyes were sharp, wary. Paul's face had the same shape, the same blond hair, the features so similar that the brotherhood was obvious. But he was docile, empty, the willing sheep to his brother's shepherd.

'The meaning of this, Constable?' Peter asked.

Nottingham took his time answering. He looked at them, unshaven, pale bristles on their cheeks. They smelt of old beer and stale sweat. He waited, his eyes travelling up and down their clothes, looking for any sign of blood.

'You're coming to the jail with us,' he told them.

Peter stuck his hands into the pockets of his breeches and tilted his head back. 'For what?'

'The murder of Isaac the Jew.' He spoke calmly, watching. Peter's face was fixed, hard, but Paul's eyes flickered with fear, and he knew he had them.

'I suppose you have proof?'

'Suppose what you like, Master Henderson. For now we're taking you to the jail to ask you some questions.'

Peter didn't turn his head, but bellowed, 'Watkins!'

The servant scurried in. Henderson didn't even turn towards the man but kept his gaze fixed on Nottingham.

'Send word to our father that the Constable has arrested us. And have lawyer Ames come down to the jail.'

As the parlour door closed softly, he said, 'You won't have us long.'

Nottingham smiled. 'We'll only need you long enough to hang you. Shall we go, then?'

The Constable gave Sedgwick quiet instructions, then followed the brothers down the street. They walked in silence, but he knew people saw them, that the word would spread that the Henderson brothers had been arrested again. He kept a good pace, forcing them to walk faster than they wanted.

For a moment he felt something, like small pinpricks on his neck, and he turned sharply. But there was no one there.

Josh was waiting at the jail, standing by the desk. Nottingham put Peter and Paul into a cell together, letting the sound of the key turning in the lock resound. Then he spoke soft words into the boy's ear and watched him hurry off at a run.

The two of them sat silent on the bed, so close their bodies almost touched. Was it to give each other strength, he wondered? He closed the door behind himself and leaned against it. Peter looked up at him, but Paul didn't move his head.

'Do you know Chapeltown Moor?' Nottingham began.

Peter leaned back against the wall. 'The races.' He paused and turned to the Constable. 'And the hangings. We like a good hanging. I laugh when they piss themselves.'

'Then we'll have to see that the pair of you make a good hanging. My guess is you'll piss yourselves even before you get on the scaffold.'

'Who was it we're supposed to have murdered?' Peter asked.

'Isaac the Jew.'

'That's the one who buys old clothes?'

'Bought,' Nottingham corrected him.

Peter shrugged. 'Bought, then.'

'Why did you kill him? The rumour that he had gold in his room?'

Peter looked at him with contempt, as he might a servant. 'We didn't kill anyone. Why do you think we did?'

'Where were you last night?'

'Last night?' Peter stretched and turned to his brother. 'The Talbot, wasn't it? We lost some money on the cockfighting.'

'That's right,' Paul agreed. Nottingham could see he looked uncomfortable, his fingers twisting together. He'll be the one to collapse, the Constable thought. All it would take would be the right thrust. 'Then you vanished with that whore for a while.'

'Money badly spent,' Peter said sorely.

'What time did you get home?' Nottingham asked.

'No idea,' Peter replied blandly. 'You'd have to ask the servants. They're the ones who got up to let us in.'

'I will.' He paused. 'And are those the clothes you were wearing last night?' He stared at Paul, who nodded in response.

Peter stood up and approached the Constable. The planes of his face, hard and sharp, burned with anger.

'I'll make sure my father destroys you for this.'

'I won't let anyone get away with murder,' Nottingham replied evenly. 'I don't care what his surname is.'

With slow, precise care, Henderson spat into the Constable's face. 'That's my opinion of you and your law.'

Nottingham brought his knee up sharply, feeling it connect hard against the younger man's balls. Almost as if time had slowed, Henderson's eyes widened in shock then he collapsed with a groan, tossed down carelessly to the floor, hands cradling his crotch as he curled up. He was gasping for air, skin suddenly pale. Paul started to rise to help him but the Constable gestured him back.

'That,' he told Peter, 'was very stupid.'

He locked the door behind them and sat at his desk, wiping the spittle from his face. He'd probably done the wrong thing, he knew that, but it had been a reaction. He'd taken a chance with the arrest. Now he needed evidence. If he couldn't find it, then Henderson would be right; the alderman would destroy him.

But he was certain the evidence was there. The sound of money, the woman had said. That was this pair. They'd be too cocksure to get rid of whatever they'd found. Now he had to wait for Josh and Sedgwick to return, and pray they'd discovered what he needed.

It was the best part of half an hour before the deputy arrived. He was carrying a pack that the Constable recognized as Isaac's, and two suits of bloody clothes that he laid out on the desk He grinned and shook his head

'Right on display by their beds,' he said. 'They couldn't even be bothered to hide anything.'

Nottingham nodded his approval. Got you, he thought triumphantly. No lawyer will be able to talk them out of this.

'Right, bring those along and let's see what they have to say. Peter might be feeling a little fragile.'

'Oh?' The deputy raised his eyebrows questioningly.

'He had a little accident. Very unfortunate.'

'Aye, it happens sometimes,' Sedgwick agreed sympathetically. 'It does.'

He knew he only had a few minutes before the alderman and his lawyer arrived, before there was another angry note from the Mayor. He needed to make the most of them.

The pair of them were sitting together. Paul had a protective arm round his brother's shoulders. Peter had been sick on the floor, and the cell was filled with the harsh smell. Traces of vomit flecked the bright peacock colours of his waistcoat and jacket.

Light, dull as lead, came through the barred window.

'So you didn't murder Isaac the Jew,' Nottingham said.

'I told you that,' Peter said. His voice was thick and he shifted his weight very carefully on the bed.

'I thought you might want more time to remember and reconsider.'

Peter's eyes hardened. 'We can't remember what we didn't do. Constable.'

Nottingham nodded sagely. 'I just wondered, since you had his pack in your room and some clothes stained with blood.'

Sedgwick came forward, holding the pack, the clothes draped over his arm.

Peter started to rise, only his brother's arms fast around him holding him back.

Nottingham leaned against the wall and folded his arms. 'That's ample evidence for me. It will be for the Assizes, too. You're both for the noose.' The satisfaction he felt as he said it almost worried him. 'Why did you do it?'

'They say the Jews always have money,' Paul answered.

'Be quiet,' his brother ordered him loudly.

'But he didn't, did he?' Nottingham said. 'Not in his pack, not in his room.' He was staring at Paul who shook his head slowly and sadly. 'So you killed him for nothing.'

'We didn't kill anyone,' Peter yelled.

'That pack and your clothes say you did. Very loudly.'

'We don't know where they came from,' he blustered.

Nottingham scratched his chin and shook his head. 'You don't think anyone's going to believe that, do you?'

The silence filled the room for a long moment. The Constable walked out, Sedgwick right behind him, letting the lock click heavily.

Nottingham sighed deeply. 'Now we just have to get them to the scaffold.'

'The alderman's going to fight you all the way.'

'There's too much here, even for him.' He gestured at the evidence in the deputy's arms. 'He'll fight until he realizes he can't win.'

'He'll hate you.'

Nottingham smiled and shrugged. 'He won't be the first, will he?'

He felt drained, a body emptied of everything. The energy and the fury had vanished now that the chase was over. He sat down heavily, the seat hard against his back.

'So what now, boss?'

'We wait for the alderman and his lawyer. Keep those things out of the way. We'll let them rant, then present them with the evidence.'

He didn't have long. Within five minutes Henderson had arrived, the lawyer trailing behind him, the master and his dog.

People claimed that the merchant had been handsome when he was younger, but there were few signs of it now. His face had turned hard and coarse, with no warmth in the eyes or mouth. An expensive wig sat awkwardly on his broad skull. He wore good plain clothes, his coat and breeches as sober as a Quaker's, but they couldn't hide the way his large body had thickened, ripened with fortune.

The lawyer, lean and long, had the feral look of an ambitious man, his gaze darting around eagerly for opportunities. His waistcoat was fine silk in bright colours, his suit deep plum velvet, a testament to his fees. He had the air of a man who spent every day around corruption and had come to relish the scent.

'Where are they?' Henderson demanded. His hands were shaking with fury.

'They're in a cell. Where they belong, Alderman.' Nottingham's reply was equitable.

'You don't treat my lads like that.'

Nottingham stood. He was taller than the merchant and looked down at him.

'I'll treat them the way I treat everyone else when they're guilty of murder.'

'Murder?' the lawyer asked. 'That's a very serious charge, Mr Nottingham.'

'With very serious consequences,' the Constable reminded him.

'You have proof, I take it?'

Nottingham gazed slowly from one of them to the other before he answered.

'I do,' he announced.

'Oh aye? Is that like that proof you've had before?' Henderson gave a short, coarse laugh. 'Evaporated like warm piss, that did.'

Money and threats will do that, Nottingham thought.

'John.' The deputy brought Isaac's pack and the clothes from the corner.

'That's the pack of the man they murdered, and the clothes they wore when they killed him.' He couldn't resist adding, 'It was Isaac the Jew they killed.'

'And where did you find these things, Mr Nottingham?' the lawyer wondered.

'In the bedroom the brothers share,' the Constable told him.

'What?' Henderson exploded, his face red, spittle flying from his lips. 'You went through my house?'

'I did.'

'And who gave you the right to do that?'

'The law of England,' Nottingham replied. 'Ask your man.'

Henderson turned furiously on the lawyer, who gave a short, embarrassed nod.

'Get them out here,' the merchant demanded angrily. 'I want to see them.'

Nottingham gestured to the deputy, never taking his eyes off Henderson. The lock clicked and in a few seconds the brothers appeared, their hopes raised by the arrival of their father.

'Did you do it?' Henderson asked bluntly.

'Of course not.' Peter held his head up defiantly.

'See there, Constable?' the merchant demanded. 'He says they're innocent.'

Nottingham had to stop himself laughing. 'The evidence says otherwise. And if you don't know the penalty for murder, Mr Henderson, I'm sure your lawyer will tell you.'

The merchant glared at his sons and gestured at the clothes and pack. 'He says these were in your room.'

'He must have put them there,' Peter said.

Henderson rounded on the Constable.

'He's accusing you.'

Nottingham shrugged.

'Ask your servants. We didn't bring anything with us. What do you think we did, bring it in by magic?' He looked at the lawyer. 'They'll go to the Assizes.'

'It won't stand,' the merchant threatened.

'He's wanted us for a long time,' Peter complained. 'He'd do anything to get us.' He sounded desperate, trapped.

The door opened. Josh walked in slowly, leading the old woman who lived in the room beneath Isaac's. A heavy coat seemed to weigh her down, her skin almost translucent. She looked around with her sightless eyes, taking in the warmth, the feel of people close by.

'Sorry, boss,' Josh apologized. 'It took us a little while to get here.'

'That voice,' the woman said.

'Which one?' Nottingham asked.

'The young one.' She spoke clearly, sounding more like a girl than a woman who'd experienced so many years of the world's cruelty. 'The one who said you'd wanted them for a long time. That's the man I heard in Isaac's room.'

It was perfect, Nottingham thought. He couldn't have asked for more. The timing, the clear honesty of her words.

'Thank you,' he told her.

'Are you going to believe that blind bitch?' Peter shouted.

Nottingham rounded on him.

'I'm going to believe the truth. And the truth is that you and your brother murdered Isaac the Jew, broke into his room, and robbed him.' He looked at the merchant, daring him to speak.

Henderson gazed at his sons.

'You stupid bastards,' he said dismissively, turning to leave, the lawyer fast behind him.

'Put them back in the cell,' Nottingham ordered. 'Thank you for that,' he said to the woman. 'Josh will see you home. You'll have to testify in court.'

She nodded, and reached out, her fingertips lightly tracing his face, feeling the cheeks, the jaw, tenderly across the mouth.

'You're a good man,' she pronounced softly, then Josh guided her away.

He slumped in the chair and pushed the fringe off his face.

'So that's that,' Sedgwick said. 'We've got them, finally. Nice and quick, too.'

Nottingham shook his head. 'You know Henderson won't let his boys walk to the gallows that easily. He's disgusted now, but he'll fight for them in court. Better lock that evidence up somewhere safe or it'll vanish before the trial. I'll go and inform the Mayor.'

'I'll walk up with you.'

For a moment the offer astonished him, then he remembered. Wyatt. The man had been out of his mind for hours. He smiled and shook his head.

'If it makes you feel better.'

Seventeen

For once, Nottingham didn't have to wait to see the Mayor. The clerk, a harried, anguished man, ushered him through as soon as he arrived. This, the Constable thought bleakly, is where the fight for the Henderson brothers begins.

Edward Kenion put down his quill, scattered a little fine sand over his words to dry the ink, and sat back in his chair. His stock was glistening white and perfectly tied, the periwig neatly powdered and fresh. But his eyes were tired, the flesh of his cheeks mottled.

'I've heard from Alderman Henderson.'

'I'd be surprised if you hadn't. I'm sending his sons to the Assizes.'

Kenion sighed. 'What charges?'

'The murder of Isaac the Jew.'

The Mayor was silent for a few moments, running his tongue across his lips.

'That's very serious.'

'I know,' Nottingham agreed. 'I have the evidence.'

Kenion nodded. 'How solid is it?'

'We found Isaac's pack and two suits of bloody clothes at Henderson's, in the brothers' rooms. And a woman who recognized Peter's voice as they ransacked Isaac's room. The jury will convict.'

'They'll hang.'

'They should. That's the law.'

Kenion looked awkward, a man caught between duty and class. 'The alderman will do everything he can to get them off. They're his sons.'

Nottingham chose his words carefully. 'As long as he stays within the law, that's his right.'

'And he'll do all he can to discredit you.'

It was a warning, but one the Constable didn't need.

'He'll have plenty of ammunition if he discovers what Wyatt's done without being caught,' Kenion told him.

'We found Wyatt's second victim this morning, too.'

The Mayor sat up sharply. 'His back?'

'The same.'

Kenion stood and started to pace, his footfalls silent on the thick carpet. He gazed down at icy Briggate from the window. What did he see there, Nottingham wondered. Did he look at the people, did he think of the way they lived?

'I'm not keeping this quiet to protect you,' he told Nottingham. 'It's for the city. We can't have a panic here. Just make sure no one else knows about this.'

The Constable nodded. Henderson wouldn't be the only one wanting someone new in the job if they discovered the truth.

'How close are you to finding this man?' He paused to look full at Nottingham. 'And an honest answer this time.'

Did Kenion really want the truth, or did he want hope? Or something in between?

'I think we'll have him soon.'

The Mayor's hand slapped his desk, the sound sharp and angry.

'For Christ's sake, I said be honest, Nottingham. I'm not a bloody fool.'

Shamefaced at his stupidity, the Constable began again.

'I've got men watching the judge whenever he leaves home. Wyatt's not going to get close to him.'

Kenion nodded his approval. 'But?' he asked.

'We've been looking everywhere, asked everyone who might help, and no one has any idea where Wyatt is. Another week and I'll have the book with the skin of the second victim.'

The Mayor sat back, thinking. Nottingham waited anxiously in the silence.

'Just get him. I don't care what you have to do.' He paused to allow the point to sink home. 'And when you find him, make sure this never comes to trial.' He looked up, staring the Constable full in the face. 'Do I make myself completely clear, Mr Nottingham?'

'Yes.'

'You find this man, I'll try to keep Henderson off your back. If you fail . . .'

Then he'd stand back and watch as Henderson tore him apart to save his sons. He nodded and left the Mayor's office. Outside the cold was bitter, but at least it felt clean.

Back at the jail he took the time to examine Rushworth's body again. His eyes had the cold milkiness of death. There were rope burns around his wrists and ankles, the skin rubbed raw all the way to dirty blood and sinew. The fingernails were chipped and torn to the quick where Rushworth had vainly tried to pick at his bonds.

The gash across his throat was a single, sure stroke. At least his death would have been quick, Nottingham thought, whatever consolation that could have been. It was impossible to judge how long he'd been dead. The winter had been Wyatt's friend; the cold kept the body longer.

On the back the cuts were confident and the murderer had peeled off the skin with even, practised strokes. Christ, he thought, how had Wyatt perfected this? How had he learnt his technique?

But then, how had he managed any of this? How would someone carry a half-naked corpse on Leeds Bridge in this weather and have no one notice?

There'd be no one to mourn Rushworth, he'd have no money for a funeral. In a day or so he'd end up in a pauper's grave where his flesh would slowly rot away, unremarked and unremembered. There would be no money for Isaac's grave either. He and Rushworth might well walk into eternity side by side.

He thought of Rose. A grave might not be much, might be nothing but bones and earth, but it gave him a place for her, where he could find something of her. Who would miss this clerk?

Nottingham let the corpse rest and glanced across at Isaac's withered body. At least the Henderson brothers would pay for that. Unless Kenion used them as pieces in his games with the corporation.

No more murders, he prayed softly. No more dead and dying this winter. Let spring come soon.

Outside, the weather mocked his words. The ground had become hard and icy, the snow a sharp crunch under his boots. The cold stung his face as he walked down Briggate. Few were out now, and those who were darted from shop to shop as if dashing between shelters. Voices and laughter came from the taverns and cookshops, where there was warmth.

Even the whores had taken their business indoors. Who could blame them, the Constable thought? It was the only place they'd find custom in this. Outside they'd just freeze into poverty.

But even now masters would begrudge heat to their servants and workers. They'd count the pennies the coal cost and eke it out like silver.

Only death, it seemed, relished the winter. So he kept his hands on the knife hilt as he walked.

Worthy was in his usual place in the untidy kitchen. Two of his men stood close to the blazing fire, their conversation ending as Nottingham entered the room. The procurer dismissed them with a sharp gesture.

'Take your coat off, laddie. You'll fry if you don't. The older I get, the more I like it hot in here.'

'I'm fine, Amos.' He leaned against the table. The pimp was

perched on a tall stool, his back against the wall. The suit was the one he always wore, threadbare, almost worn through at elbows and breeches sagging at the knees. The brocade of the cuff had long since worn away and years of stains covered the fabric. The procurer's belly bulged against the faded, elaborate pattern of the long waistcoat, his hose was blotched with grime, and the leather of his shoes scuffed dark.

'You think you'll get the Henderson lads to swing?' he asked.

Nottingham wasn't surprised that he'd already heard.

'I have the evidence. I don't see what the alderman can do to stop it.'

Worthy shook his large head sadly. 'Stop fooling yourself, Constable.' He reached out with a thick, scarred hand and pointed. 'He's not going to let it happen. The family name depends on it. He's going to use all his influence to stop you, and that's a lot of power in this city. You mark my words on that.'

'I haven't forgotten, Amos.'

'Still, that pair is best off the streets,' he said dismissively.

'You haven't mentioned Rushworth,' Nottingham said flatly.

Worthy shrugged and spat on the flagstone floor. 'It's why you're here, isn't it, laddie? I know you don't like my company enough to come by for gossip.'

'You've heard we found his body.'

The pimp have him a withering look. 'I won't ask about the skin. I don't need to, it's all over your face.'

Nottingham nodded. 'Have your men found anything?' he asked.

'Not a bloody thing,' Worthy answered bitterly. 'And it's not for want of trying, either, lest you were wondering,' he added. 'I don't know who this bugger is, but he's not relying on anyone. He just seems to vanish.'

'No one vanishes.'

'No?' The procurer raised a bushy eyebrow. 'Neither of us can find him. You tell me what that means.'

'It means he's cleverer than us.'

'No, laddie, I don't believe that. Between us, we know the place in a way he never could. He's been gone a long time.'

'He's been planning this for years, Amos,' Nottingham said insistently. 'He lived here before, he had time to know Leeds.'

'You have men on the judge,' Worthy said. It was a statement, not a question. 'And I have men on your men.' He looked at the Constable with a question in his hard eyes. 'But who's looking out for you?'

'I'm prepared. I can look after myself.' He brought out the knives and laid them on the table.

'A handsome arsenal, Mr Nottingham,' he said sarcastically. 'And fine if you get a chance to use them.'

'I'll be ready for him.'

Worthy stood up and walked around the table until he was face to face with the Constable. 'Laddie,' he said quietly, 'you've been going round with your head in a cloud. You're not ready for a gust of wind, let alone Wyatt. I could take those from you in a moment.' He paused for a moment. 'What would you think if I told you I'd had a man on you for days?'

Nottingham's eyes gave him away.

'My lad's good, but so is Wyatt. When he comes for you, he'll take you,' Worthy warned.

'We'll see. Amos, I don't care how we get him, or who gets him. Just so long as we stop him quickly.'

The pimp nodded.

'And take your man off me. I want to flush Wyatt out. You think what you will, I'll be waiting for him.'

With a curt nod, the Constable left the house, back on to Swinegate. He glanced around, but saw no one waiting in the shadows. The businesses had their doors closed, precious candles burning inside as they hoped for customers. Even the smith's hammer seemed to fall at a slower pace. Normally cramped, a cauldron of noise, the street looked wide as a river in the expanse of snow.

He walked past the apothecary where strange and wonderful things hung in the window, past the cabinet maker where the sweet smells of wood and varnish filled the air in summer.

The cold was like a harsh wall against his face as he turned on to Boar Lane and felt the thrust of the wind blowing down hard and thin from the East. Holy Trinity Church stood tall on the other side of the road, its lines still new and sharp, the glass of its windows reflecting a milky light.

Maybe he should feel triumphant. He had Peter and Paul Henderson in the cells with good, hard evidence against them.

But with Wyatt still loose it was hard to know anything but failure.

He turned suddenly, but all he saw were one or two servants braving the weather to carry messages for their mistresses and an old man with a stick, tottering cautiously on the snow and ice. The world had become an upside-down place, the weather like an unleashed beast.

At Briggate, first he thought to turn and head back to the jail. Instead his footsteps took him in a different direction, towards Timble Bridge and home.

It was dark when Josh reached his room, the key turning awkwardly as ever in the lock. The darkness and cold inside surprised him. Normally Frances would have had a light burning and the smell of food would fill the place. Groping for tinder and a candle, he called her name softly. She might be sleeping, the way she sometimes did at odd hours, curled and quiet like a small child, tiny under the covers.

The flame took, guttering at first as it threw strange shadows and then strengthening. She was in the bed, just her face showing, pale as the moon. A patch of deep colour, shiny and dark, stained the sheet.

'Frances,' he said, and her face turned towards him, eyes half opening.

In a voice hardly more than a whisper, tears on her cheeks, she said, 'I've lost it. I've lost the baby.'

He knelt by the pallet, stroking the cold sweat from her forehead with his hand. Her hair was matted and soaked. Slowly he pulled back the covering to see the thick stream of blood that had collected between her legs. A heavy metallic tang filled the air. He reached out and ran his finger through it. Still warm.

'Jesus.'

It was half exclamation, half prayer. He knew nothing about babies, but death was an old companion and he could feel him in the room. He squeezed Frances's hand tenderly.

'How long ago did it happen?'

She gave a tiny shake of her head. 'I don't know.' It sounded as if each word was an effort. Inside, he felt the fear rising, the taste of terror in his throat. He kissed her lips softly, feeling them cold and clammy.

'Hold on,' he told her. 'I'm going to get someone who can help.' As he began to rise, he said, 'I love you.'

Eighteen

Outside, in the freezing darkness, his breath came quickly as panic took his mind. He could rouse the apothecary, but he wouldn't come for a lad with no money. Who else was there?

John might be able to help. He fixed on the thought and began to run, slipping and sliding as he tore out of the court and down Briggate. Please God, he asked, let him be home.

At the house he pushed open the door and ran in, his footfalls loud and urgent. He hammered on the wood, silent prayers slipping from his head to heaven.

Sedgwick answered finally, his face slack with sleep, hair wild.

'It's Frances.' The words tumbled out. 'Help me. She's bleeding.'

'Come in, lad,' Sedgwick said.

'No, you have to come,' Josh pleaded. 'She's bleeding.'

The deputy pulled him inside by the hand. A candle illuminated the room softly. His woman was in bed, her sharp eyes focused. A small boy slept on a pallet.

'Where's she bleeding?' Sedgwick asked.

'There.' Josh pointed.

'The baby?'

He nodded and saw Sedgwick exchange an anxious look with the woman.

'She needs someone,' he told the deputy.

'I'll come,' the woman said quickly, climbing out of bed and beginning to dress, taking quick, calm charge. 'John, you get next door to watch James then go fetch the apothecary.'

Sedgwick nodded, took Josh's address, and put on his clothes.

'Show me where she is. You're Josh, aren't you?' She wrapped a heavy shawl around her shoulders. 'I'm Lizzie, love.'

Outside she hurried along, holding on to Josh's arm for support on the ice. 'What did you say your lass's name was?'

'Frances.'

'We'll take care of her,' Lizzie said reassuringly. Josh blinked back his tears and believed her. She seemed so calm and capable.

Their footsteps clattered on the rickety stairs and he opened to door to the room. Frances lay where he'd left her, eyes closed, face white as bone.

He watched as the woman walked over to the bed, smiling gently.

'Hello love,' she said, 'I'm Lizzie.' She stroked the girl's head and turned to Josh. 'Build up the fire,' she ordered, 'and get your lass something to drink. She'll be parched.'

He did as he was told, putting valuable coals on the hearth and watching the glow rise to a small blaze as he poured some small ale into a cracked mug he'd taken from the back of an inn.

Lizzie was examining Frances and he couldn't look. He couldn't bear to see the blood caked and cracked on her, or the way her legs seemed splayed like a corpse. He was scared. The woman was talking quickly and quietly to the girl, her words too soft to hear.

Finally she stood and drew Josh into a corner away from the candle's light. She put her hands on his shoulder. He could feel his body shaking under her touch.

'John'll be here with the apothecary in a minute.' She sighed. 'She's lost the babby, but I've seen worse. There's no meat on her. She couldn't nourish what was growing inside. Do you understand that?' Her voice was warm. He nodded. 'How old is she?'

'I don't know,' he answered truthfully. 'Will she . . . ?'

'Die, you mean?' Lizzie raised her eyebrows. 'God willing, she'll recover. The apothecary will give her something to make her sleep. That's what she needs now, rest so she can heal. Can you look after her?'

'What do I need to do?' he asked eagerly.

She ruffled his hair. 'I know you're a Constable's man, Josh, but you're nobbut a boy.' She paused. 'Look, tomorrow we'll get a couple of lads to carry her over to our room. I can take care of her until she's on her feet again. How's that?'

'But—' he began, before realizing he had nothing to say. He couldn't care for Frances, he was gone more than he was here. He looked at Lizzie, her mouth quite relaxed, her eyes warm. 'Yes,' he agreed.

'Good lad. Don't worry, you can come over and be with her all you like.'

The door opened and Sedgwick arrived with the apothecary, a wizened old man who was wheezing from the climb. He shrugged off his greatcoat, showing how he'd thrown on his clothes when the deputy roused him. The tiny room seemed suddenly full of people.

'She's lost a lot of blood,' Lizzie told him.

'Skin and bone,' the apothecary muttered.

'She's strong. But she needs sleep.'

The man nodded and rummaged in the bag he'd brought, finding a small bottle and a battered spoon. He fed Frances a little of the liquid.

'Thank you,' Josh told Sedgwick, and the deputy smiled and shrugged self-consciously.

'Thank Lizzie, lad. She knows what to do. You can trust her.'

The woman came and touched the deputy on the arm, taking him into the corner where she'd talked to Josh. He watched as she whispered insistently into his ear. John's eyes widened and for a moment he looked as if he was about to protest, then just nodded his agreement and returned to the boy.

'I can't afford to pay,' Josh said.

Sedgwick put his arm around Josh's shoulders. 'You don't have to. You work for the Constable, the apothecary looks after us for nowt. You just take care of your lass tonight. I'll have a couple of the men take her to our place in the morning.' He squeezed Josh's thin flesh affectionately. 'Don't worry, lad. Lizzie says she looks as if she'll be fine. She's just going to need some time.'

Relief filled him. He began to cry. He bowed his head and covered his eyes with his hands, but he knew he was hiding nothing. The years of living by his wits and his sly fingers slid away and he felt like a small child again, helpless and utterly lost.

Arms hugged him tight and Lizzie's breath was soft against his skin.

'You have a good cry, love.' Josh buried his face against her shoulder and let the tears come, tasting their salt in his mouth, while hands stroked his back like the mother he couldn't remember.

'Does Frances own another shift?' she asked.

He didn't know. Home was just a place he saw when he wasn't working. Frances kept it warm, had food on the table, a quiet smile on her face and loved him. He gave her his wages. That was all he knew of the place. He shrugged.

'What about another sheet, then?' Lizzie said. 'Do you have one of those?'

He shook his head. Lizzie gently pushed him away and kissed his forehead.

'Never mind, eh? We'll make do. I've cleaned her up a little, so you just watch her tonight. Josh?' He raised his eyes to meet hers. 'If she starts to bleed again or if she seems worse, just come and get us.'

'Yes,' he replied. 'Thank you.'

'I'll get the men over to move her first thing,' Sedgwick told him. 'Don't come into work until they've been.'

They left, the candle flame swaying wildly in the draught from the door, shadows dancing madly on the walls. He sat on the bed, trying to keep his eyes away from the dark bloom on the sheet, and took Frances's hand. She was asleep, her breathing low. She seemed fragile and brittle under his touch, as if death still had hold of her other hand.

He loved her. He'd said the words for the first time in his life, and understood what they meant. He'd sit and watch her all night and keep her safe.

Nineteen

Nottingham was pacing the room when Sedgwick arrived. Dawn had barely broken to the east, pale light crackling up from the horizon. He'd lit a fire after he reached the jail, but the warmth hadn't filled it yet and he'd kept his greatcoat on. His calves were cold, even under wool stockings and heavy boots.

He'd barely slept. Any joy in yesterday's success had evaporated quickly, leaving only anxiety about Wyatt. All too soon, he knew, there'd be another book coming, another taunt, another threat, another horror. He'd held Mary, her body warm and comforting, the rhythm of her breathing softening as she slipped into rest, but his own thoughts wouldn't give him peace.

He'd risen early, the chill wind licking at him as he walked into the city. Sounds travelled in the darkness, making him start and grab for the knives. But it was just a dog searching for food, and he felt foolish for his sudden fear. A month earlier he'd have given it no mind.

Sedgwick brought a flurry of freezing air with him. His face was drawn, deep shading under his eyes.

'Morning, boss.' He shrugged off his coat and threw it over a chair. 'I checked the night men. Nothing to report.'

Nottingham nodded.

'You don't look well. Bad night?'

'It's Josh. His lass lost the baby last night. He came and fetched us.'

'How's his girl?'

'A couple of the men are going to move her to our room so Lizzie can look after her. We told him she'll be fine, but . . .' He let the words fail. They both knew the truth, that she'd be lucky to survive. He shook his head. 'There's nothing to her.'

'How's Josh?'

'Cried like a baby that she was still alive.' Sedgwick sighed sadly. 'He's beside himself with fear, boss. I told him not to hurry in this morning.'

Nottingham nodded. 'I'll make sure he's busy. Keep his mind off things.'

'Anything more on Wyatt?' the deputy asked.

'Nothing.'

'Do you think someone could be helping him?' Sedgwick asked. 'I was thinking about it last night. After all, we know he's here somewhere. There has to be some reason we never see him.'

Nottingham considered the question for a moment. 'Who? He was gone eight years.'

'Didn't you said he had a woman when you arrested him?'

The Constable shook his head. 'That was years ago, John. How would he have kept in touch with her?'

'He can read and write. Maybe she can too, maybe he sent letters. And we know he's resourceful,' Sedgwick insisted. 'It's possible.'

Nottingham turned over the idea. There was some reason in Wyatt having an accomplice. It would explain why he seemed invisible. Someone to buy things, even to help dispose of the bodies.

It would answer some questions, but it raised even more. Who would help someone like Wyatt? He'd barely returned to Leeds. How could he have met someone so quickly that he could trust so completely?

It was impossible to believe it could be the woman. Women could be violent, they murdered, he knew that. But what Wyatt was doing went far beyond that. Still . . .

'The idea of someone helping him makes sense,' he conceded. 'I should have thought of it.'

'What about the woman?'

'I don't know,' he replied slowly.

'What was her name?'

'I don't know.' Nottingham gave a small shrug. 'It was Wyatt we were after, not her.'

The silence rose between them.

It supposed a great deal, but it could possibly be the woman, he was reluctantly forced to admit to himself. All he could recall was that she looked different, darker. But he'd only ever seen her briefly, and that had been over eight years before. If she really had waited for Wyatt she'd certainly have the anger after all this time. But what were the odds?

'It's possible,' he acknowledged finally. Why hadn't he ever found out about her? Quite simply, because she hadn't mattered back then. They had the evidence against Wyatt, and they wanted him convicted as quickly as possible. That was all that counted. She hadn't been important. Then.

'We can try looking for her,' he said. 'The only things I can remember are that her skin wasn't pale like most people and she had a strange air about her. Foreign, perhaps.'

'Was she? Foreign?' Sedgwick asked.

Nottingham pushed the fringe off his forehead. 'I don't know, John. I never talked to her. She was nothing. We were just after Wyatt.'

'There wouldn't be many here who look like her,' the deputy suggested. 'Anyone with darker skin.'

'That's true.'

It was so little, but at this point he'd try anything that might bring him to the murderer. And the simple fact was that, unlikely as this was, they had nothing else.

'Have the men keep their eyes open. If they see someone who might be her, they should just follow from a distance. That was good thinking.' The deputy grinned in appreciation and started to leave. 'And John, this doesn't mean we're not still watching for Wyatt, too.'

'I know, boss. I'll remind them.'

Nottingham walked over to the fire and held out his hands, as if trying to cup the warmth and bring it close. He was proud of his deputy. Sedgwick had come a long way in the last two years. He used his head, he was brave, and in a few more months his reading and writing would be good enough. Then all he'd need to become Constable would be more experience.

Nottingham had waited ten years for the position. He'd served his old master well, spending seven years as Deputy Constable. At first he'd felt the weight of responsibility heavily on his shoulders. He'd wanted to prove himself, to show how much he deserved the position.

As time passed, it became a job like any other. He took over more of the work, making decisions as Arkwright the old Constable became happy to fade into the background. By the end all that was missing was the title, and when that came it seemed perfectly natural. He was old enough, with ample experience and confidence.

He had no doubt that Sedgwick would become Constable in good time; he'd recommend him himself, just as he'd promoted him to deputy. The old order would pass and the new one come in.

Nottingham was still thinking when Josh arrived. There was a pearl light coming through the window, pale and gentle. The boy looked as though he hadn't slept.

'John told me,' he said. 'I'm sorry.'

Josh look embarrassed.

'Have they moved her?'

He nodded. 'Lizzie says she's a little better. She was sleeping.'

He told Josh about Wyatt's woman. For a swift moment he considered sending the lad home, but decided against it. In his room he'd just brood. At least here he'd be doing something. It was a feeling he'd come to know all too well himself in the last weeks.

'I need you to check on the men around the judge,' he said. 'Make sure they stay alert. Keep your own eyes open, too. Wyatt's going to be planning and watching.' He paused. 'Or it could be the woman doing it,' he added as a sudden revelation hit him.

'She could be following you, too, boss,' Josh pointed out.

It was true, he realized. He'd been expecting a man, looking for one. His eyes had passed over the women without thought.

'Let's worry about the judge,' he said with a smile he didn't feel.

He watched through the window as Josh ran off up the street. The boy was in pain, but he still had plenty of energy.

They had another road to follow now, another chance to track Wyatt. Somewhere out there he was finishing the next part of his book. Very soon it would arrive.

Twenty

It came that afternoon. Once again it was wrapped in a sheet from the newspaper, delivered by a young boy who'd been paid to bring it and couldn't give any worthwhile description of the man who'd instructed him.

Nottingham laid it on the desk unopened. His throat was dry. He knew he had to read it, that it could tell him important things about Wyatt. But first he'd see Rushworth's skin, debased, used. He'd have no choice but to touch it, feel it, hold it.

Slowly, he sat down, and carefully removed the paper. The book lay there, the cover staring back at him. Slowly, with a mixture of revulsion and sadness, he reached out and ran his fingertips over the rough skin. The poor bastard, he thought. To die and have a memorial like this.

He pulled the cover back, seeing the sharp copperplate of Wyatt's writing. *The Journal of a Wronged Man, Volume Two of Four.* The paper had been roughly cut and carefully sewn into the binding.

Nottingham held the pages apart with his fingertips, trying to keep his touch clear of the skin, and began to read.

My arrival in Leeds, all those years ago now, was far from auspicious. I was young and naïve and I honestly believed I had the chance to make my fortune here. I arrived with nothing. Truly with nothing. I had the clothes I wore and, if I remember it properly, three small coins. But I believed in the power of Fortune to look after me.

The journey from Chesterfield had taken me five days. What little money I had set out with was spent on food and lodging along the road, pitiful as that was. Thin stews with hardly any meat, gruels, beds alive with fleas. But it was all that was on offer, and it was better than hunger and cold.

At first, Leeds justified my faith. Within a single day I had a job, making far more money than I ever had in Derbyshire. My decision seemed like a good one. I worked for a tanner. As jobs went, it was a step up from what I had known, more clerking and putting together the wages. The hours were long, and much was expected of me, but I could manage all that with ease. I was young, I had energy, I still held my dreams of running my own business and watching clerks as the owner watched me.

I had a room in a lodging house, but it was clean and neat. I had ample to eat, even a little money in my pocket for the first time. But soon I discovered that others were making more than I was. Nights in the taverns and conversations over a jug or two showed that the tanner was taking advantage of me. I had been a country boy and easily satisfied, but no more. I was suddenly wiser. I left my position and sought another that would pay me what I was worth.

But I quickly found that Leeds was a cruel town. Because I had left one job, others were reluctant to take me on. I believed, as I still do, that the tanner had told others about me. I was a clerk with a good hand, I could spell, and I could think, but I could not find a job. After a month, all my money exhausted, I began work in a shop.

Some might have said I had been humbled for my pride, yet that would be a lie. I had simply understood my worth, I had rightly demanded it, and I had been hit back down. For my trouble, now I was selling flour and other comestibles to servants.

It kept body and soul together, but little more than that. The injustice of it stung me every day, but I had my plans. I had had another setback, but I had overcome it. I knew that in my heart. I would have my revenge, too. In the end I burned down the tannery. The only pity was that the owner was not in it. He should have been, but something happened, I do not even recall what now. Still, I took satisfaction from the fact that it bankrupted him. If he had paid me a proper wage, he would have prospered and so would I.

The shop work was degrading to someone who could easily do a clerk's work. I determined I would come through it, my time in the wilderness. It was intended to try me, to make me stronger and prepare me for the future.

In the end, it was a period that lasted for two long years. I hated every day of it. But I did have the opportunity to discover how stupid most people are. They would pay for something and never count the change. I was able to supplement my wages a little. That was just as well, because the shopkeeper paid me next to nothing.

But I knew things would improve eventually. I kept my faith in myself. There were jobs, and I kept applying. Finally one came along, a proper clerk's job with a merchant. I worked hard, and he paid me well for all I did. Within twelve months I had become his head clerk. He saw my worth and rewarded it.

He was older, though, and I had barely had my high position for a year when he decided to retire. There was

no one to take over the business. If I had had the money,
I would have bought it from him. But I could not have
raised the sum he needed. Not yet. I knew no one who
would take the risk of backing me. No one with money.
That was the secret, of course: a connection to money.

The stock was sold off, and those of us who worked
there were let go. I had a good reference, and a little extra
money, but that was all. Once again, I had been cheated of
my reward.

I was able to find another job. It was only my due, after
all. Graves employed me. He promised me a lot. The other
merchant had recommended me highly. I would start at the
bottom, Graves said, to learn his ways, then as soon as I
showed my mettle I would become his head clerk.

He lied, of course, as they all do. Instead, he received
my services for far less than they were worth. He gave me
increases each year, but they were miserly. He could afford
more. I knew that because I kept the accounts for the business. After four years of this, of still being a clerk and Graves
waving me away each time I reminded him of what he had
said, I met Charlotte.

Nottingham carefully closed the book. There was more to read,
but he needed to think on Wyatt's words for a while. How deep
was the well of bitterness inside the man? It seemed endless.

He had a very faint memory of a fire at a tannery, years before.
Even back then, it appeared, Wyatt's warped sense of justice could
be ruthless. Each grudge, each affront went into his ledger, never
forgotten, never forgiven. The Constable sat back, stroking his
chin.

Was Wyatt a madman? He had to be. No one in his right
mind would do what he'd done. He stared at the book's cover
and felt his gorge rise. A man's skin. That had to be the true
sign of insanity.

He poured a mug of small ale from the jug and drank quickly,
letting the liquid wash the dryness out of his mouth. The silence
of the room gathered around him. He knew he had to look at
the remaining pages.

But not for a minute yet. Everything connected with this man disturbed him. He was calling the tune, and the Constable and his men were dancing like fools. Even Worthy had found nothing.

And meanwhile Wyatt laughed.

These books were the proof. He gloated. This wasn't his story, it was his boast. Nottingham glanced out of the window. A few people straggled along Kirkgate, their breath blossoming on the cold air.

Inside, intimate with Wyatt, he could have been in a different world, a close, horrifying world. Very carefully, using his fingernails, he prised the book open and found his place.

> Since my time in Derbyshire I had foresworn women. In one way or another they were all whores. They took your money, they took your life. I had my plans, and if I wanted a woman she'd come later, when I was established, once I had my fortune.
>
> I had bought a shirt that was too large for me, and needed it altered. I was good with a pen, but I had no skill with a needle. Charlotte was a seamstress who lived in the same court. Since she was so close I took it to her.
>
> There was something unusual about her. She looked different, a deeper colour to her skin, but it was more than that. She was reticent, as genteel as a lady for all she dressed in old clothes and didn't have two pennies to her name.
>
> She had no idea where she had been born or about her background, but her family had ended up here, then died. She was the only one to survive. Something about her touched me. Unlike the girl who had tried to ruin me or the prostitutes who wanted my coin, she was honest. I wanted to look after her, to give her a better life.
>
> She moved into my room.
>
> But meanwhile, you will also want to know what happened to Mr Rushworth. Of course, you already know.
>
> He was so easy to take. A soft word, and then he recognized me. I knew your man was behind him, but there was no challenge in tricking an oaf like that.
>
> Then I had him away. He was such an unassuming man in life, a man who sensed his lot. The only time I ever heard him speak up was against me. If he had not done that he

could still be content with his ink and paper. Maybe there
will be some to miss him. I never asked.

In the short time I held him with me he spoke more
than I heard in those long years we worked together. He
apologized for all the trouble and pain he had caused me,
of course. As well he should. He begged. Yes, he begged
most volubly. It should have been satisfying but it quickly
became tiresome to hear his wheedling voice, praying to me
for his life. In the end I finished him sooner than I really
wanted just to quiet him.

By that time I found that there was very little satisfaction
in killing him. But it was a job that had to be done, a small
task to be completed. It was best done quickly.

Gingerly, he slid the book into the drawer on top of its companion.
He'd read it, he had no desire to ever open it again. If he could,
he'd have burned them both immediately and let the blaze carry
away all the hatred, all the fury that Wyatt had packed inside
himself over his life.

Wyatt would be in his middle thirties now, and all those years
of simmering anger were boiling over. After all these words he
might know more about Wyatt's history, but the man himself
remained elusive, more apparition than flesh. He'd told enough
about the past, but beyond the killings he'd said nothing of the
present. He was a clever, cautious man, hinting at so much but
giving away nothing.

Charlotte. At least they had a name now, although there was
nothing more about the woman to help them.

What troubled him most was the confidence Wyatt possessed.
He wasn't writing a confession or apology, there was no sorrow
in his words for anything he'd done. He truly didn't believe he
could be caught. Was he really so certain of himself?

The Constable poured more of the small beer and swilled it
in his mouth before swallowing. He felt like throwing the mug
against the wall just to hear it smash, but what would that prove,
other than his own frustration?

Who would he go for next? The judge, Nottingham thought.
He wanted the challenge, to prove he could do it. He wanted
to show how good he was, how deep his revenge could run.

And he'd want the Constable alive to read about how he'd done it.

Some of the men watching the judge were obvious; they were meant to be. Others were good, more adept at hiding themselves. He was certain Worthy had his men there, too, watching the watchers. A second ring of defence. When Wyatt came, they'd have him. One way or another. And if he came for the Constable instead, he was ready.

Twenty-One

If it wasn't for the cold he'd have fallen asleep. The fear for Frances poured through him. He felt sure Lizzie would look after her, but he'd noticed the dark, worried look that flashed between her and John, the concern in their eyes.

He could lose her.

He'd checked the men, seeing each was in position, and told them to watch for a woman with darker skin. Some of them had taken it in immediately, others had been confused and he'd patiently explained it to them.

Two were waiting by the Moot Hall, where the judge had finished the Petty Sessions, and two more were close by the house at Town End. Josh circled around, his eyes open and alert for the woman, even as his heart fretted.

He'd seen so many die in his life, but what he was feeling now for Frances was different. She'd been with him for four years now, arriving from nowhere, so quiet she might have been a shadow. She was a patient girl, and shy, hardly ever meeting people's eyes. Sometimes he wondered what had happened to her before they met, but she'd never mentioned anything about it.

From the corner of his eye he caught a movement, but he didn't turn to look. Instead he slowly crossed Briggate, the ruts of ice hard from cart wheels and hooves. There was someone half-hidden in the entry of a court. He didn't stop, but a single short glance was all he needed. Someone else was watching. From what he'd seen, though, it couldn't have been Wyatt; the man's skin had the paleness of too many English winters. He'd tell the boss later.

He settled in a spot a little further down Briggate that allowed him to watch the man without being observed. A wall kept the worst of the wind away and he crouched, hands deep in his pockets. This was work he could do well, tucked away, waiting, unseen, following. It was why the Constable had taken him on. He had the patience to do the job well. But as soon as he settled his thoughts returned to Frances and the anguish came back to his mind.

The idea that she might die terrified him. Over time she'd become part of him, her smile, her presence. He'd looked after her, but her warmth had comforted him too, first when they were children and now in different ways. It seemed impossible for Josh to imagine his life without her in it.

As soon as he finished work he'd go over and spend time with her. Lizzie had said he could stay as long as he wanted, as long as he didn't tire her. But he'd be happy to simply sit and hold her hand. There didn't even need to be words.

Two men walked by, heavily wrapped against the cold, barely wasting a glance on him. All they'd be worried about would be their money, Josh thought. He could have been another beggar boy, or the cutpurse he used to be. Two paces on they'd have forgotten about him.

He kept his face carefully angled, looking down but still able to watch the man across the street from the corner of his eye. His thoughts made their inevitable way back to Frances, feeling the sparrow touch of her small hand in his, the way she'd looked as she was carried to John's room.

For a moment he wondered if he'd see her alive again and panic rose quickly through him. He wanted to run to her. But he stayed where he was. There was work to be completed. Duty was something he'd learned in the last few months; there was a job to do and he'd see it through.

Time passed slowly. The iciness of the ground seeped through his shoes and into his feet. His limbs ached, and even deep in the pockets, his fingers were stiff.

Suddenly the man moved. Josh waited a moment then slid to his feet. His legs were stiff and for the first few steps he stumbled like an old man, knees not wanting to move.

The man was further up Briggate, easy to spot as he walked in short bursts, stopping to inspect shop windows as he slyly cast his eyes ahead to the judge and the Constable's men who followed.

It wasn't Wyatt, Josh was positive of that. The man moved too confidently, like someone who'd known the ground well for years. The judge crossed the Head Row, a small body plunged deep into a large coat. He was going home to eat, Josh knew, and then he'd sleep in his chair for an hour. It was his daily ritual, as he'd learned in the days he'd had to follow the man.

Nottingham's men did their work well, staying nearby until the judge was safe behind his own door. They'd leave for a while now, to warm themselves in an inn, and return later to follow if he went out again.

Josh waited until they'd gone. Knowing he had time, he ran around, through the courts and by the Grammar School, to reappear higher up Town End, hidden by a gatepost. No one would look there, and he could see the entire street.

The man waited a few minutes, pacing restlessly and stamping his feet to stay warm before turning on his heel and marching away. Josh followed carefully, keeping distance between them as they moved on to lower Briggate, then on to Swinegate. There Josh moved quickly, his suspicions sharp, arriving in time to see the man vanish into Worthy's house.

He ran back to the jail, eager to tell the Constable, but he'd left. Josh stood on Kirkgate, the wind harsh against his face. He'd have to give the boss the news later.

He needed food, something hot inside him. He hadn't eaten since the day before. There was no market, so there were no stalls, but Michael at the Ship would feed him.

Walking quickly he headed back up Briggate. By the Moot Hall, he was about to turn into the small court with the inn when he felt a hand on his sleeve. He turned to see a child, barely five, urgently pulling at his coat. The boy's face was grubby, hands filthy, and he was dressed in a short, ragged jacket and torn breeches, calves bare, shoes held together with twine. For a moment Josh thought he must be a beggar, then the boy said,

'They want you to come. They think they've seen your man.'

Twenty-Two

The boy took off at a run, as if he had no doubts that Josh would follow. And he did, sliding and slipping on the snow and ice, but quickly catching up and keeping pace. The boy knew his way around the streets, taking short cuts and dashing through small spaces.

They ended up in the Ley Lands. Looking ahead, Josh could see where the city petered out and gave way to cottages. Here, though, there were still courts and yards where people simmered and stewed, survived or died. Even in this weather he could smell the stink of misery, as if it had become part of the houses themselves.

The boy led him around a corner. A man waited there, so deep in the shadows that he looked to blend in with the wall. He was wearing a long cloak, the hood pulled close over his head.

For one horrifying moment Josh wondered if he'd come into a trap, then the man pushed back the cowl. It was the young man from the group of Gypsies.

'We think we've seen him,' he said without preamble.

'Where?'

The man didn't move.

'There's a house in the court with most of the roof missing. It looks empty, but there's a man with darker skin who goes in there.'

'Thank you.' The words didn't seem grateful enough. If they caught Wyatt from this, the man would have a good reward.

The man smiled wryly. 'You'd better go and tell your master, boy.'

'Yes.' Josh began to turn away.

'And make sure you remember our part,' the man warned.

'I will.' He started to run back to the jail, hoping that the Constable had returned.

When he arrived, Nottingham was sitting at his desk, a slice of pie at his side as he worked. After running hard through the cold, the heat of the room seemed close, and Josh felt clammy cold sweat drying on his face.

'Wyatt,' he said, drawing in lungs full of air. 'I think I might have found him.'

The Constable sat up sharply, his eyes quickly alert. 'Where?'

'In a court by the Ley Lands.' Josh sat, slowly regaining his breath.

'Are you sure it's him?'

'No,' Josh admitted. 'I was told.'

Nottingham pushed the fringe off his forehead, fierce concentration on his face.

'Have you seen him?'

Josh shook his head.

'Do you believe the information?'

'Yes, I do,' Josh answered firmly.

Nottingham nodded. 'Go and find John and a couple of the other men and come back here. We'll go and see if this is Wyatt.'

'Do you think it could be?'

The Constable shrugged. 'I hope so.' He smiled. 'We won't know until we see, will we? But we're going to be prepared. Get John.'

It took a full hour before the men were assembled at the jail. Nottingham and Sedgwick took primed pistols, and the Constable armed the others with knives. Josh led the way through the afternoon streets, the party moving silently. The wind had finally dropped and more people were around, heavily wrapped, stepping back in fear and hurried whispers as the men passed.

They halted outside the court. Only Josh and Nottingham ventured in, keeping out of sight as the boy pointed out the house. Two of the men were detailed to go around and watch the rear. There would be no chance of Wyatt escaping, if Wyatt it was. Five minutes later the Constable raised his hand. Flanked by Sedgwick and Josh, their weapons drawn, he walked to the house with the missing roof and pushed heavily on the door.

With a mild groan it gave way and they entered. Sorry grey light filtered down through the rafters and broken joists, casting deep shadows. They stopped to listen, waiting as the place filled with a deep, sad silence. Walking slowly, they moved from room to room. Half the doors were missing, glass gone from the windows, floors deep in dust, cobwebs and rat droppings. It was a place that begged to be taken down and opened to the sky.

At the end of the hall stood the last door, closed and dark. Nottingham turned the knob slowly and pushed it open. The faint light showed stairs down to a cellar. He walked slowly, feeling each step with his foot, the others close behind him.

The floor under his feet changed from wood to packed dirt. The air smelt of stale food, sweat, shit, of life. Someone ate and slept down here. He tightened his grip on the pistol, slowly letting out his breath.

The Constable waited, letting his eyes adjust to the heavy gloom until he could make out the walls. He could feel his heartbeat, the fire of dryness in his mouth. Very slowly he edged his way along, fingertips on the walls, touching the rough finish of bricks and mortar.

After a few yards there was wood. He traced the frame of a door, old, dry, splintering. His hands moved further until he found the door itself, sliding down to the knob. Nottingham could sense the others behind him, tense and waiting.

Slowly he turned the doorknob, then pushed the door wide and stepped into the room. The blackness felt as absolute as death. He had no idea how big the room was, or where Wyatt might be in it. He needed light. And they had none.

'Who's in here?' he shouted.

He could hear John moving around the room. Glancing back he could pick out Josh at the door, faintly highlighted, standing like a ghost.

Nottingham moved to the wall and began working his way slowly around the room. Suddenly there was a small flare of light, and a glow gradually filled the room. Sedgwick had found a candle.

In the opposite corner a man cowered in his bed. His eyes were wide and terrified. There was a wet spot on the dirty sheet where he'd pissed himself, and the scent of urine wafted across as he cowered.

'Who are you?' Nottingham asked. His pistol was pointed straight at the man's head.

His skin was darker. That much was true, but he looked nothing like the Wyatt of the Constable's memory. This man was squat, his shoulders wide, his hair little more than a shadow on his skull. A thick moustache, the bristle hair turned to grey and white, covered his top lip.

'Who are you?' he repeated.

The man looked from Nottingham to Sedgwick and to Josh. The Constable could see he was scared for his life.

'Your name?' Nottingham asked, trying to soften his tone.

'I—' He looked around helplessly, petrified.

'What's your name, please?' Nottingham asked again, this time more gently, lowering his weapon.

'I'm Tom.' The man spoke the word tentatively, the fear full in his voice. 'Tom Walker.'

Nottingham looked around the room, for what it was worth. The bed was old straw and an even older sheet, with a small travelling chest standing at the foot. Besides that the place was almost bare, the floor swept clean.

'What are you doing here?'

'I was a sailor. I'm on my way home.' The Constable caught an accent he couldn't quite pinpoint in the man's voice. 'I've no money and I found this place.'

'And where's home?'

'Newcastle.'

'Where are you travelling from?'

'Portsmouth. Paid us off and let us go, like.' He squinted hard, the shock and surprise starting to fade. 'And who are you, then?'

'I'm the Constable of Leeds,' Nottingham told him. Walker stared at him.

'Is there anyone else living in the house?' the Constable asked.

'No one I've seen. But I've only been here a couple of days, like. I'm on my way tomorrow. Just needed to rest up.'

Nottingham smiled.

'We'll leave you, then. Have a safe journey, Mr Walker. Josh, go and tell the others we've finished.' He paused. 'But good work.'

Upstairs, the light seemed to flood in on them, leaving Nottingham blinking. He felt the tension of the last few minutes seep out of his bones, leaving him tired.

He shrugged himself deeper into his greatcoat and they left the house, the pistol in his pocket. He'd hoped this had been it, that he could have taken Wyatt quickly and simply.

'How are the men around the judge?'

'They're staying close,' Sedgwick answered. 'But not so close he knows they're there.'

'Good.'

Josh arrived at a run, his face anxious.

'Boss?' he asked.

'Go on.' He ruffled the boy's hair. 'I know it wasn't Wyatt, but he was dark. Just a sailor. But well done.'

Josh beamed. 'I was out earlier, and someone was following our men who were after the judge.'

'What?' Sedgwick asked. 'Who?'

'And did he go back to Worthy's house?' Nottingham asked.

'Yes.' Josh sounded deflated.

'Don't worry, lad. Worthy and his men want to find Wyatt. Worthy claims he owes Graves a debt and this is his way of paying it off.'

'You don't believe that, do you?' Sedgwick scoffed.

The Constable made a dismissive gesture. 'I know full well that Amos Worthy has never done anything without his own reasons. Still, it's good to know we have another line of defence around the judge.'

They were close to the jail, just the other side of Kirkgate. The light was waning, the bitterness in the air more acute.

'Go home,' he said. 'Josh, I hope your girl is a little better.'

The boy reddened. Nottingham waited until they'd turned the corner then started down the road. He needed his hearth, too.

In the distance was the Parish Church. He knew he should stop and see Rose's grave. It seemed like days since he'd talked to her and he was beginning to feel as if she was slowly slipping away, to become part of the past, not the present. In his head the line between the living and the dead was becoming firmer. She was growing less substantial, drifting into mist like a ghost.

He could still feel her in his heart, the love as strong as when she'd been a little girl. But maybe Mary had been right, that work was who he really was, that only his job brought him truly alive.

Nottingham stopped at the lych gate, running his hand along the wood, his nail idly chipping off a fragment of ice. For a moment he considered turning the handle and taking his apologies, his sorrows, to Rose. But maybe it was better for both of them for him to let her rest a while, to let her die.

Slowly he walked on, looking ahead to the warmth of home.

Twenty-Three

It was simple enough to glide through the city unnoticed. Wrapped heavily against the weather he could be any one of the anonymous figures on the street. He'd seen the men placed so obviously around the judge and followed their movements.

He'd even spotted the others surreptitiously watching the watchers. That gave him pause. He knew the judge's routine by now and where all his guards would be, although Dobbs himself seemed unaware of their existence.

Spiriting him away wouldn't be easy, but with care he could manage it. He had ideas, a plan that would leave them all wondering what had happened. But that was for when he was ready.

It amused him to walk past those meant to catch him. Bundled like this, with just his eyes showing, he was almost invisible. The weather had been his friend this winter, its cruelty matching his own. As long as he was careful – and he was always careful – he had the freedom of Leeds.

He'd followed the Constable too, at a wary distance. He knew the man's routines, he'd seen his family, discovered his loss. By watching and waiting, exercising the patience that had served him so well these last years, he'd been able to build up his picture, to put all the pieces in place. Soon the time would be right again. Soon.

Twenty-Four

'How is she?' Josh asked in an eager whisper. Frances was curled on a pallet, sleeping softly, two tattered blankets covering her thin body.

'She's been sleeping a lot,' Lizzie told him kindly. 'But she needs that. She lost a lot of blood and her body needs to get strong again. Poor little thing.'

Josh sat on the floor by Frances and took her hand in his. She didn't even stir as he touched her, and her skin felt cool in his fingers. For an urgent moment he looked across, watching her face carefully to check she was still breathing.

'You stay with her.' Lizzie put her arm around his shoulder and squeezed it lightly. 'Don't worry, love, she's doing well.'

'Thank you,' he said.

'We're going to take the lad out for a while,' she continued. 'You just spend some time with her.'

He nodded and stroked the pale hand.

Sedgwick had James by the hand, pulling back with a smile as the boy tried to run from him. Lizzie watched them lovingly, and even in the cold the deputy felt happy.

'How is she really?' he asked.

'She's stronger than she looks,' Lizzie told him. 'I thought we were taking her in so she wouldn't die on her own.'

'Do you think she'll live?' He hoisted James up on to his shoulders then above his head, the boy squealing with pleasure.

'She might,' Lizzie answered cautiously. 'Who really knows?' The hem of her skirt shushed over the packed snow. 'When's it going to get warm?' she asked.

'Not bloody soon enough.' He let the boy down, but kept a tight hold on his hand. 'Be good to feel warm again. Do we have to stay out long? I'm tired.'

'Give them a few minutes, love.' She put her arm through his. 'You remember what young love's like. And who knows how long they might have?'

He nodded grudgingly as they walked down to the Aire. The light had fallen away and twilight lingered on the horizon, a thin band of pale blue below the thick clouds.

'I've told you we're keeping men on Judge Dobbs,' Sedgwick said thoughtfully.

'Yes.' She held his arm as they followed the path down to the river bank, James's tiny legs pumping hard on the grass.

'There's a part of me that wishes Wyatt had got him first.'

'John!' She hit his chest lightly. 'That's a terrible thing to say about anyone.'

He shrugged. 'Well, it's true. He's no more interest in real justice than James here has. I've seen him transport men for next to nothing, and hung at least two I know of who weren't guilty, just because the merchants wanted it.'

'That's the way. You should know that by now.'

He kicked at the snow. 'Doesn't mean I have to like it.' He paused, looked around, and turned to her. 'He's a bastard. Most of the justices are. They don't care about the evidence. All they do is give the verdicts and sentences the Corporation wants. If one or two of them ended up dead, it'd be no loss for the law.'

'Be careful,' Lizzie warned him in a hiss. 'Anyone hears you talk like that you'll lose your job.'

'I know that. You're the only one I've ever told.'

'What about Mr Nottingham? How does he feel?'

Sedgwick shook his head. 'It's not something we've talked about.'

'For the best, if you ask me.'

'Aye, mebbe.' He put his arm around her. 'Don't worry, I like my work, I want to keep it.'

She pulled him close for a swift kiss. 'Then make sure you do. Come on, we can go back now, we've given the lovebirds some time alone. You look as if you're perished.'

'I've been outside all day.'

He took James by the hand again, the three of them making their way back to the Bridge.

'John?'

'What?'

'Please, don't ever say things like . . . you know . . . again. It's dangerous.'

'I won't.' He gave her a gentle smile. 'I promise.'

The fire burned high, the crackle of coal soft in the room. Nottingham felt the heat all through his body, soaking his flesh and caressing him inside. Mary sat close by, sewing a new dress for Emily; the girl was across the room, bending to write in the notebook he had bought her for Christmas, a candle flickering dangerously low next to her.

For the first time in months, since the grip of winter on the city's throat, he felt real contentment. All the problems remained, but for tonight at least he'd been able to leave them behind.

He reached out and lazily stroked Mary's wrist, watch her lips curl into a small smile as her hands worked. Apart from small domestic noises, the room was quiet. He felt as if he could happily let sleep take him.

Mary pushed the needle into the fabric and set it down on a stool. 'It's late,' she announced. 'Time we were all in bed.'

She stood, and slowly he followed her, stretching as he rose. Emily finished her sentence, blowing on the ink to dry it before she closed the book. A normal night, he thought as he banked the fire for the night, the way things used to be. Maybe they could slowly find their way back to some kind of happiness, to a new normality. It would be different, changed, smaller, but at least it seemed possible.

The bedroom was cold, with frost already on the window glass, the scratchy fabric of the sheet chilly as he pulled it back. But not for too much longer, Nottingham thought. No matter how cruel this winter had been, it would pass.

In his shirt he could feel the air nipping hard at his skin, and he held Mary as she came into the bed, her hair loose and brushed. She curled into his arms, shivering slightly. He could feel her breath against his cheek.

Slowly, shyly, they kissed. He was sure that with every move, every gesture, she'd pull back, scared. But she stayed, her touch welcoming, her hands chilly on his skin. Tenderly, still cautious, he began to explore her. It wasn't with eagerness, but softly, almost breathlessly, a homecoming after so long away.

He looked into her face, seeing her eyes warm, happy, finally alive again. Relief and joy surged in his blood and he pulled her close. After, he could feel his heartbeat gradually slowing, her hair soft and ticklish against his face.

Rolling on to his back, he put his arm around Mary, her head resting on his shoulder. They lay together in silence, and he listened as her breathing quieted before letting himself fall into the darkness.

Waking came too soon. The night was still full. Mary had her back to him and he moved without disturbing her. He dressed rapidly, while the heat of the bed still clung to his body. In the kitchen he washed his face and hands in a bowl, the cold water sharp.

Nottingham took bread, stuffing it into the large pocket of the old draped waistcoat, and a swig of small beer from the jug on the table. Outside, as he pulled the greatcoat tight around his waist, the air seemed a fraction warmer. The snow was softer, squeezing down under his feet. That made the short journey longer and harder, his boots sliding over the surface as he tried to walk.

By the time he reached the jail he was exhausted, legs aching from the effort. But even that couldn't take away his feeling of contentment.

Sedgwick was already there, feeding coals to the fire. His coat lay over the chair and he turned and stood as Nottingham entered.

'Morning, boss.'

'John.' He slipped off his coat and hung it from the nail in the wall. 'How's Josh's girl?'

'Still sleeping when I left.' He poked at the blaze to send it roaring. 'You know, he spent the whole evening sitting by her, stroking her hand, making sure she drank some water. Didn't say a word, either of them.' He shook his head in astonishment and respect.

'What does Lizzie think?'

The deputy shrugged. 'She says Frances might survive. The lass has no strength. Looks like she lost the baby early, but there's nothing to her. She's like a twig, wrists as thin as bobbins.'

Nottingham nodded. 'What if she dies? What do you think Josh would do? He seems to trust you.'

Sedgwick shook his head again slowly. 'No idea. He keeps everything inside. I like him but it's impossible to guess what he's thinking.'

'He's been doing some excellent work.'

'You mean that tip yesterday?'

'Yes. And noticing one of Worthy's men following ours. People have come to know him. I don't want to risk losing him.' Nottingham settled into the chair and began looking at the papers on his desk. There was only one urgent item, the remainder just the workings of a growing city that needed more and more things written down and signed.

Sedgwick was putting his coat back on, ready to go and check the men.

'Don't tell them they have people watching them,' the Constable warned. 'See if any of them notice for themselves.'

The deputy grinned. 'Right, boss.'

Left to himself, Nottingham sat back, took the bread from his pocket and began to chew slowly. There was a deep joy in his soul now, a sense that he and Mary would come through this. They'd be poorer at heart, there was no avoiding that, but they'd also be stronger.

On top of that, the other worries had returned, cascading on him like water. Wyatt. The Henderson brothers. And now Josh and his girl. According to the letter he'd received, Alderman Henderson intended to apply for their release until they went on trial, and was offering a surety for their behaviour. Did the Constable have any objections?

Objections, fears . . . how many could he list? More to the point, would anything he said make any difference at all? Henderson had wielded power on the Corporation for years. He knew who he could manipulate, and more importantly, how to do it. The judges dined at his house and listened intently when he spoke.

Nottingham had no doubt about what would happen if Peter and Paul were let out. Within a day there'd be many souls all too happy to confirm they'd been drinking with them until late, and any witnesses would be intimidated or simply disappear.

But he dared not state that blatantly. It would be a slur on the Alderman. He needed to be circumspect with his words, to express his concern at how grave the crime had been, that justice demanded they remain in jail. He added that Isaac the Jew had been known and respected, and that his friends might seek revenge; the Constable and his men couldn't be everywhere to protect them.

It didn't sound convincing, even to him. Unless there was a rare judge in Leeds who'd begun to respect the law, they'd be home very soon – and Henderson would make sure the judge was one of his cronies.

Nottingham would keep the evidence close, where the Hendersons and their friends couldn't find it, and he'd need to find the old woman a new room, somewhere safer, where the brothers wouldn't find her. That would be a job for Josh. At least they'd be able to make a good case when it all came to trial.

He finished writing, sanded the document dry and rolled it up. Eating the remainder of the bread, he prepared for the day. First to the Moot Hall, then it would be time to talk to Worthy again. It seemed impossible that between them they couldn't find Wyatt in a city the size of Leeds. In London, Norwich, or even in York he could understand it. In those places humanity roared like a flood. Here, he'd once been told, there were only around seven thousand people. Every day he saw familiar faces, he could give names to many of them. How could one person, or even two, hide so well?

The question vexed him as he walked over to the Moot Hall. More people were out, their progress along the street slow as the ice gradually oozed into slush around their feet. But the air had certainly turned, with the faintest hint of spring in the breeze. Pray God it wasn't another false hope.

The clerk took his paper and yawned as he glanced over the writing. It was just one more document in an endless series that he'd read today.

'The judge has already been appointed to the case,' he said in a bored tone.

'Who is it?' Nottingham asked.

'Judge Dobbs.'

The Constable smiled wryly as he walked away. Of course, who else could it be? This was God's little irony. Dobbs and Henderson had been friends for years, and Dobbs had never been celebrated for his impartiality. Justice would stand a greater chance in a crooked gaming palace. The Henderson brothers were as good as home.

He walked down Briggate, water squeezing out under the soles of his boots. The surfaces were slick, and several times he had to catch his balance against the wall. He watched others fall; one of them didn't get up again but rolled around and bellowed in pain, clutching his ankle.

By the time he reached Worthy's house he was aching and tired. Nottingham couldn't remember the city streets ever being this treacherous. There was nothing he could do about it, except hope the temperature would keep rising so this would pass quickly. Two women had tumbled with great embarrassment; their skirts flew up and the boys and apprentices roared their comments.

The kitchen was hot. The heavy faces of the pimp's men were shiny and patches of sweat stank under their arms. They left eagerly when Worthy dismissed them. The Constable waited until the two of them were alone, drawing off his greatcoat and standing by the long table.

'Heard you almost had someone,' Worthy said.

'The wrong man.'

The procurer shrugged. 'Did he know owt?'

'Just someone passing through.'

'So we're no closer to Wyatt.'

'No.'

Worthy began to pace around the kitchen, the heels of his shoes clicking sharply against the old flagstones. 'What do we do, laddie?'

Nottingham watched the pimp as he moved. He was a large man; his protruding belly pushed the dirty waistcoat out in front of him. It was all firm, though; Worthy was a strong man, with voracious appetites for everything.

'I still don't understand your interest in all this, Amos.'

Worthy turned to look at him, his scarred hands resting flat on the tabletop and speaking firmly. 'I told you once, I owe Sam Graves a debt. This is the only way I can repay it now. You understand?'

There was a dark intensity in his eyes that Nottingham finally believed.

'Judge Dobbs has been given the Henderson case,' the Constable said.

Worthy spat on the floor. 'You know what'll happen.'

'I'll have the evidence, and I'll look after my witness.'

'Aye, and it still won't make a damn bit of difference.'

'If I don't present a case, they won't have one to answer.'

'Don't be so daft. With Dobbs there won't be a case anyway. He's lived in Henderson's pocket for years. They'll be out of the courtroom before you have chance to draw breath.'

Nottingham shrugged. Of course Worthy was right, but he

had no choice but to follow the law. He had to present the facts. However he felt, what happened after that was beyond his control.

'Wyatt,' he said.

'He's smarter than the pair of us,' Worthy said with faint admiration.

'I wonder if a woman was waiting for him,' Nottingham said.

The pimp tilted his head in curiosity. 'What woman is this?'

'He was living with someone when we arrested him. Her name's Charlotte, according to his new book.'

'So why would you think all this, laddie?'

'Think about it. We can't find him. He has to buy food somehow, he's not living on fresh air. So maybe someone is helping him. It could well be her. Who else would he have?'

'Why would she wait?' Worthy countered. 'He was gone a long time.'

'I don't know,' Nottingham admitted. 'It's all guesswork. But it makes sense. We haven't seen him at all. She could be running the errands, even help him carry the bodies.'

Worthy considered the idea for a few moments, rubbing the back of his hand across his greasy mouth then down the grimy material of his waistcoat.

'I suppose it's possible,' he agreed grudgingly. 'But it's a lot of guessing and hoping with bugger all facts.'

'I know that,' Nottingham argued passionately. 'Still, I don't care how clever Wyatt is, he can't have arrived here with nothing and then just started doing this all by himself.'

'We don't know how long he's been in Leeds.'

'From the sentence he had, it can't be that long. He has someone helping him.' He looked up. 'It feels right.'

Worthy nodded slightly. 'Mebbe, laddie, mebbe. So what do you know about her?'

'Beyond what I told you, nothing, really. Her skin was a little darker, black hair. That's all I remember.'

'Not a lot.'

'I've had my men out looking, but there's been nothing yet.'

'I'll have mine keep their eyes open. But what we're really saying is we're nowhere and grasping at straws.'

Nottingham smiled wryly. 'I hope not,' he said.

The door opened and one of Worthy's men appeared. 'That lad of the Constable's is here. Needs to see him.'

Nottingham stood up. 'I'll be off.'

'I'll have them look for her.'

The Constable nodded and left. After the gloom of the kitchen, even the greyness of Swinegate seemed bright. Josh was waiting by the door, his body tense, eyes darting from side to side.

'What is it?'

'We had a message, boss. Your wife is ill.'

Twenty-Five

'What? Who told you?' Nottingham felt the shock, the numbing dread, rising in him. Not like Rose, please God . . .

'A boy came. Said your neighbour had sent him,' Josh answered nervously.

'How long ago?'

'About half an hour, I think, maybe a little longer. We've been looking for you.'

The Constable nodded curtly, his thoughts dashing ahead of him. 'Tell Mr Sedgwick he's in charge for the moment. I'll send word when I know more.'

'Yes, boss.'

Nottingham ran along Swinegate, a few more people moving on the street, with hawkers treading warily as they shouted their goods. His heels threw up small spurts of slush, boots sliding every few steps.

He cut through The Calls, where small brick lodging houses advertised their empty rooms, and the tanners and shoemakers had their works, the air low with the dank stench of piss and leather.

Nottingham began gasping for breath. He needed to be home, to see Mary. The thought of her falling ill . . . at least Emily was there. His thoughts roared wildly: Mary was dying, he'd have to live without her.

By the time he reached Timble Bridge the fear was pushing

him faster, trying to outrun the darkness at the back of his mind. Home was close enough to see now, and he breathed deeply to try to quell the panic.

Along Marsh Lane trees lined the road, winter-bare and stark. Nottingham started to run harder. The slush was thick, the layer of ice slick underneath. His left foot slipped and he began to fall, hands flailing at the air as his body arced forward.

He was still in the air as something struck his shoulder, the pain sharp enough for him to cry out even before his body hit the ground. Without thinking, he rolled to the side, sliding unsteadily on to his feet, trying to keep his balance.

The man was facing him, legs apart, a heavy, shiny cudgel swinging in his hand.

So this was Wyatt. Under an old tricorn hat, he wore a rich brown, full-bottomed periwig – probably taken from Graves, the Constable thought. A scarf covered the lower part of his face, leaving only his eyes showing, calculating and pale in skin the colour of old wood. Nottingham could see the edge of a branding, T for thief, on the man's cheek. His hands were large, their backs covered with dozens of tiny scars.

The Constable had knives in his pockets. He just needed to reach them. Reach one, anyway. His left arm was useless, numb from the blow. He began to edge backwards, feet testing the ground at each step. Wyatt said nothing, standing still, his intent gaze never leaving Nottingham's face. He was smaller than the Constable, but a full decade younger, hardened and muscled by years of labour.

Nottingham tried to move his left arm. Harsh pain sprang through him, so sharp he had to compress his lips to stop crying out. Wyatt had been clever; he'd played on his fear, played on his love for his family. Worry had made him stupid. He hadn't even taken any precautions for his own protection. He'd thought about death so much in the last few weeks and now he was looking directly at it.

For once, though, the long, cruel winter had been on his side. If he hadn't slipped the cudgel would have cracked his head, and Wyatt would have taken him silently. Now he had a chance. Home was just a hundred yards away, down an empty road, with no one in sight.

If he tried to turn and run, Wyatt would be on him. He could shout, but who would hear with doors and windows shut tight?

Nottingham took another step backwards, his boot heel coming down softly, shifting the weight to his left leg. A droplet of sweat ran down his spine. He hardly dared to breathe, his eyes fixed on Wyatt.

Beyond the two of them, the world ceased to exist. Wyatt kept swinging the cudgel gently to and fro.

Wyatt would know exactly where he lived, Nottingham thought, how far he had to go to safety. He'd play with him, let him feel hopeful, and then pounce. The cat with the mouse.

The Constable knew that his only chance was to end this. Throw himself at Wyatt, knock him from his feet, then run. If he allowed Wyatt to keep control, he was lost. Those eyes were imprinted on his memory now; they'd visit him in his dreams, leave him awake in his bed.

He'd have to make his move soon, but he couldn't offer any warning of it. To fool Wyatt, it had to be a complete surprise.

'Papa!'

Nottingham tensed at the sound of Emily's voice behind him. She must have come out from the house and seen him.

'Papa!'

The Constable didn't turn. His gaze remained firmly on Wyatt. The murderer's eyes shifted to Emily, then back to Nottingham. He began to raise the cudgel and Nottingham drew in his breath. Then silently Wyatt turned and slipped into the woods.

With a long sigh Nottingham sat on the ground, the icy wetness of the slush soaking through his breeches. He moaned and reached across to touch his shoulder. As his fingers pressed lightly on his coat, pain raced down his arm.

'Papa!'

He heard Emily running down the road, but he was too fatigued to turn and look at her. His right hand was shaking.

'Papa, what's wrong? Who was that man?' Emily knelt by him, her gaze dark and fearful.

'He's someone who wants to kill me,' he answered her softly. He felt as if his mind was floating, that none of the last few minutes had been real, as if he'd conjured them from his imagination. 'Thank you,' he told her.

'Why?'

'If you hadn't shouted, I might be dead.'

Her face turned pale. He reached out and stroked her arm.

'It's fine now, love. He's gone.' He held out his right hand. 'Come on, help me up.'

He leaned heavily against her. It was just a short distance home, but by the time they reached the door he felt as if he'd marched too many miles. His body was weary, the pain in his shoulder intense and sharp.

Inside, he stumbled to his chair and slumped as Mary came out from the kitchen. She knelt by him, running her hand over his face, and he tried to smile for her.

'Richard . . .' Her voice was fearful, suddenly husky.

'Don't worry,' he told her. 'I don't think anything's broken.' He smiled gently at her. How many times had she seen this before? All too often over the years he'd returned with his wounds, scaring her, bringing the tears rolling down her cheeks. The words had become a litany between them.

She took his hand, parting the fingers and sliding her hand between them.

'Can you send next door's lad to the jail?' he asked. 'Get John to come here and bring the apothecary.' Mary nodded, slipping out quietly.

Emily reappeared with a mug of the good ale, walking carefully, supporting it with both hands so not a drop spilled. He drank deep, suddenly realizing how dry his throat was, just how much this had taken from him.

'Why does he want to kill you?' she asked. Her face was fretful, and her voice had the edge of anxiety. He'd always attempted to keep his work apart from his family, and far from his girls. Now it had fallen on her like a weight.

He considered the answer and decided to be honest. She deserved that.

'I was there when the old Constable arrested him a long time ago. He was transported to the Indies. He's come back and wants to kill all those he thinks are responsible for what happened to him. Since the old Constable is dead, he's after me.'

She furrowed her brow. 'What had he done?'

'He stole from his employer. He was guilty.' He paused and

shook his head. 'Don't try to understand it, love. There's no sense to it. Whatever happened, it's turned his brain.'

'How do you feel, Papa?'

'Not so well,' he admitted, then smiled to try to reassure her. 'But I'll be fine.'

The edge had gone from the pain, dulled by the ale running through his blood. He'd survive, although these days it took him longer each time to recover.

Mary returned, ready to minister to him like a mother to a child. She made him stand, steadying him as she carefully pulled off his coat, then the waistcoat and shirt to expose his flesh.

The wound was swollen, the skin flaming, with small spots of blood starting to dry on the point of the shoulder where Wyatt's cudgel had broken the skin. She washed it clean, the dampness of the cloth bringing a curious mix of relief and pain.

Slowly Nottingham tried to flex the muscle, shifting his arm very carefully. The numbness was beginning to fade, ebbing like a tide. If he moved slowly, with effort he could open and close his fingers.

He drained the ale and settled back on the chair. The fear and the thrill of the encounter had vanished, leaving him empty and exhausted. He closed his eyes, needing to rest for a moment.

When he reopened them, Sedgwick was standing there, watching with concern. The apothecary, old and huffing from the walk out of the city, stood at his side, peering at the wound through a pair of battered spectacles.

'John.' His voice sounded thick and he cleared his throat.

'What happened, boss?' The deputy was confused, glancing between Nottingham and Mary. 'I mean . . .'

'It was Wyatt,' he explained. He took his time, trying to be clear. He didn't have the energy to repeat himself. 'He was the one who sent the message. He knew I'd run home, that I wouldn't be thinking of anything else. I was lucky, I slipped on the ice just as he tried to hit me. If I'd been upright, I'd never have stood a chance.'

The apothecary was touching his arm, making him wince as he probed with bony, sweating fingers.

'Did you see him?'

Nottingham blinked at Sedgwick. 'Not all his face, but enough. And I won't be forgetting him in a hurry, I'll tell you that.'

The deputy waited, then said, with a tinge of embarrassment, 'Tell me what he looked like. While it's still fresh in
your mind.'

Nottingham smiled. He'd said those words so often himself,
and now he was a victim he was forgetting the obvious. Before
he could open his mouth, though, the apothecary pronounced,
'You'll be fine. There's nothing broken. It's going to hurt for a
few days. Just keep it well bandaged and try not to use the arm
for a while.' He gave a short, sharp bow and let himself out.
Nottingham rolled his eyes and grinned.

'Well, the City's just paid to learn something we already knew.'

'Better safe than sorry. You know that, boss.'

The Constable nodded, then focused his mind on the image
of Wyatt.

'He was a little shorter than me, but heavier. Hard to tell, but
a lot of it seemed like muscle. And he had a lot of scars on the
back of his hands.'

'What about his skin, boss? Was it dark?'

'Darker,' Nottingham said thoughtfully. He shifted on the seat,
careful to keep the pressure away from his shoulder. 'More like
the coffee you see in Garroway's after you've added milk. He
wasn't burnt. There's a brand on his cheek, a T. That must have
been done before he was transported.'

'No one could miss that.'

'No,' Nottingham agreed and attempted a smile. 'So you were
right. There must be someone aiding him.'

'Anything else?'

The Constable closed his eyes to picture the man.

'He had a piercing stare. He was holding a cudgel, swinging
it gently, and he was just staring at me.' He stopped, looked up
and shook his head.

'How did you get away?'

'I didn't,' Nottingham admitted. 'If I'd tried to reach for my
knife he'd have had me.' He tried to shrug, but stopped as pain
bit into his shoulder. 'Emily came out, saw me and shouted. He
just trotted off, calm as you please.'

'At least we've got a good description now.'

'It's not worth anything unless someone sees him.'

'Aye.'

'He's going to go for the judge now. He's got to. Keep the men close by him. He won't try for me again for a while.'

Sedgwick nodded.

'Lizzie sent word just before I left. Josh's lass is a bit worse.'

'Have you told him?'

The deputy shook his head.

'Send him to her, John. God knows, it might be the last time he has with her. We can make do for a little while. I'll be in soon.'

'No, you won't,' Mary ordered firmly. 'You're resting until tomorrow.'

Nottingham looked at the deputy and raised his eyebrows. 'Looks like you're in charge until the morning then, John.'

The door closed with a deep, solid finality.

'Go to bed, Richard,' Mary said.

'I'll be fine.'

She smiled indulgently. 'You're not twenty any more.' She took his hand gently. 'Neither of us is. The apothecary left something for you to drink. And you need to sleep.'

He surrendered without another word. She was right, and he knew it. His joints were stiff as he stood, aches and pains beginning to set in to his bones. He climbed the stairs slowly, feeling the years far beyond his age.

If ever he became old, it would be like this. His body would be frail. Walking into town would become an effort, a journey to plan. The thought didn't cheer him as he settled into the bed. The softness cushioned him and he breathed out softly, relaxing.

'Drink this,' Mary said quietly. Even sweetened with wine, the liquid tasted foul, but he thirstily drained the cup in two swallows. She stroked his forehead, kissing him with loving tenderness, then left him to drift along in the dark country of dreams.

Twenty-Six

At the jail, Sedgwick organized more men to watch the judge, to keep a presence close by both day and night. It would leave them stretched, but he knew the boss was right. Now Wyatt had failed to take the Constable, he'd be searching for some opportunity to grab Dobbs. They couldn't afford to leave the slightest chance.

He understood how lucky the boss had been. One step another way and he'd have been gone. No one would even have known until night, and then they'd have been scrambling, lost.

He shook his head. If he'd been a praying man, he'd have given his thanks to God. For once things hadn't gone Wyatt's way. Maybe the tide was starting to shift, and they could gain a little headway.

Now they needed to find him. He wasn't infallible. It seemed as if they'd searched everywhere, but Wyatt was hiding in some corner. All they had to do was discover it.

He was still thinking when Josh arrived. As always, he was out of breath from running along the streets, his shoes soaked, old stockings discoloured by damp. He shook his head, with nothing new to tell.

'That message from the boss's wife, it was a trick.'

'What?' Josh stood stock still, his mouth open wide.

'It was really from Wyatt. He tried to grab the boss on his way home.'

'The boss?'

'It's all right, lad, he didn't get him. The boss is a little hurt, but nothing bad.' He ruffled the boy's hair.

'Are you sure?'

'Aye, I am. I saw him a little while ago.' He paused, trying to sound casual. 'Look, why don't you go and see Frances? There's nothing more you can do for now.'

'Shouldn't we be hunting Wyatt? After him attacking the boss.'

Sedgwick sighed, folding his long body awkwardly into the Constable's chair. 'Believe me, if I even had an idea where to look we'd go after him. But I don't have a clue. Do you?'

'No,' Josh admitted.

A sense of failure hung in the room.

'Look, lad, you go. If I need you for anything, I know where you'll be.'

'All right.'

Alone, Sedgwick listened to the city outside the walls. There was the creak of carts as they turned from Briggate on to Kirkgate, conversations of people passing like the soft drone of bees. It seemed as if the city was beginning to come alive once more, a gradual rousing as the snow started to disappear.

After shivering and freezing and false starts, the fresh hope of spring was welcome. There'd been so much death in the last months. Among the worst he'd seen were the twins, pretty girls no more than a month old, swaddled in old, stained linen and left out in a doorway with a note saying 'I hav no muny. I hav no fud. I hav no milk.' The babes were already dead when he found them, their flesh chilled and waxy against his fingers. For the first time since he'd taken this job, he'd cried.

For so many, the weather had meant no work and no money. They'd starved, trying to scavenge grass and roots from under the snow wherever they could. He'd seen men begging and pleading for something to eat for their families.

But the memory that stood out from all others had come in January, when the cold was deepest. An infant, barely old enough to walk and talk, had been toddling down the street, stumbling in the ice, falling and then standing again. He was dressed in a shirt that was too large for him and breeches with no coat, his thin shoes soaked and full of holes. When Sedgwick had asked where he lived, the boy had lifted one small fist. His knuckles white from the strain of grasping it tight, he produced a small piece of metal, rubbed shiny by years of use. It was a sign to hang over a bottle's neck, reading Ale.

'Mama gave me,' he said proudly. 'My name. Hungry.'

The boy had no idea where he lived or who his mother was. All he owned was this worthless piece of tin with a word stamped on it. Sedgwick had found the lad a home, but if he hadn't he'd have taken him back with him, a younger brother for James. Within a day, frostbite started to blacken the boy's toes and fingers. Inside a week he had died, his screaming hoarse and terrified.

The pictures were trickling through his memory when the door of the jail opened and a clerk from the Moot Hall entered. He was a small man, with an ungainly limp where a broken leg had once been badly set. He nodded briefly, took off his battered tricorn hat and in a friendly tone said, 'Still getting a bit warmer. Happen we've seen the last of all this, eh?'

'Maybe,' the deputy agreed cautiously. He'd seen the man before, always ready with gossip or a lengthy joke in the Ship.

'Mr Nottingham here?'

'He had some things to do,' Sedgwick lied. The boss didn't need what had happened with Wyatt bandied around. 'I don't think he'll be back today.'

The man shrugged. 'Tell him his Worship wants to see him. Nothing too urgent. It's about the Henderson brothers.' He rolled his eyes. 'Be better if they just hung the pair of them. But you never heard that from me,' he added hurriedly.

Sedgwick grinned and the other man turned to leave.

'You got money in this city you can do anything.'

'We keep trying,' the deputy said.

'You can't fight wealth,' the man told him with a shake of his head, as if the words had been written by the Church. And they might as well have been, Sedgwick reflected as the man closed the door. Money did what it wanted and walked roughshod over everything else. It didn't care what bones it broke or the injuries it left.

He despised it. Once, back in the days when he was starting out with the Constable, he'd believed he could change that, that he might be able to bring proper justice to the poor. Time had kicked those ideas from under him. The rich made the rules. If those rules conflicted with the law, then all it took was a word, a little money, and the law was forgotten.

The Hendersons would walk free. It was as certain as tomorrow. All their evidence, their witness, it would mean nothing. He'd never paid much attention to Isaac the Jew himself, but letting them go would be the same as pissing on his grave. It wouldn't be the first time, or even the second. And it certainly wouldn't be the last.

He gathered up his coat, locked the door as he left the jail, and made his way up Briggate. Time to check on the men around the judge's house. After what had happened to the boss, they couldn't take any chances. Wyatt couldn't be allowed to come close to Dobbs.

He felt the air against his face. It was warmer than it had been a couple of hours ago. Glancing up, the skies were still grey, but the leaden tinge had vanished. Perhaps things might improve, after all.

To his surprise, the men were set and alert. Only one had vanished to go drinking, and Sedgwick dragged him out of the tavern and back to his post, scarcely able to stand. There was just enough of a chill in the air to keep him alert and awake, especially after night fell.

Slowly he made his way home, walking the circuit of places to check every evening, from out by the old manor house to the banks of the Aire, under Leeds Bridge and along by the warehouses.

It added time to the day, yet he found satisfaction in it. Sometimes he felt like a lord, walking the boundaries of his property and exulting in all he saw. Occasionally, after the day had seemed like hour after hour of pain, it was a way to calm down, to let his long legs stretch and stride out. Somewhere in the distance he could hear a drunken voice trying to sing a verse of *Black Jack Davy* as a fiddle scraped along after a fashion.

The song dug up distant memories. He'd been thirteen, maybe a little younger, and up by the Market Cross with his father. They were part of a crowd watching a travelling troupe. Someone had sung that, and the story of a lady leaving her husband to run off with a Gypsy had seemed so wonderful. He'd hunted around until he found someone who knew the words, and then sung it for years when he was on his own, walking outside the city. Those days were long gone, but he found himself humming the tune again as he completed his rounds.

By the time he reached his room he was tired, ready to turn his back on the world for a few hours and enjoy his family. As soon as he opened the door, he knew that wouldn't happen.

Lizzie rose from her stool, James quiet in her arms. Josh was kneeling by the bed, head in his hands, and the sheet had been pulled over Frances's head. One more victim, he thought. Leave him a minute, Lizzie mouthed, shaking her head as he moved towards the lad, and he knew she was right. Everyone needed their own way to say farewell.

Instead, Sedgwick took James, feeling the life of the boy as he wriggled in his grasp, smiling and happy to see his father. The joy flowed through him, a contrast to the scene across the room. Lizzie drew him aside and whispered, 'I'll wash her and prepare her. Poor mite wouldn't have a clue what to do.'

He didn't need to ask if she'd done it before. By her age almost every woman had. They'd buried parents, husbands, babes, and seen the cruel endings of life. He kissed her on the forehead and let James slide gently to the floor. The boy wandered to the corner to play with a wooden horse that Sedgwick had awkwardly carved.

'Can you make sure she's buried soon?' Lizzie asked.

He nodded. The boss would look after it.

He held Lizzie tenderly, her warmth comforting against his body. Josh had barely moved, but it was time. Time for him to go home, to see that life continued. The deputy took him softly by the shoulders, raising him to his feet. The lad's face was wet with silent tears, and Sedgwick wiped them away with his sleeve.

'Come on,' he said tenderly. 'She's gone now. There's no more pain for her.'

Josh gave one long, last look as the door closed.

They walked, absorbed in their thoughts. Sedgwick kept his arm draped over the lad's shoulder, for the contact, to keep him close to this world. When they reached the room, Josh's hands shook so much that he couldn't push the key into the lock. The deputy took it from him, turning it, knowing how Josh would be fearing the night ahead, and the procession of days to follow.

'Make sure you're at work tomorrow,' he said. 'We need you.'

He lit a tallow candle, its acrid smell quickly filling the place with a circle of light. Shadows clung to the corners, the inviting places outside time. The lad was sitting on the bed, his face stunned, gazing around the room as if he hoped to find Frances alive there.

'Look,' Sedgwick began. 'It hurts, I know that. It's going to hurt. But all you can do is face it.' He paused. 'Come in to work in the morning,' he repeated. 'It'll be better than being here by yourself. Trust me.'

He waited until the boy nodded absently. Maybe he'd heard, maybe he hadn't. The morning would give him the answer. He patted Josh's shoulder sympathetically, then left.

Twenty-Seven

He raged around the room. In his fury, he kicked over the desk and an inkwell spun into the corner, spraying a crazed blue stream. He picked up the small knife he used to delicately remove skin and plunged it into the table.

The veins in his neck were bulging, the way they always did when his temper flared. He let out a long yell of frustration, knowing none could hear him. After his failed attempt to ambush the Constable he'd bolted back here, to the one place he was safe.

The weather, the fucking weather. He'd fooled Nottingham so perfectly. He'd have him strapped to the chair now if the man hadn't slipped on the ice, if the girl hadn't appeared in the doorway.

If.

The Constable had been completely unprepared. He'd expected more of him than that. It had taken so little to convince him, to catch him off his guard. Those hours spent watching quietly, of asking small questions to learn names and relationships, they'd all paid off.

Now he was here alone. All his planning had crumbled, and his anger filled the room like water, roaring loudly between the walls. He couldn't come close to the judge for all the men around him, but the Constable had been so cocky . . .

He closed his eyes and laid his left hand on the table, pushing the palm against the wood. He took a deep breath, letting it out slowly, forcing everything from his lungs before he drew air back in. With his right hand he drew the knife from the table, holding it lightly.

He waited until his breathing had steadied, until he began to feel in control again. The knife was firm in his grasp. Lovingly, he stroked the blade lightly across the back of his left hand.

He didn't even feel it cut the skin. The pain arrived with the first ooze of blood. He gasped for a moment, the way he did every time. He'd let it flow for a minute, then staunch it with a cloth.

This was his ritual of failure, his way to chastise himself. Every scar on the back of his hand was a reminder of a time he hadn't succeeded. Some were for things so small he could no longer recall them, while others held deeper, harder memories.

He'd begun it in the Indies. He'd watched an overseer slice open a slave's back to serve as a bloody reminder that he'd failed to escape. In the heat and sweat there any wound could quickly fester. That was part of the attraction. Every failure brought the possibility of death. Each cut was a lesson, and he'd try to learn from every one.

The blood had trickled over his hand and on to the table in a dark, tiny puddle. The red stood out, garish, against his flesh. Finally he reached out for the cloth and pressed it on the wound, watching the rich colour spread.

He felt calmer now. Nottingham was still out there, rather than here, where he should be. At least he'd hurt the man, he knew that. It was some tiny consolation. And he'd have him here, sooner or later, just as he'd have the judge. He already had much of the third volume of his book written, the sheets now scattered across the floor.

The isolation of the house helped him. Down in the cellar they could scream as loud as they liked and no one would hear, no one would come. Charlotte had done well to find this place. He'd managed to send her money he'd embezzled from his masters in the Indies. They were just small scraps, irregular, but she'd hoarded them with care.

She'd kept her faith in him. She'd always believed he'd return. She was the first woman to return his trust, to love him completely. When he reached Leeds after his long journey from Jamaica she'd been exactly where she promised she'd be every night, waiting for him and nursing a single glass of gin in the Ship.

Wyatt had never asked how she'd survived all the years he'd been gone. He was scared that he'd hate the answers, that he'd look at her differently. She'd be back soon with food, walking the half-mile out from Leeds to this place in the empty valley below Woodhouse Hill. There was a grand house farther up the slope, but its owner had closed it up for the winter.

The Bradford road ran a quarter of a mile to the south, distant enough that no sound could reach it. From there a track led to the house, running across flat land. No one could come close without being seen.

He heard the solid clunk of the door and knew Charlotte had returned. She'd hurry down, eager for a view of the captive Constable. Her footsteps rang over the floor above his head and he imagined her putting things away, her eyes alive with anticipation.

When he'd explained to her about the revenge he'd planned, she'd gripped his hand tightly, smiled, and hissed, *yes*. The hatred on her face as he listed their names, counting them off on his dark fingers, had seemed like love to him. It was worth every second, every drop of sweat under the sun on the other side of the world.

She'd helped him with Graves and Rushworth, taking delight in their torment. She enjoyed hurting them; she revelled in their screams and cries as much as he did. But she gave him the pleasure of the death and then left him to cut and cure the skin. And she'd been the one to dispose of the bodies. She was far stronger than she appeared. No one looked twice at a woman helping her drunk man home in the early morning. All it took was a few scolding words to the corpse if she saw anyone. Then she'd lay the body down, take his coat and hurry away.

He righted the desk and gathered the papers, sorting them into order. The bleeding had stopped, and he peeled the cloth from his hand.

'Do you have him?' Charlotte shouted from upstairs. He could hear the eagerness in her voice.

'No,' he yelled back. 'The bastard got away.'

'What?' She hurried down to him, and he saw the anger flash bright across her face. 'I thought you said you had it all planned.'

'I did. He slipped on the ice as I hit him. Then when I was ready to finish him, his daughter came out of the house.'

She slapped him hard across the face, the sound echoing around the thick stone walls. Colour rushed into her cheeks, darkening her skin even further. It had always been this way when he displeased her. She'd lash out until her rage had run. He stood still, letting her hit him again and again. He'd had worse from the overseers. Telling her it hadn't been his fault, that the Constable had had luck on his side, would make no difference.

She'd always angered quickly. But she loved him later. In the silent aftermath she'd bathe the scratches she'd left, kiss the bruises and the welts. She'd trail her hair, still black and lustrous, across his chest.

Finally she stopped, panting for breath, her lip bleeding slightly where she'd bitten it.

'So what are you going to do now?' She spat the words out so he wasn't sure if it was a serious question or a taunt.

His face stung from the blows, his cheeks burning from pain and from shame. He let his hands hang by his sides, the cut on his hand still a vivid slash.

'Nottingham's going to be prepared now,' she continued. 'He'll be wary. And he'll have more men on the judge, too.'

He nodded. She was right, every word was right. It was going to be difficult now.

'You'd better think,' she told him, her voice suddenly becoming husky and intimate. 'We need to finish this.'

Twenty-Eight

By morning the snow and ice had melted into soft, mushy pools. At first the Constable tried to pick his way around them, but he gave up long before he reached the Parish Church. His boots were sodden, his feet cold and wet.

He could move the fingers on his left hand, but he could still barely raise his arm. Mary had helped him dress, fussing when he winced as the coat touched the wound. His shoulder throbbed, the pain sharp when he moved it. But he'd survived worse before. A pistol was primed and ready in each of his coat pockets, next to the knives. He'd not be a fool again.

Sedgwick was already at the jail when he arrived, the signs of a sleepless night heavy under his eyes. He stood up hastily as Nottingham entered.

'Are you all right, boss?'

'Just walking wounded, John.' He grinned. 'I'll be fine in a few days. How's Frances? Is there any improvement?'

The deputy was quiet for a long, awkward moment before he answered.

'She died.'

The words hung in the air. Nottingham shook his head sadly. 'Oh Jesus. I'm sorry. How's Josh?'

'I took him home last night. Told him to come in this morning. It'll take his mind off things if he's busy.'

The Constable nodded his agreement. 'If he doesn't come in, go and check on him.'

'I will.' He sighed. 'By the way, someone from the Mayor's office was here yesterday afternoon. The Mayor wants to see you. About the Hendersons.'

'More trouble there. Wait and see, we'll be lucky if it comes to court.'

'Boss?'

'What?'

'Lizzie asked if you could arrange the funeral for Frances.'

'Of course. Does she need any help?'

'I don't think so.'

'I'll take care of it.' He grimaced. 'I'd better see what His Worship wants. But at least the day can't get any worse.'

Sedgwick laughed. 'Don't say that, boss. You'll only tempt fate.'

'It doesn't need any bloody temptation around here.'

He had other places to visit before going to the Moot Hall. The young curate at the Parish Church, heartened by the change in the weather, was swift to agree to a funeral the next morning.

On Swinegate, people were out, chattering, buying, selling, a gabble of voices that filled the air and the pavement. The better shopkeepers had cleared the slush outside their businesses, hoping to entice folk to stop and look. After too many weeks of starved trade, there was a brisk hunger about the city, an eagerness. Servants and housewives had wildness in their eyes as they touched the merchandise, then rushed the coins from their purses before grabbing the goods as if they were something illicit.

Down the street, the old door, its layers of paint peeling, stood closed. He went through, feeling the heat from the kitchen washing out through the house. Worthy was in his customary spot, messily eating bread and drinking small ale. He swallowed the food he'd been chewing and wiped his mouth with his sleeve.

'Mr Nottingham. What can I do for you, laddie?'

The Constable slumped on to a stool. 'Wyatt attacked me yesterday. I was lucky.'

Worthy was suddenly alert. 'How did he do that? Didn't you have your weapons handy?'

'I had no chance to reach them.'

'And I thought you were an intelligent man, Constable.' He spat out the title. 'You know he could be anywhere. You said yourself how clever he is. And here you are, telling me we could have been looking for you now if it wasn't for sheer bloody luck?'

'Yes,' Nottingham admitted guiltily.

Worthy shook his head and spat on the flagstones. 'Christ, but you're a stupid bastard.' The pimp looked at him, his voice slowly rising. He brought a fleshy fist down on the table, making the dishes jump. 'If I were you, I'd not be coming here to admit I'd made such a mess of things.' His face was darkening, the colour rising from his neck. 'I told you to always be on your guard. What did you think, that I was joking?'

Nottingham stood up. 'Finished ranting, Amos?' he asked calmly. 'I'm not one of your men. You don't intimidate me. I came down to tell you what Wyatt looks like. If you want to know, that is?'

'Go on,' Worthy said grudgingly.

'He's not quite my height, and a little heavier than me. There's colour to his skin, but not too dark, and he has a T branded on his left cheek. Oh, and lots of tiny scars on the back of his hands.'

'That it?'

'That's all I could see. You can tell your men. It might help.'

'Where did he find you?'

'Just near Timble Bridge.'

Worthy nodded slowly. 'If he's that good, how did you get away?'

'I told you – luck. I slipped on the ice.' He looked abashed. 'He'd have cracked my skull if I hadn't. As it was, he hit my shoulder.'

The procurer glanced at the arm. 'Hurt, does it?'

'Yes.' He knew what was coming, but he didn't mind. That was really why he'd come here, to be reminded of his stupidity, to have it ground into him so he'd never make the same compla-cent mistake again.

'Serves you bloody right, laddie.' There was no irony or sympathy in his tone. In his world the forgetful, the thoughtless, ended up dead, with little mourning. He'd been lucky, and he knew it. This was just the harsh reminder. 'I'm not one of your Papist priests,' Worthy told him. 'You're not going to find any absolution here.' He gave a quick, sly smile and smoothed the grimy stock at his throat. 'You can confess everything you like, though. I've got all day.'

Nottingham stood. 'I need to go, Amos. I just wanted to tell you about Wyatt. I've got more men on the judge, but we need to find this bastard soon. So far hardly anyone knows what he's done to those he's murdered, but that can't last.'

'And do you have any bright ideas about what to do?'

The Constable shook his head sadly. 'If I had, don't you think I'd be acting on them?'

He took his leave, following the street to Boar Lane on his way to the Moot Hall. He'd needed the disdain and the withering comments. He was human, he made mistakes, but when mistakes could be lethal, he needed to learn.

Even in the slush and the grey grime of late winter, he could feel the city beginning to blossom again. The dead would go in the ground soon, their memories alive, and spring would come soon.

He was shown straight through to the Mayor's chamber. With each month since he'd taken office, Kenion's room had become more crowded with documents and books. Pristine last September, now there were clutters and piles in the corners and on small tables.

Edward Kenion was seated behind his desk, eyes close to the paper he was reading. He needs spectacles, Nottingham thought, but he's too vain to wear them. The Mayor looked up.

'Do you have anything new on the murderer?' he asked without preamble. There was a husky bark to his voice.

'We know what he looks like now.' The Constable was carefully vague in his admission.

'But you don't have him, do you?'

'No,' Nottingham admitted. 'Not yet.'

'Then do something about it, Constable.' He sounded frustrated. 'Find him.' He fluttered his hand to wave the matter away. 'Anyway, that's not why I wanted you here. Alderman Henderson's sons.'

'Peter and Paul.'

Kenion nodded briefly. 'We've decided not to put them on trial.'

'What?' Nottingham stood up sharply, the outrage flaring on his face. 'They're guilty of murder. They killed a completely harmless man.'

'How much proof do you have?' the Mayor asked, his voice calm. He didn't meet the Constable's stare.

'We found his pack at their house. Both of them had bloody suits. Someone else identified them as being in the dead man's room. How much do you want?'

'From what I'm told, your witness never saw them. She can't see, I believe?'

'She can hear well enough, though.' He breathed deeply, trying to stop his temper from blazing through. 'And what about the pack?'

'They claim to have found it on their way home.'

'The clothes?'

'They were in a fight.'

The Constable began to pace, his boots sinking into the thick rug. 'You don't believe that. You can't.'

'The Corporation has discussed the matter,' Kenion announced flatly. 'We had a judge set, but we've decided not to proceed. They've been released.' He sat back, daring Nottingham to speak.

The Constable knew he should say nothing, that he should accept the announcement and leave. He couldn't change things. But the thought of Isaac the Jew, lying broken and alone on the frozen ground filled his head.

'If they get away with this, those two will kill again,' he warned. 'They'll believe they're immune from anything.'

'The Corporation believes they're innocent of the charges, Mr Nottingham,' the Mayor told him coldly.

The Constable brushed the fringe off his forehead, running his hand back through his hair. 'One day they'll go too far and someone will kill them.'

'That won't happen, Constable. We pay you to keep this city

peaceful. Make sure you remember that.' It was an order, pure and simple.

He wanted to punch the wall in frustration, to shout through gritted teeth. As it was, he had no choice but to bow his head, to take the blow and leave. Outside, in the bustle of Briggate, he let the street swallow him.

The air was filled with the iron smell of blood from the Shambles and the heady dark richness of shit from the horses pulling carts up and down the street. Leeds was returning quickly from the winter, battered and with fearful memories.

He stepped out, his face angry, fists clenched in his pockets. He passed the market cross, then turned at the Head Row, walking past Burley Bar, where the houses petered out into scrubby countryside. The road had turned to deep mud, churned by hooves and wheels.

His shoulder ached viciously, leaving him sweating in the chill air, but the pain was good; without it, the fury would be boiling over in his head.

As ever, the Corporation was protecting its own. He wanted to release all the frustrations of the last months in one long scream of rage. This was his city. It didn't just belong to the rich. It was as much the home of Isaac the Jew, of Rose, of all those who'd died during the winter. Leeds was bigger than all of them. His job was to keep them safe, every one of them, and to arrest them when they flouted the law. The justice he upheld was meant to work for them all, not only for those with the jingle of coins in their pockets.

He knew how stupid it was to come out here alone to this place, beyond the houses, where the land offered plenty of cover. He was prey to Wyatt again, a bird flapping with a single wing. But the pistols were ready, and he needed this.

He turned to look back up the hill. There was the Red House, its bricks like a bloody stain against the sky. The smoke from the city's chimneys hung like a dark cloud in the air. But it didn't matter how much he hated the place sometimes, his life was there.

Very slowly, Nottingham drew deep breaths in and out until he was ready to go back. A few minutes, a chance to exorcize the fury, that was what he'd needed. He stayed alert to movements, hand in his pocket, as Leeds embraced him again, its streets like arms around him.

Nottingham arranged the coffin for Frances. The undertaker did work for the city, and made enough from it to furnish his grand house across the river on Meadow Lane. After a few spare words he agreed to supply something, just cheap deal boards hammered together. His apprentice, solemn and shiny in his new coat and hat, arranged to collect the body that afternoon.

At least Frances would go into the ground with dignity. Josh deserved that. She deserved that, she'd been loved in life, and she should be cared for in her death.

Sedgwick had gone from the jail. He'd left a note in his awkward, uneven scrawl, explaining he'd gone to investigate a theft by a servant. The usual business of life. The Constable settled in his chair.

The Henderson decision had been made, and he had to accept it. Nothing he could say would alter it now. It would eat at him, he knew that, one more humiliation, but it served as another reminder of the limits of his power. Like a man secured by a chain, he could only roam so far, no matter how ambitious his reach.

He'd see the brothers again on the streets, watch them strutting with the invulnerability of privilege. They'd commit more mayhem and crime, and taunt him with the knowledge that there would be nothing he could do to stop them.

His face was still set hard when Josh came in. The boy's shoulders were slumped, his eyes staring without seeing, stunned.

'I'm sorry, lad,' Nottingham said quietly. Josh turned towards him, flesh pale except for the deep smudges under his eyes. 'I know what it's like.' He paused, waiting for a reaction that never came. 'What was her full name?' he asked, 'For the funeral.'

'Frances. Frances Amelia Ormroyd.' The words came out painfully, like bone breaking skin.

'Come on, sit down. Have something to drink, you'll feel a little better.'

Josh did as he was told, hardly noticing as he gulped from the cup of small ale Nottingham placed in his hand.

'Josh,' the Constable said, waiting for the boy's attention. 'We're going to bury her tomorrow. If you like, you can spend tonight at my house, or with Mr Sedgwick.'

Josh shook his head.

'It's up to you. But you know where we both live, if you change your mind later. You know you'll be welcome at either place.'

'I can't,' Josh said in an empty tone, swallowing more of the liquid. 'The room's so empty, but I can still smell her everywhere.' He glanced up. 'It's why I came here. I didn't know where else to go.'

'It's going to be that way for a long time,' Nottingham warned him sadly. 'You'll see her. Hear her, too.' His voice softened. 'For a while, it's comforting, like they haven't really left.'

'But it's so strong.' The boy sounded confused. 'It's . . .' He shook his head, lowering it so the Constable couldn't see him crying.

'It'll get better eventually.' Nottingham knew the words wouldn't sound comforting now. They wouldn't even sound hopeful, but he had nothing better to offer. 'Do you want to work? It'll take your mind off everything.'

'What do you want me to do?'

'Go and check the men round the judge's house. There are more of them since . . .' he rubbed his shoulder.

Josh flushed, his face reddening with embarrassment. 'I'm sorry, boss.'

Nottingham smiled kindly. 'I think you have bigger things on your mind. Go on, check them all. If any of them aren't there, you'll know where to find them. Make sure they go back.'

'Yes, boss.' The boy rose and made his way to the door.

'Josh?'

'The funeral's tomorrow at nine. If you don't want to spend the night at my house or his, I'll send Mr Sedgwick round for you.'

'Yes, boss,' he answered dully. 'Thank you.'

Nottingham sat and brooded for a few minutes. Then he gathered up his coat and marched down Kirkgate. More of the slush had melted, and in places he could even see bare dirt under the puddled water.

He went into the churchyard. A thin grey layer of slush still covered the ground, but he didn't need his eyes to know where Rose was buried. He stood there, letting memories rise to the surface. Rose, three years old and laughing as she watched her father try to juggle. At sixteen, modest and beautiful, walking into town with her mother. Ten, hair bleached by the summer sun, eating an apple. Rest with God, he said under his breath. He said the prayers he knew, staring at the earth, trying to see through it, to see her, even though he knew nothing of the real Rose remained there. Finally, reluctantly, he turned away and walked slowly home.

Twenty-Nine

A light shower of rain spattered down from grey clouds during the funeral. Nottingham stood by Mary and Emily, with Sedgwick, Lizzie and Josh on the other side of the grave. He looked about eleven, the Constable thought as she studied the lad's youthful, transparent face, a boy dressed up in a man's life before he was ready for it.

He knew the lad could do a man's work, but inside he was still so young, not ready to have loved like this. Soil trickled from the boy's hand, landing hollow on the wood as the curate finished the service. Nottingham put an arm around the boy's shoulders as they walked away.

'Come on home with me,' he said. 'Mary'll look after you.'

Josh shook his head, a grim smile on his lips, eyes blank. 'I can't, boss,' he replied. 'I'll be fine. I promise.'

The Constable stood, hands in his pockets, cradling the butts of his pistols, as the boy slipped quietly through the lych gate and up the street into the city. He understood what the lad was thinking, the grief coursing through his veins, but he was powerless to stop it.

From a walk, Josh broke into a run. He needed to get away from there, from the church, from death. The coffin had just been a box. It was only when he threw the earth that he really understood he was saying goodbye to Frances, and her face filled his head.

He needed to be somewhere that didn't bring her flying from the shadows in his mind. He ran until he could run no more, through cuts, along the river, dodging people, lungs aching, shoes soaked. When he stopped, he was across from the Old King's Head. There were coins in his pocket left from his wages, money he hadn't spent on food, and he walked in to use it on ale.

He hadn't eaten in over a day and the drunkenness hit him quickly. He'd wanted to fall into it slowly, to feel its caress on him, loving him as it pulled him away. Instead, he tumbled and dove headlong into his oblivion.

It was night by the time he left, his feet stumbling and awkward, stepping into water and not caring. The drink hadn't made the pain vanish, but he had managed to hold it at bay for a few short hours.

As he walked, he felt the sickness rising suddenly and turned to puke against the wall, wave after wave rising as he choked and spat. He felt a little better afterwards, but no clearer. His sight was blurred and his feet wavered. It didn't matter. Nothing fucking mattered any more.

Josh was aware of voices on the street as he moved, and from the corner of his eye he could sense the shapes of people, their outlines and the colour of their coats. He groped his way into the cramped entry to a court, leaned over and puked again, coughing and spitting until all he could taste was bile.

Then he was on his knees. There was a pain in his back, and without thinking he started to crawl away from it through the vomit and the slush.

'It's the Constable's little whelp.' He could hear the voice distinctly behind him. He'd heard it before, but he couldn't give a name to it.

'Wonder what his master would say if he saw him like this?' It was a different voice, but similar to the first. Josh tried to crawl a little faster, but could barely move. The voices stayed close behind him. Just a little further and he'd reach the court. Something pushed him and he sprawled forward, a puddle of cold water a vivid shock against his face.

'He should keep a tighter lead on his boy. Show him how to

behave in public and not annoy his betters.' There was an intake of breath and a boot landed hard on his ribs. He retched again, crying out. He tried to climb to his knees.

A club cracked sharply down on his back, sending him sprawling once more. Then boots began to hack at him, against his legs, his stomach. Josh tried to curl and protect himself, knees up against his chest, fingers laced over his skull. Things remembered from childhood.

These two had plenty of time, and they were relishing it as a private luxury. One kick would land, the spot carefully picked. As the pain burned through him like fire, they'd select the next place, in no hurry, making it hurt.

He was painfully, chillingly sober now. He was trapped. Even if he could reach the court down the passageway, it was a dead end. He'd never be able to push past them to escape; he lacked the strength and the speed. Shouting and screaming wouldn't help. In a place like this there were no Samaritans. All he could hope was that they'd stop before they killed him.

The blows and boots kept coming, delivered with rough precision, enough of a gap between them to tease him with the vain hope of mercy.

He had no idea how long they continued. Time became something unknown. He thought he saw Frances, but he knew she was dead. Finally, thankfully, there was oblivion.

By the time he came back, pain filled his body. They'd gone, he didn't know when. It was still full velvet darkness. He tried to straighten his legs, moving them fractionally, but tears flowed from the pain. He felt something in his mouth and opened it to spit out blood and broken teeth.

The thought danced at the edge of his mind that if he died here, he'd be with Frances. He started to smile, but it was agony.

He tried to think. He was here until morning, or until someone found him. Some of his bones were certainly broken, and there was probably damage inside. The Henderson brothers, he realized. The voices had been theirs.

His mind began to swim and he forced himself to focus. What could he do? He tried to speak, but all that came out was a whisper that no one would hear. He needed to stay awake, not to give in to this.

The others would be asleep in their beds. They'd have worried about him during the day. The night men would be out, as much as they ever were, but they'd never glance down here. Even if they did, he was just another shape on the ground, lost in the night.

He began to think about Frances, tracing the shape of her face in his head. He remembered the things she'd said, the quiet smile of her brown eyes. He'd loved the way she'd reach for his hand in a crowd, scared of losing him and being on her own. That had always been her fear, right from the time he'd met her, and she'd spend her days fretting when he was gone. At night she'd cuddle close, as if she was afraid he'd vanish before the dawn.

She'd just been a child when she joined the others. She'd drifted in one day, there like a shadow haunting the edge of things, a silent sliver of a girl. His thieving had supported them, and slowly she'd just become part of things. They were a large family, looking out for each other, helping. She'd done her share, quietly, unobtrusively. They didn't speak much. Frances kept her own counsel, spending words reluctantly, keeping them like valuable coin.

He'd liked her shyness, the way she kept her head bowed. Back in the days when he was a cutpurse, sometimes he'd save a coin and pass it to her. He remembered the delight he felt when she finally used the money to buy a dress. She'd blushed when she noticed him looking.

Josh tried to move again. He steadied himself for the effort, using his hands to drag himself forwards. The pain seared through his arms like fire. He managed to pull himself a couple of feet. In spite of the cold he was sweating, panting as if he'd run across the city, tears running down his face.

He let himself fall again. Maybe it wouldn't be so bad to die. He'd see Frances again, hold her tight and see that smile blossom, first in her mouth, then all across her face. She'd been the first to care about him. The only one to ever say she loved him.

He was so tired. He felt ready to close his eyes and sleep, to leave all this behind. But he forced himself to remain awake. He was still that way as the first light arrived, breathing slowly, and still in the same position when the night man heard a soft groan and glanced down the passage. Only then, found, could he let himself fall.

Thirty

Josh woke at the jail. He could smell it, so strong and familiar around him that he felt he must be dreaming. He struggled to open his eyes, but he couldn't; the lids felt stuck together. He fluttered and forced them apart, but there was just blackness still. He panicked. Had he gone blind?

He let out a quiet cry, and then there was the soft, comforting voice of John Sedgwick in his ear.

'Don't worry, lad,' he said. 'You're safe now, you're with us. I'll sit you up, you can have something to drink. You can't see, there are bandages over your eyes.'

A hand between his shoulders raised him. He didn't mean to, but he couldn't stop the cry that came with touch and the movement.

'Just breathe lightly,' the deputy advised. 'It'll hurt less. Someone did a good job on you.'

Josh drank, swallowing gratefully. A mouthful at first, then another, before he greedily drained the cup, letting the liquid swirl away the taste of blood in his mouth.

'There's something in it,' Sedgwick told him. 'It'll help you sleep.'

'Do you know who did this?' It was the Constable. From the sound of it, he was over by the door.

'The Henderson brothers.' It was difficult to speak, to make his mouth form the words.

'You were lucky the night man spotted you,' Sedgwick told him.

'The apothecary looked at you while you were unconscious,' Nottingham informed him. 'It's not good, but it's not too bad. You've got several broken ribs, and you're going to hurt all over for a while. That's the worst of it. You must be tougher than you look, lad. He doesn't think there'll be any lasting damage.'

'My eyes?' Josh asked.

He could almost hear the boss shrug.

'The apothecary suggested it. They kicked your head a lot. He wants your eyes bandaged for a couple of days. We'll look after you. I promise you that.' He felt Nottingham's hand on his. 'We put some dry clothes on you.'

Josh felt one of the rough jail blankets drawn up around him.

'Get some rest,' the Constable said.

'He's right, lad,' Sedgwick agreed. 'It's the best medicine. We'll only be in the office.'

'Don't,' he began, then had to clear his throat. 'Don't close the door,' he asked, each word an effort.

'We won't,' the Constable assured him. He felt warm breath against his cheek and quiet words in his ear.

'You're going to be fine, I promise.'

The footsteps faded on the flagstones and he lay there, slowly letting relief fill him.

Nottingham's face blazed with rage. He was pacing the office, grinding his teeth as Sedgwick sat by the desk. 'I'm going to kill them.'

'Boss—'

'You heard him.' The Constable continued, waving an arm in the direction of the cells. 'The Henderson brothers. I'm not going to let them get away with almost killing one of my men.'

'But the Corporation won't even put them on trial when we have proof. What do you think they'd do if we presented them with this?' Sedgwick asked soberly.

'I didn't say anything about a trial, John.'

'Don't, boss.' Nottingham stopped and turned to look at him. 'You said the Mayor warned you that if anything happened to them, you'd get the blame.'

'Christ, man, you saw what they did to Josh.' The Constable's face was red with fury. 'He's still a boy, he didn't have a chance against them. Are you willing to let that lie?'

'No,' the deputy admitted.

'He'd barely buried his girl, for God's sake.'

For several seconds neither of them said anything.

'Look, we both care about him, boss,' Sedgwick said gently. 'The first thing to do is see he gets well again. You heard the apothecary, he was worried about the way he'd been kicked in the head. Once Josh is back on his feet we'll decide what to do.'

'When he can move, I'll take him home with me,' Nottingham offered. 'He'll need someone to look after him.'

'Lizzie would do that, but . . . I don't think it would help him to be where Frances died.'

'No.'

The Constable knew he needed to calm himself. When one of the men had arrived at his house to tell him Josh had been attacked, his stomach had lurched. This wasn't a man who could fend for himself in a fight, this was a lad who didn't even look his age.

He'd sent the man for the apothecary and hurried off to the jail, arriving just after they'd brought the boy, carrying him carefully on the old door. Sedgwick was already there, fear playing over his face.

The two of them stayed close by as the apothecary made his inspection. They'd helped cut off his soaking clothes, showing his thin, white frame. Fists clenched so hard that the nails hurt his palms, Nottingham had watched the ribs being bound, the broken nose reset. Two fingers had been smashed, and they were carefully bandaged with a splint. It was for the best that the boy had passed out. Bruises were blooming like dark flowers all across his flesh. He prayed Josh would live and sat holding his hand until he woke, willing the next breath, the next heartbeat. He needed to know who had done this.

It was full daylight outside, a market day. On Lower Briggate the coloured cloth market would already have ended, its business conducted in near silence as thousands of pounds changed hands on a promise. Trestles would be dismantled and labourers would be carrying cloth to warehouses, bent double under the weight. Later, in the White Cloth Hall down the road, everything would be repeated as the lengths of plain material were bought and sold.

Traces of snow remained deep in the shade. Where the slush had finally vanished, the streets had become heavy, dark mud, holding fast and thick to horses' hooves and men's boots. He could hear the clatter and shouting of people beyond the window, the life and laughter and flaring arguments.

Winter was passing, but the pain still lingered. Rose had died, carrying his heart with her; Frances had died; so many others. Josh had survived, but from the look of him that was mostly luck.

The Constable sighed. What could he do about the Hendersons? Sedgwick was right, official action was impossible. And the Mayor had already warned him against taking action outside the law. Never mind that they were murderers, that they'd beaten his man, that the pair of them and their father believed no justice applied to them. He was powerless.

He rubbed his shoulder. Much of the pain had vanished, and now it simply ached. He could move it a little more freely, though awkwardly and with a wary slowness.

He pushed his fringe back and sighed. He needed progress. He needed everything. They had to find Wyatt quickly. The net they'd thrown around the judge was good, but sooner or later a clever man would find his way through it. They had to stop Wyatt before that happened.

How could they manage it? They needed luck, the kind of luck that had deserted Leeds this whole winter.

Once they had Wyatt, he could concentrate on what to do about the Hendersons. There would be something: accidents that couldn't be blamed on anyone. No one was going to treat his men like this.

The deputy was sitting with Josh, watching over him. The boy would survive, the apothecary had promised that. Nottingham just hoped the boy would want to continue in the job. He was good, a natural at this work, with a kind of imagination that was rare.

But he'd need his confidence. He had to believe in himself and come back from these injuries and the setbacks with his faith still strong. Josh was a boy, he'd just lost his girl, he was too young to understand and accept it all. His world had opened up around his feet.

Was there a return from all that? All he could do was wait. Josh had been a find, a gamble, the thief who'd successfully become a Constable's man. Finding another like him would be hard. Losing someone he liked, who felt like family, that would be harder still.

Two hours later he was still sitting, trying to think of ways to find Wyatt. Every path came to a dead end. Sedgwick had left, and Josh was still sleeping, giving soft little cries as he moved while he rested.

John Sedgwick drifted up Briggate, long legs moving slowly, eyes assessing everything. He checked on the men around the judge. Two of them were by the Moot Hall where Dobbs was presiding over the daily petty sessions. Another pair waited by the man's house up at Town End.

Thoughts clicked through his brain as he walked. He'd been terrified when he'd seen Josh looking more dead than alive. There had been blood all over his face and hair, his clothes soaked through. Sedgwick wanted revenge for that just as much as the Constable did, but it had to be smoothly done. For himself, he'd as soon kill the Henderson brothers as look at them and remove the problem forever.

He'd never been a violent man, but sometimes it was necessary. Anyone who killed had to die himself. That much he believed from the Bible: an eye for an eye. If someone hit him, he hit back.

Wyatt was one who certainly had to die. Someone like that was filled with the devil; he didn't deserve to live. And he understood that it needed to be done quietly. Wyatt's woman, too. She was part of it. Once the pair of them had gone and the books destroyed there could be no danger of word ever leaking out.

He'd never imagined words could be dangerous. But Wyatt and his books had made him think. He'd read them, working his patient way through both volumes when he was alone at the jail. He understood their power and their horror. As he learned to read and write he'd developed a respect for words. Now he wasn't so certain. He needed the skill if he was ever to advance to Constable, but it was one to exercise carefully, he decided.

He moved down the Head Row and along Vicar Lane, where old houses stood cheek by jowl with new buildings. The street was busy with folk, carts filling the road, smoke from the chimneys hanging low over the city. Already people were forgetting the winter, consigning it to bitter memory before it had even left.

The deputy was too wary to be sanguine. The weather could

still have a sting in its tale. He'd heard some of the weavers talking over their breakfasts before the cloth market. Up in the hills all the snow was melting into the streams and rivers. There was too much water. Any rain and there'd be flooding.

He'd seen it before, the Aire spilling up from its banks. The Calls had been knee deep, the bottom of Briggate impassable to man and beast. Not that, he hoped, not after this winter . . .

The season brought his mind back to Josh. The boy would need plenty of care for the next few weeks. He'd be better with the Constable and his family. Recovery was hard enough, he knew that. He'd been beaten himself once, not long after he became a Constable's man. Within a month his body had been fine, but it had taken a full year for his nerve to recover.

Sedgwick stayed at the jail that night. Josh had woken a few times during the day, a little better but not well enough to be moved. He checked on the boy and dozed in the chair, a full pie and a jug of Michael's best ale from the White Swan by him on the desk. He was warm and fed but ready for his own bed when the Constable arrived with first light.

Once Sedgwick had left, Nottingham settled. There were reports to write but first he spent a little time with Josh, feeding him a bowl of broth he'd brought from home.

The boy still found it difficult to speak, his mouth swollen. But he seemed more alert; that was good news, and the bandages had come off his eyes.

Mary had been reluctant to take Josh in, and he knew her objections made sense. They had no room for him, no truckle bed to pull out. And they were still grieving themselves, missing Rose. But compassion had finally won out over reason and she'd agreed. She'd set up a pallet in the living room. Later today he'd have Josh carried to the house on Marsh Lane.

The lad had fallen back into his rest when Nottingham checked again. Now there was time to write, and come up with some plan to find Wyatt.

He'd been working for an hour when the door opened and three men walked in, glancing around uneasily. One was large, the others much smaller, but their faces showed they were brothers, the same shape to their mouths and noses. They had skin a few shades deeper than his own, much the same colour as the woman Charlotte in his memory. He stood up, cautiously assessing them. Their clothes were old and patched but still serviceable, and they wore good, heavy boots.

The Gypsies. With everything else this winter he'd forgotten they were in Leeds. They'd been coming so long, since well before his time, that they were part of the seasonal landscape. They kept themselves to themselves and they rarely caused trouble. Nottingham thought that the face of the biggest man looked faintly familiar, but he didn't believe they'd ever spoken before.

The large man pulled off his hat, showing thick white hair.

'We look for Josh,' he said hesitantly.

Thirty-One

'I'm Richard Nottingham. I'm the Constable of Leeds.'

The big man smiled widely under his heavy moustache. The other two stood emotionless behind him.

'Josh, he tell me about you.'

'You know him?' Nottingham's eyebrows rose in astonishment. He wondered how the lad could have met these men.

The man nodded merrily. 'Yes, yes, of course we know him. We are friends.' He spoke with a strong accent the Constable couldn't place, all his words slow and considered. English wasn't his native tongue, that was obvious, but there was a deep, pleasant music running under it all, nonetheless. 'He come to see us since he was little. We know him well for long time.' The man held his hand at waist height. 'Now he work for you. He help us, we help him.'

'And who are you?'

'David Petulengro,' the man replied, pointing at himself. 'These are brothers, Thomas and Mark.' Mark had serious, deep eyes and skin heavily scarred by the pox, while Thomas was much younger, wirier, with a shadowed face, his features sharp and dour. Petulengro frowned. 'We hear what happen to Frances.'

'You knew her as well?' the Constable asked.

'Yes, yes,' the man answered in surprise. 'Josh bring her to see us many times.' He held up his hands for emphasis. 'We liked her.' His brothers nodded in agreement. 'We want to tell him our sorrow for her.'

The Constable nodded.

'When you bury her?' Petulengro asked.

'Yesterday.' He looked apologetic. 'Josh never mentioned you . . .'

Petulengro shrugged. 'A man hurts, he don't think. We want to tell him how we are . . . sorry. To ask what we can do,' the Gypsy repeated. 'You know where we find him?'

'Josh . . .' the Constable began. Should he tell them? For a moment he was doubtful, but their concern seemed genuine. 'Josh was badly hurt. He was beaten two nights ago.'

Petulengro's eyes narrowed, and Nottingham could see the disbelief fight with confusion in his face.

'But how?' he asked, not comprehending. 'Why?'

'Because of his job,' the Constable replied coldly. 'They hurt him a lot.'

Petulengro paused to explain to his brothers in his own tongue. They both looked curiously at Nottingham.

'You know who?' David asked.

'Yes,' the Constable admitted.

'And you arrest them? In jail?'

'I can't. It's . . .' How could he explain it so it made any sense? 'I can't.' He left the words, knowing how futile they sounded.

'Why not? They do this to him, yes?' Petulengro's dark eyes were focused on him.

'Yes. But they have money. Power.'

The man nodded. That was a protection he understood.

'And Josh, how is he?'

'Bad,' Nottingham said. 'He'll live, he'll be fine, but he's going to need time and care to heal.'

'Where is he? Who look after him?' There was urgent concern in his voice.

'He's here.' Nottingham watched the men's eyes widen. 'He's in one of the cells for now. Later I'll take him home with me.' Suddenly his mind took a leap and he said, 'Were you the ones who told Josh about the foreigner?'

Petulengro gazed down, an embarrassed flush growing across his face. 'Yes,' he said. 'Josh, he ask us to look for someone. We saw this man, and we don't know.' He shrugged an apology.

'It doesn't matter. You tried to help.'

'We can take Josh,' Petulengro offered suddenly. He turned to his brothers and spoke a few sentences. They both smiled widely and nodded. 'We have room, we have people, they look after him.'

'He'd be better with people he knows,' Nottingham countered. He realized he understood little about these people. How could he trust them? 'Somewhere warm, somewhere he feels safe.'

'He know us. He hurt inside, too,' the Gypsy said quietly and tapped his chest. 'His heart.'

'Yes.' But whose heart wasn't hurting this winter, Nottingham thought.

'We look after him,' Petulengro offered again. 'We take care of him.'

'No,' Nottingham began, then stopped. What right did he have to say that? He wasn't the lad's father. Josh was old enough to make his own choices. 'We should let him decide,' he said.

Petulengro gave a broad smile. 'We have women. They know herbs, make him better. Body and here.' His fingers traced his heart again and then his head.

'He needs that,' the Constable agreed.

'We see him now?'

'Yes.'

With so many people the cell was cramped, the candles flashing shadows like lightning against the walls. He could smell the breath of the other men, the reek of horse from their clothes.

Josh had his eyes open. Nottingham stood by the bed and took his hand. 'Well, I've seen you look better, lad.'

The boy tried to smile, then stopped as he felt the pain of movement. The Constable poured a little water into his mouth, a few drops at a time. Looking down, seeing Josh bandaged, helpless as a bairn, the ache in his shoulder seemed like nothing. He'd see that the Hendersons paid for all they'd inflicted. For Josh, for Isaac, for all the others.

'You know these men, Josh?'

'Yes.' The word was little more than a faint sound accompanied by the tiniest nod of the head. 'Good friends.'

Petulengro came forward and took Josh's hand gently.

'Frances . . . we so sorry.' There was a quiet, paternal concern in the man's voice that seemed to reach the lad.

'Thank you.' For the first time in too long Josh gave a small smile.

'We will miss her,' Petulengro continued.

Nottingham watched the two of them, the Gypsy talking softly and Josh's face reacting. There was a closeness between them, he realized. The other men looked on, staring at the lad, horrified by his wounds. And there was nothing he could do to avenge him. At least not yet.

The Constable let Petulengro talk for a few minutes, then said, 'They've offered to look after you while you mend, lad. But it's up to you. You can stay with me, at my house, if you want.'

For a long time there was no answer, and Nottingham wondered if Josh had drifted back into the peace of unconsciousness. Finally there was a single word, a mumble.

'Them.'

After seeing Petulengro with the boy he wasn't surprised, but he still felt stung by the answer. He'd come to think of Josh almost as his own, the boy he'd taken in and given hope to. Not a son, but maybe something close.

'I'll see to it,' he agreed, trying not to show his feelings.

In the office they made the arrangements. The brothers would take Josh, swathed in blankets and strapped to a door.

He was aware that a time was ending. He felt certain now that Josh would never return to work, even if the lad barely knew it himself yet.

'Don't worry,' he assured Josh as the boy was carried out. 'I'll be up to see you. So will Mr Sedgwick. We'll have you back in no time.'

And then he was gone.

Petulengro waited by the doorway. 'Thank you,' he said.

Nottingham shook his head. 'I just want him well again.'

'He will be,' the Gypsy promised. 'It take time, and love. We know Josh many winters, we care for him.' He turned to leave then hesitated. 'There one thing more.'

The Constable waited.

'We see something strange. I see it myself. A woman who look like one of us, but she not one of us. It make me think.'

'Like one of you?' Nottingham asked quickly. 'How do you mean?' He could feel the surge in his blood, a sense of something special, the luck that would lead them to Wyatt.

'Her colour.' His tongue tripped over the word. 'Her skin.' Petulengro rubbed his face with his fingertips. 'We not know who she is.'

'Where did you see her?'

'Woodhouse Hill, at the bottom, yes?'

'I know the place,' Nottingham told him with an encouraging smile.

'A house there. All alone. She come and go, come and go.' He made a backwards and forwards motion.

'You've seen her more than once?'

'Yes.'

'What does she look like?' the Constable asked. He could hear the undercurrent of urgency in his voice and hoped the other man didn't notice it. His heart was beating hard behind his breastbone.

'She is . . .' Petulengro searched for the words, thinking hard. 'She is not so tall. Hair very dark.' He smiled at his own greyness. 'Not like me. She not thin, not fat.' He shrugged. 'I only see her from far away.'

'Did you see anyone else? A man?'

The Gypsy shook his head. 'But that house. Very strange.'

'What about it?'

'It's like she live there and no want anyone to know. Shutters closed. It look . . .' Again he struggled for the word before shrugging and settling for '. . . dead.'

Nottingham could feel a vein beating in his temple. 'Can you point the place out to me?'

Petulengro nodded. 'We go now?' he asked.

They marched out along the Head Row, well past the edge of the city at Burley Bar, neither of them speaking. Nottingham was tangled in his thoughts, looking ahead and looking behind. Finally, with Leeds behind them, Petulengro stopped.

'There,' he said, and pointed. The house was a good quarter of a mile away, sitting on the flat land at the bottom of a hill.

'And you say you've seen her there yourself?'

'Yes.'

'But never a man?'

Petulengro shook his head.

The Constable stared at the building, willing himself into the place. This was it. It had to be. He knew it as firmly as he knew his name.

'Thank you.'

Petulengro nodded and turned to walk away.

'Look after Josh well,' Nottingham said. 'I'll be up soon to see him.'

'He our friend,' the Gypsy replied simply.

Sedgwick was waiting at the jail when he returned. The deputy was pacing fretfully across the floor, boots clattering awkwardly on the flagstones.

'Boss.'

'I know. Don't worry. Josh is in good hands.'

'He's at your house already?'

'No, he's with his friends. Friends of his we didn't know about.' As the deputy opened his mouth, Nottingham raised a hand to prevent the torrent of questions. 'He wanted to go with them, it was his choice. I told him he could stay with me. He preferred to be with them.' He paused deliberately to let the deputy take that in. 'I'll tell you all about it later. First, call in as many of the men as we can spare.'

Sedgwick glanced at him questioningly.

'We're getting Wyatt and his woman tonight.'

Thirty-Two

The deputy had managed to round up five men, a ragtag collection of sour souls from the shadowy places of the city. Nottingham wouldn't have trusted most of them, but now he needed them.

He had to keep men around the judge until Wyatt had been caught. Those had to be the sharper ones, alert, able to think for themselves. That left him with those he used only in desperation, who'd claim the coin and drink it away as soon as they had it. The Constable knew all too well not to pay them until the job was done.

'We'll go when it's dark,' Nottingham instructed them. 'The house sits by itself, so they won't be able to see us. There's open ground all around it.' He paused and waited for them to show their understanding. 'There's a man and a woman, they should both be there. You can't miss him; he has a T branded on his cheek.' He pointed swiftly at four men. 'You'll each cover one corner of the house. You,' he said, looking at the fifth, 'look for a back door and guard it. Mr Sedgwick and I will take the front door. It's simple enough: we want both of them.' He looked around the faces and said seriously, 'I don't mind their condition. Any questions?'

A heavy silence followed his words.

'Right, be here at six sharp. We won't wait for anyone who's late. And you won't be paid if you're not here,' he added. It was all the incentive they'd need.

They dispersed and he was alone with Sedgwick. The close smell of unwashed bodies and stale beer still hung in the air.

'Do you really think it's them, boss?'

'I do, John. Don't ask me how, but I know it is. I can feel it in my water.'

Sedgwick stretched, his long arms almost touching the ceiling, then slumped on a chair. They had more than an hour to pass before the men returned.

'So who has Josh?' he asked, trying to make it sound like an idle question.

'Friends of his. Gypsies.'

'What?' He sat up quickly. 'You let Gypsies take Josh?'

'Calm down,' the Constable told him. 'I didn't *let* anyone take Josh. He wanted to go with them. He knew Mary and I would have looked after him. He chose this. You know they come here every winter. Josh has been friends with them since he was little. He trusts them.'

'He didn't know what he was saying,' the deputy complained.

'I was there. He knew full well what he was doing. He'd taken Frances out there often – they'd only just heard she'd died and came to pay their respects. They want to look after him.' His tone softened. 'Think about it. When he looks at us, he's reminded of all the bad things that have happened.'

Sedgwick nodded reluctantly.

'It's probably for the best, John.'

'I'll still want to see him, check on him.'

'So do I. I promised him we would. They're only camped up by Woodhouse.'

'They the ones who told you about Wyatt?'

'They said they'd seen the woman going into the house a few times. Said she looked like one of them, but they didn't know who she was. They were puzzled. They were going to pass it on to Josh.'

Sedgwick considered the information then asked, 'What are we going to do about the Hendersons?'

The Constable shrugged, feeling a twinge in his shoulder. 'We'll never get them to court, you know that.'

'That's not the only kind of justice.'

'I know.'

'So what, then?'

Nottingham sighed very quietly. 'All in good time, John. Let's get Wyatt first and take care of that.'

'And then?'

'We'll let things blow over, bide our time.'

'But how long?' Sedgwick asked angrily. 'They could have killed Josh.'

Nottingham could hear the frustration in his voice, the impotence. He'd felt it often enough himself before. 'I know,' he answered calmly. 'Once the time is right, we'll do it together. Just you and me.'

The deputy smiled, satisfied, and Nottingham stood up.'Why don't you go next door and have something to eat and drink? We'll be off soon enough.'

'You coming, boss?'

'No, I have an errand first.'

Worthy was sitting in the Talbot, two of his men on the opposite side of the bench, hands resting on dagger hilts, their eyes constantly scanning the crowd. It was a loud place, booming with voices, the floor slick with split ale, the air harsh with smoke and the smell of cooked food. The pimp was chewing a chicken leg, wiping the juices from his chin on to his coat as he ate greedily.

Nottingham settled next to him and poured himself a mug of ale.

'Help yourself, laddie. Never a need to ask.'

The Constable ignored the jibe. 'Can you get your men out tonight?' he asked.

'If you have a good enough reason,' the procurer said through his food.

'Wyatt.'

Worthy put down the meat, wiped his hands again and turned to face the Constable. He was slow to speak. 'You thought you had him before.'

'This time I'm certain.'

Nottingham felt the hard eyes on him, weighing the words for truth and belief. He took another small drink and waited.

'All right, Constable, I'll trust you this time,' he answered finally. 'I can give you four of them. And I'll come down myself. If you get him, I want to be there.'

'There's a house at the bottom of Woodhouse Hill, between that and the Bradford road.'

'Aye, I know it. Nobody's lived there for years now.'

'Wyatt and his woman are there.'

'And how do you know this?' Worthy asked cynically.

Nottingham tapped the side of his nose. 'Information, Amos. Information. I'll have my men there.'

'Well then, Mr Nottingham, if you have it covered so well, why do you need us?'

'I can always use more help. Just in case. Have two of your men at the top of the hill and two on the road.'

'Aye, I heard you'll be shorthanded for a while. The Hendersons did the boy.'

'Yes.'

'What are you going to do about that?' Worthy raised a thick eyebrow. His forehead was scarred, the pale line disappearing under his short, dirty wig. 'People have to see who's in charge, or they'll think they can get away with anything.' He threw the bones on to his plate and stood up, his men following quickly.

As he left, he looked back at Nottingham and gave a brief, emphatic nod.

'We'll be there, laddie.'

The rain had begun while he sat in the Talbot. By the time he left it was coming down so hard it bounced off the paving stones on Briggate. There was no point in running; after just a few yards he was drenched.

The downpour was cutting into the last of the slush, leaving more water on the ground, puddling faster than it could soak into the earth. Still, there was one good thing about it; Wyatt and his woman wouldn't be looking for visitors on a night like this.

The men had assembled, coats steaming in the heat from the fire. All had shown up, ready to earn their money.

'They say it's been raining like this up in the hills for the last day,' Sedgwick told him.

'The Aire will be flooding soon, then,' Nottingham said. 'All we need.' He opened a drawer and then closed it again. 'No point in taking pistols, we won't be able to prime them in this weather.'

He stood by the door and shouted for silence.

'Right, I told you earlier what I need you to do. If you see anyone trying to run from the house, take them down. Do what you have to do,' he told them. 'Let's go.'

There was little talk as they walked up Briggate and turned down the Head Row, then out along Park Lane. The rain had let up slightly, but still teemed down, runnels sluicing down the edges of the road.

The Constable halted by the path that snaked up to the house No lights showed from the building. He took a deep breath, feeling the raindrops hit cold against his face.

'No talking from here unless it's vital. You won't be able to see much in all this. Just remember what I told you.'

He marched off along the track, Sedgwick close behind. The mud pulled and sucked at his soaked boots. He was ready for this, ready for it to be over, never to see the books again, to touch the covers made of human flesh.

Nottingham looked ahead to the building, a blurred smudge between earth and the heavy sky. He was breathing slowly, no longer even aware of any pain in his shoulder. In his right hand he held the dagger.

As they neared the house he could start to make out its shape, squat, the tiles of the roof missing in one corner. It looked abandoned, but deep inside himself he knew this was the right place.

The rain dripped in a heavy stream from his hat. A fence, long destroyed, brought him into what had once been the kitchen garden, now bare and waterlogged. He turned and waited as the slow snake of men caught up to him.

'Are you all ready?' Nottingham asked quietly. 'Take your positions – and be ready.'

With Sedgwick at his side he rounded the building, reaching out to touch the stone, rough under his fingers. They stood by the front door for a moment, then the Constable nodded and Sedgwick raised his boot.

Thirty-Three

The wood gave only a little at first, then more on the second kick, groaning on its hinges. At the third attempt it exploded open. Nottingham rushed in.

A candle sat on the table, burning bright, the room full of light. The shutters were closed. The room was clean, floors swept, the bed in the corner neatly covered with a sheet.

She was there, half hidden in a crouch behind the table. She wasn't quite the woman of his memory. Her face was older, harder, the hair dark but missing its deep, unusual sheen. A large knife lay at her side, but she made no move to pick it up.

'Where is he, Charlotte?' Nottingham asked. She glanced up at her name, and the candle glow reflected off the tears running down her cheeks.

'You get her, John,' Nottingham ordered. 'I'll see what else is in the house. He's here somewhere.'

He found a candle stub and lit it. Raising his arm sent a shudder of pain from his shoulder, but he needed light and he needed the dagger. The door by the stone sink had to lead outside. Another, though, seemed to go somewhere else. Cautiously, he opened it, standing back as he pushed the wood against the wall.

Stairs went down to the cellar. This is the place, he thought. The stench rose to meet him, a sickening, heady blend of piss, shit and blood. He descended carefully, keeping the flame out ahead of him.

There was the table, with a neat stack of paper, a quill and an inkwell. Close by, a chair and another table with leather straps, and several knives. Barrels stood in the corner.

But there was no Wyatt. He turned around, letting light play into every corner and crevice, but there was no one. At the far end of the room another door stood, barely ajar. Beyond it he could hear the rain. He went out and called for his men.

'Did anyone come out this way?'

He was greeted with blank stares and shakes of the head. They'd missed him. He'd managed to escape. He ducked back in the house and examined the door. The lock was new, the key still in it. Now he was out and loose in the city.

The Constable took the papers from the desk and slid them into a large waistcoat pocket.

Upstairs, Sedgwick had Charlotte's wrists tied behind her.

'Where did he go?' Nottingham asked urgently. He took her chin in his hands so she had to face him. He kept his grip tight enough to hurt her. 'Tell me and you won't have the gallows.'

She closed her eyes and said nothing. He pushed her away.

'Take her to the jail,' he ordered. 'Have one man stay in case Wyatt returns. Send another down to watch the bridge. We're going after him.'

By the time Sedgwick caught up to him with his long stride, Nottingham was halfway down the track that led to the road. The rain slashed at his face and ran down his neck. He slowed to a fast walk.

'He must have got out without the useless bloody men seeing him,' the Constable blazed. 'Worthy's men buggered up, too. They were supposed to be by the road.' In the darkness he pointed at the city. 'He's out there. He won't be leaving Leeds. He's dreamed about this place and what he'd do for so long that he doesn't have anywhere else to go.'

'So where do we start?'

'I don't know,' he admitted, 'but he doesn't have another bolt-hole. And that means we'll find him.'

'Where?'

Nottingham made a quick decision. Where would he be if he wanted to hide in Leeds?

'We'll begin by the river and work out from there.'

They marched on grimly, up the Head Row then down Briggate. The only sound was rain pounding on the cobbles; all the snow had finally melted. The water soaked through his coat and his shirt, leaving his skin cold. His boots squelched and he felt as if the world was liquid.

Wyatt was somewhere, somewhere close. At the stairs by the bridge Nottingham stopped. Below, the water was loud, at least two feet higher than usual. For a short moment the moon came through the clouds and he could see the torrent gushing deep and forbidding. The rain in the hills, Nottingham thought, and all this melted snow. Something went by in the river, a large branch, a body, it passed too swiftly for more than a guess.

The Constable glanced upriver. In this weather a regiment could hide in the woods there and never be noticed. The other way, down among the warehouses, were shadows deep enough to engulf a man. Before dawn any search would be hopeless.

He let out a long, slow breath. It was time to admit defeat for now.

'We'll start again at first light. Go and get some rest.'

Once Sedgwick had left, dashing away gratefully, he stood for another minute. Tomorrow it would happen.

He burrowed into the bed, the blanket close about him, still feeling the chill all the way to his marrow. As soon as he'd walked into the room he'd stripped off his clothes and stood close to the fire, trying to take in its heat.

Lizzie had rubbed his body with a piece of rough cloth and fed him a bowl of warm soup. It took the edge off everything, but he was still cold. The blanket helped, and the closeness of Lizzie's body. A few feet away James was already asleep, his breathing soft in the air.

'Don't you go and come down with something, John Sedgwick,' Lizzie said with a chuckle. 'You'll want me waiting on you every minute of the day.'

He laughed quietly. She could always do this, come up with

the right words to make him forget everything else, to make him happy. He reached for her, but she rolled away with a teasing giggle. 'That's not the way to get warm and you know it.'

'There's a right way and a wrong way, is there?'

She sighed. He didn't need to see her to know she was rolling her eyes. 'Men. Don't you know anything?'

'If we did, you'd have nothing left to teach us.'

'You cheeky bugger.'

But she gave in readily enough, and enjoyed it as much as he did. Later, as sleep was slowly overtaking him, she asked, 'How's Josh?'

'Some people are looking after him. Gypsies,' he said uncomfortably.

'What?' He felt her sit up. 'I thought he was going to stay with Mr Nottingham.'

'The Gypsies came. They're old friends, apparently. Known him since he was a nipper or something. And he wanted to go with them.'

'He could have come here,' Lizzie insisted, 'with folk who care about him.'

'I know.'

'Better off than with a bunch of Gypsies,' she grumbled.

'If it's what Josh wants.' He was surprised to hear himself defending the decision.

'Maybe,' she agreed cautiously. 'But what are you going to do about those Hendersons? I remember them, they're a nasty piece of work.'

'We'll do something. The boss promised.'

'Good.' She snuggled close. 'I love you, John. Now let's get you warm so you can work tomorrow.'

At the jail Nottingham built up the fire and stripped to his shirt and breeches. Charlotte was in a cell, shivering, the sodden dress hugging her close. He left her. Let her grow cold and scared, he decided. Maybe she'd talk then.

Once he was warm he settled at the desk with Wyatt's manuscript. The third book, it would have been. The one wrapped in his skin.

Seven years in the Indies. That was the judge's pronounce-
ment. Judge Dobbs, telling me I should be grateful that he
was not going to hang me, and all because I knew enough
to recite a Bible verse. But if Graves had kept his word and
Rushworth had not peached there would have been none
of this. I only took what I had been promised, and a little
more for my trouble.

The voyage was months of hell. We were chained below
decks, like the slaves I would see later. It was no matter to
the captain if we lived or died; he would be paid all the
same. Before we left Liverpool they branded my cheek with
a T. A thief for all to see and know. I smelt my flesh as it
burned and decided then I would come back for those
responsible.

The Indies were all the agonies that man has described,
and more. The heat never faded. Even the nights brought
no relief, only time to think and sweat. They worked us
from dawn to dusk, often beyond. In the season we would
be bent over, hacking at the sugarcane with sharp knives.
One slip and the blood would flow and insects flock to its
scent. Some died that way, others from the yellow fever. It
would take them suddenly, pulling them into a delirium.
Few came back from that.

The overseers were cruel men who knew how to work
us hard. The whip fell every day. Twice it fell on me, and
I still carry the scars.

But I knew I would survive it all. I used those hot, sleepless nights well and began to plan. I was different from those
other convicts. They were stupid men, bred to labour like
oxen. The fields were a good place for them, alongside the
slaves from Africa. Truth to tell, other than colour and
tongue there was little to mark them apart. I had education,
reading, writing, arithmetic. Once the plantation owner
learnt that, as I made sure he did, I was plucked away and
put in an office.

I had better meals, better quarters. By the end of three
years I made sure I was trusted, and after another twelve
months I was indispensable. It was simple enough work to
salt away small bits of money that the owner would never

miss. For a coin or two a sailor would start a letter on its journey to Charlotte.

I could have any slave girl I desired, and a few times I succumbed. I was the owner's right hand, dependable. I pointed out where he was being swindled and helped him increase his profits. I worked well, for myself as much as for him. My stack of coins increased. It was no fortune, but it was enough.

My plan grew slowly. From a faint outline it took shape. I thought and considered. Mere killing seemed inadequate. Anyone can murder, it takes no skill, there's no statement in it. I wanted something that would lodge in the mind, something that would make you remember me.

It all fell into place when I talked to a French trader from the Antilles. He told me of the custom in his homeland. When a man was condemned to be executed, the notes of his trial were bound in his skin. At first it shocked me and I thought the French barbaric. But then I realized it was the perfect thing. I could leave the accounts of my vengeance in the skins of those who had wronged me.

A sugar plantation is a self-sufficient place. I had time and I had the position to persuade the tanner to teach me his art. One thing I learned remains with me still: each creature has just enough brain to tan his own hide. Curious, is it not? The brains are rubbed on the inside of the leather to cure it, and there is just enough to work the whole skin.

But that was too much, even for me. There were other methods and I learnt them well. The true technique is in the cutting and I practised on slaves who died. Their bodies were worthless anyway.

As my time ran out the master asked me to stay on as a free man. His offer was tempting, but the need to make men pay was deep in me. The salary he suggested would have made me a rich man in Europe, but I knew I had to do this. I had made my promise to Charlotte that I would return. She would be waiting. I had my sack of money, enough to keep us until my job was done.

But whoever reads this – perhaps you, John Sedgwick,

> although your knowledge of your letters is poor – will want
> to know how I took the Constable.

It ended there.

And no more to be written, Nottingham thought. In the morning they'd find him and that would be the end of it all. He put on the clothes that were still damp but warm against his flesh.

As he unlocked the cell Charlotte glanced up. Her face was pale, body shaking from the chill. Good. This was how he wanted her, weak, vulnerable.

'I have all the evidence I need against you,' he began.

She kept her dark eyes steady on his, saying nothing.

'We'll find him when it's light.'

'And kill him?' she asked. Her voice quavered.

'Yes,' he told her bluntly. 'No trace, no record.'

'And me?'

'You too.' He waited, letting her digest the words. She was silent and he continued. 'I'll burn the books. None of this will ever have happened.'

'But it did, didn't it? You'll remember, you'll know.'

'I live with a lot of things, Charlotte. Good and bad. But I still sleep at night.'

She ran her fingers through her wet hair like a comb. There was a bitter ugliness on her face.

'What do you want from me?' she asked.

'To try and understand him.'

'Why? Do you think he's mad?'

'Yes,' Nottingham admitted. 'I do.'

She shook her head wildly, sending droplets of waters spinning across the room. 'He's not. Not any more than you or me. He wanted things for us. A good life where we weren't always hungry. A place where we could live decently. They stopped us having that.'

'They?'

'The people who cheated him, the ones who broke their promises.' Her eyes flashed with life. 'He could have been successful. He's a clever man. But they wouldn't let him. They only want their own kind to have money, not people who want to better themselves. We had ideas above our station.'

'Do you really believe that?'

'I know it.' She stood, a tall woman, suddenly proud. 'I saw it every day when he came home. His work, my sewing, and we could still barely make a life. He was smarter than all of them. He fooled Graves for a long time. If that man had done right by him he'd still be alive.' She paused. 'And if not for luck, you'd be dead. Think about that.'

'Where has he gone?'

'Do you think I'd tell you?' She laughed. 'Even if I knew, do you honestly believe I'd tell you?'

'I don't know,' the Constable said. 'But I'm certain he hasn't left Leeds.'

'He won't go anywhere until his business is finished,' Charlotte told him. 'He'll leave then, whether I'm alive or not.'

'Do you want to die?' Nottingham asked her.

She glared at him. 'Have you ever waited for someone? I don't mean for an hour or two, but for years? He was the first man to value me, to treat me well. I look different.' She stuck out her hand to display the deeper colour of her skin. 'You see that? I've been called all manner of things in my life, but I don't know what I am. My mam died when I was born and she never told anyone who my father was. A tinker, a sailor, a Gypsy? I don't know. But *he* didn't care what I was, it never mattered to him, he loved me for me. He said he'd return, so I waited for him. I was faithful to him. But all those years without him were like dying. I already know what it is.'

He said nothing.

'Your daughter died, he told me.'

'Yes.' He kept his voice low and even.

'And did you feel like you'd died yourself after that?'

He didn't answer.

'Imagine that feeling tenfold, a hundredfold. That's what I've had.'

'You know we'll catch him.'

'If you're good enough. You haven't been so far.'

'He doesn't have anywhere to hide now.'

She turned away. In the quiet he could hear the rain beating down outside.

'Even if I could, I wouldn't give him up.'

'Not even if I offer you your life?'

'No, Mr Nottingham. Not even for that.'

Nottingham stared out of the window. The thick line of grey clouds rolled all the way to the western horizon. The streets were awash, mud clinging to each step. It wasn't a good time to have men after you and no place to go, he thought with satisfaction.

He opened the drawer and took out the two books, the bindings rough under his fingertips. He needed to see them again, to touch them again so he could remind himself of the evil behind all this. He'd barely put them back out of sight when Sedgwick arrived.

'Our man's been on the bridge all night. He swears Wyatt hasn't gone that way,' the deputy announced. 'The river's over its banks now, too. It's going to be a bad one, boss.'

They'd had floods before. The engineers worked, made their calculations and built their walls. But nature was stronger than anything they could devise, and when the force was powerful enough, the waters returned.

At least there was little to concern them in that. Houses might be ruined, a few would drown, but none of it was crime.

'If you were Wyatt, where would you try and hide?' Nottingham wondered. 'You're soaked, you're scared, your woman's been taken. Where do you go?'

'Somewhere I can build a fire,' Sedgwick responded.

'You need dry wood for that. Where do you find dry wood when it's been raining like this?' He stopped suddenly. 'Come on.' The Constable buttoned his greatcoat and jammed the hat on his head.

'Where are we going?' Sedgwick asked as they strode down the street.

'Graves's warehouse,' Nottingham answered briskly. 'Think about it. Where does Wyatt know in Leeds? There's his house, and he daren't go back there now. And there's the warehouse. He worked there for years. The place will be empty overnight. It has a stove. He'll think he's safe there for now.'

'The workers will be arriving soon.'

Nottingham shook his head. 'Not today. It's down by the river. No one with any sense is going near those places today.'

'Which is why we're going there.'

The Constable grinned. 'True, John. But we're hunting.'

'Off somewhere?' Worthy was standing at the corner, right hand resting on his stick, upright, indifferent to the weather. 'You'd better not be going without me, laddie.'

'Come along then, Amos.'

'Your men let him get away,' Worthy said. The Constable saw Sedgwick glance uneasily at him, then blankly across at the pimp.

'They did,' he admitted. 'Seems he was ready, just in case. He must have gone as soon as we entered the house. But your men didn't catch him, either, did they?' Nottingham added pointedly.

The procurer acknowledged the fact. 'Won't happen again. I've already made sure of that. You know where he is?'

'I believe he's in Graves's warehouse.'

'That's possible,' Worthy agreed after a moment's consideration. 'And if he's not?'

'Then we'll look elsewhere until we find him. I'm going to have him today.'

By the river they stopped. The water was a full two feet above the bank, sucking at the earth and pulling it away. The noise as it flowed was overwhelming, the biggest sound in the world.

The current was pulling everything along. Nottingham saw large branches, too heavy for a man to lift, bobbing like twigs. Dead animals were carried by the water, a few sheep, a cow, and then they were gone, so fast that they seemed like imagination.

He'd seen floods before, too many to remember, and this was one of the worst. Leeds depended on the river. It sent the cloth down to the ports and brought back other things the city needed. Floods were the reminder that it couldn't be trusted, that it wasn't always so docile.

The damage would be extensive this time. The Constable was thankful that the bridge was strong, its foundations deep. It had been widened only a couple of years before; it would withstand all this.

But some of the buildings along the river weren't so strong. Water like this could undermine them. Yesterday the warehouse staff would have sweated, moving the cloth to a safe height, protecting the investment. Cloth was worth more than workers in Leeds.

'There's only one door,' Nottingham told the others. 'We'll go
in together. Amos, you stay back and guard that. Mr Sedgwick
and I will go and flush him out.'

Worthy seemed about to protest, but then closed his mouth.
The plan made sense, Nottingham knew. They were younger,
more agile. Worthy's sheer size and violence would make him an
impassable obstacle.

Now they just had to find Wyatt there. It was right, it made
sense. He'd go to the only place he knew, somewhere he might
feel safe.

The three men followed the muddy track, rain squalling against
their backs. Nottingham hunched down into his coat, right hand
clutching the cudgel, the dagger tight in his left. His shoulder
ached with the tension, one more reason to want Wyatt found
and punished.

As they drew closer to the building he began to pray that he
was right. He held his breath, only letting it out when he saw
that the lock had been broken. Excitement roared through his
blood, louder even than the river.

'He's here.'

Thirty-Four

'You go to the left,' the Constable told Sedgwick. 'I'll take the
right.'

'He'll not get out of here,' Worthy promised.

'I know, Amos.' Nottingham smiled grimly. 'Just remember,
he's got nothing left to lose.'

'I owe him for what he did to Sam. You remember that,
Constable.'

'Let's find him first before we start talking about revenge, shall
we?' He took off his hat and ran a hand through his hair. His
eyes moved from Sedgwick to the pimp, then he leaned against
the door, forcing it slowly open.

As soon as the space was wide enough he darted in, the deputy
close behind. Light filtered through the high windows, grey and

pearl-pale. Water had seeped in, leaving long, shallow puddles like wet fingers on the flagstones.

He moved cautiously along the wall, eyes sharp for any tiny movement, ears pricked for sound. After a few yards he stopped, taking time for his breathing to slow. He could hear the water outside, muted but still deadly.

Slowly he continued. The cloth had been placed up on shelves, on top of cupboards and cabinets, anywhere the flood couldn't reach it. The air was filled with the smell of wool, the stink of Leeds money.

Wyatt was in here.

Nottingham reached the corner. The river was louder here, just beyond the brick. He saw Sedgwick at the opposite corner, shaking his head. No sign. He gestured and began to edge forward. He brought his feet down lightly, watching where he stood, attempting to make each step silent.

His palms were sweaty and he adjusted his grip on the weapons. For a moment he thought he heard something, some faint noise. He halted, waiting for it to come again. But there was nothing and he began to move, looking forwards, upwards, anywhere a man might hide.

He covered half the length of the warehouse. It had seemed to take hours, but he knew only quick minutes had passed. Nothing. Could Wyatt have already left, he wondered fearfully?

No. The man had nowhere else to go.

The long creak ran around the walls. He couldn't place where it started. It was followed by sharp silence and then the violent splintering crash of wood and stone. From the other side of the room Sedgwick yelled.

The Constable was already running, soles slapping against the stone, heading in the direction of the sound.

'He's going for the door,' Sedgwick shouted, and Nottingham changed direction in mid stride. He could see Wyatt now, ready to pull back on the knob, crouching, but too far away to catch.

The movement was so swift and smooth that it blurred, like part of a dance. Wyatt tugged, thrust with his free arm, and then rolled through the opening. He was out into the morning, on his feet and running, not looking back.

Worthy was down, clutching at his thigh. A blossom of blood

stained his breeches and began to spread down his hose. His mouth was set, refusing to acknowledge the pain. Nottingham raced past him, barely twenty yards behind Wyatt, the rain dashing like needles against his face.

He stumbled in the mud, arms flailing and came close to losing his footing. His boot slid until he could find traction on some gravel and he forced himself forward. Wyatt had gained a precious yard or two, dull light glinting off the dagger in his hand as he moved.

Nottingham dared not think of Worthy or of Sedgwick. He had to keep his mind on his quarry, to go faster, to catch him. When that was done could he go back. He'd help where he could and count the cost where it was too late.

Nottingham was panting hard, feet pounding on the soaking ground. His lungs burned, mouth open wide as he gulped in air. Ahead, Wyatt slid, put out a hand to steady himself and dropped his knife. But he kept moving, never glancing behind.

He was close enough to hear Wyatt straining, his breathing loud and pained. Neither of them could run much further. Wyatt stumbled again, and Nottingham drew even closer, pushed himself harder. He wiped the rain from his face.

He was the huntsman. He had weapons.

His foot slid wide on the slippery ground and before he could save himself he was sprawling face down in the mud. He pulled himself up quickly, his lungs hot as fire. Wyatt had gone.

He felt the panic start to rise. It was impossible.

He was by the pumping engine, just below the bridge. Normally it would be pushing water from the Aire up to the reservoir by St John's Church, but it was closed now because of the flood. The building stood tall, its small windows set like eyes high in the wall. With careful footsteps the Constable walked to the door. It was unlocked.

Nottingham eased his way in, and immediately the full stench of death caught in his throat, making him retch. It was inescapable. All around the room, stacked across the floor like forgotten wood, were awkward bundles of white: corpses laid out in their winding sheets.

This was one of the places the city had used to store its winter dead, a place to leave them until the ground was soft enough for burying. Now, as the thaw took hold, they were putrefying, and the charnel house smell was like the opened gates of hell.

Wyatt lay among them, a dark shape, and the only one moving. Outside the river raged. In here there was only the rank stillness of death. The Constable moved closer, the knife tight in his hand.

'You've been lucky twice now, Constable.' Wyatt's voice was ragged and breathless, with an edge of desperation. 'I fell over a corpse.' He laughed bitterly. 'I twisted something. I can't get up.'

'Everyone needs luck,' Nottingham told him. 'You've had your share. But luck runs out.'

For the first time he could see Wyatt's full face. The man had thin hair, barely enough to cover his scalp, plastered against his head by the water. His skin was the colour of aged wood, the price of so many years of sun. The T branded on his cheek was bright and loud.

Wyatt gingerly touched his ankle. 'Fuck, that hurts.'

The Constable simply stared, wondering how many times Wyatt's victims had complained and screamed from their pain before he killed them and took their skin. He was tempted to kick the ankle to see if it made him yell, so he could experience a tiny portion of the agony he'd inflicted. Instead he kept his distance, wary of a ruse and any weapons the man might have.

'Get up,' he ordered.

'I can't.' Wyatt shouted the words, his face contorted.

'Then you're going to have to crawl.'

Wyatt tried to roll over, letting out a sharp moan as his foot touched the ground. It was convincing, but the Constable stayed back.

'I don't care how you do it, but you're going to move,' he said sharply. Slow drips of rain fell from the tip of his dagger. He'd recovered from the chase and breathed normally again. He kept his gaze fixed on Wyatt.

He should kill the man right here, slice his throat open, just the way Wyatt had done with Graves and Rushworth. Kill him and send him down the river. Wyatt had to be erased from history, as surely as if he'd never come back to Leeds.

The man extended his arm as if he was going to pull himself along, fingers curling to prepare for the effort. Wyatt's eyes flashed with pain, then his arm whipped out towards Nottingham's leg.

The Constable stepped back neatly, leaving Wyatt clutching at air.

'Get up,' he said again.

'Not going to kill me?' Wyatt's voice was a sly taunt. 'Maybe your shoulder still hurts too much? Or do you want the trophy?'

'You'll die. I can guarantee that.'

The man looked up with the furtive gaze of an animal. 'I'm used to it. I was dead inside from the time the ship left until it returned. Then I came alive again. A resurrected man, Constable.' He gave a short, sharp bark of a laugh. 'Dying again doesn't scare me. I could slide out of here and into the river.'

'Then why don't you?'

'Because I'd rather make you kill me.' He moved slightly and twisted his mouth at the pain. 'But you won't. Not in cold blood.'

Nottingham said nothing. The man was right. He relished the idea, but he couldn't do it. Not like this. He heard a noise and half-turned, watching Wyatt from the corner of his eye.

Sedgwick and Worthy stood in the doorway. The pimp's thigh was coarsely bandaged, an old piece of grimy cloth wound tightly around it. He was limping heavily, using his stick and dragging his boot as he hobbled. He seemed aged, suddenly vulnerable, his large body bent and deflated. The creases and folds of his face were deeper and rougher, showing the old man he usually hid so well.

At least Sedgwick looked unhurt. His eyes were fixed on Wyatt, burning with hatred.

'So you got the bastard,' Worthy said. He might have looked smaller but his voice still had power, and the anger flowed in his words.

'He's too scared to kill me,' Wyatt taunted. 'He's a man of principle, is Mr Nottingham.'

'But I'm not, laddie.' Worthy pronounced the words flatly, as if it was a perfectly understood fact of life. He reached under his greatcoat and pulled a long knife from its sheath on his belt. 'You stabbed me. I'm not going to let anyone do that and get away with it.'

'There's always a price, isn't there?' Wyatt sounded fatalistic, almost content at having been given a final sentence.

'Aye, there is.' Worthy spoke softly. 'And it has to be paid in full.'

Nottingham stood and watched. He knew Worthy too well. The man had announced he'd kill, so Wyatt would die. And Nottingham would do nothing to prevent it. All he felt now was relief that he wouldn't have to complete the task himself.

'Do you know who I am?' Worthy asked.

'No.' Wyatt shook his head, eyes moving between the three men standing above him. Sedgwick hung back, uneasy, but the Constable ignored the glances he gave.

'You're not with them, that's for certain.' Wyatt moved his leg and gritted his teeth.

'A man ought to know who's killing him,' the pimp told him. 'I'm Amos Worthy. That name mean anything?'

'Nothing. Should it?'

'Sam Graves was a friend of mine. I admired him.'

'You never worked for him, then.'

'That's as mebbe.' Worthy cut off the interruption. 'But he helped me when none of the other sods in this place would.'

'Good for you.' Wyatt raised his head then hawked and spat. 'He destroyed my life.'

'The way I've heard it, you were caught stealing from him. So don't tell me you didn't have it coming. And you didn't just kill him, laddie, you desecrated him.'

Wyatt didn't respond.

'A real man wouldn't need to do that,' Worthy said with venom. As the anger rose in him he stood more erect and seemed to grow younger, chest jutting out menacingly.

'Boss . . .' Sedgwick said, but Nottingham waved him to silence. Wyatt looked up at the Constable. 'Charlotte?' he asked.

Nottingham shook his head. She'd disappear too, so there was no lingering vestige of what had happened. The Mayor would have a discreet word with Graves's widow, and there was no one to care about Rushworth.

'You'd better kill me, then,' Wyatt said with finality.

'Think you deserve a quick, easy death, do you, laddie?'

'Does what I think matter to you, old man?' It was a goad, and Worthy reacted.

He was swift with the blade, slicing across Wyatt's neck. The blood gushed up in a shining arc. As his breath gurgled, Wyatt turned to the Constable. There was no fear in his stare, just triumph.

Nottingham held the murderer's eyes until the life had gone from them. It was over in a moment but it seemed to last forever.

Worthy wiped the blade on his coat and returned it to its sheath.

'We'd better get him out of here.'

The words roused the Constable. It made sense. Even in this village of the dead a bloody corpse would raise questions. He turned to glance at Worthy.

'Put him in the river, laddie,' the pimp said, emphasizing each word slowly as if addressing someone simple.

Nottingham took the corpse by the collar, dragging it slowly over the ground. Outside the rain continued, but the air smelt clean and fresh, of life.

'Let him drop,' Worthy ordered, and the Constable released his hold. Putting his weight on the stick, the procurer limped over. He raised his leg and pushed at Wyatt, grunting with effort and pain.

The body began to roll and tumble down the slick, muddy surface towards the river. The water flowed violently as Wyatt slid inexorably towards it.

The river took him quickly, the current pulling him down like a lover and dragging him under. Nottingham waited, wondering, half-hoping he'd surface, but there was nothing, just the flow surging downstream.

'Looks like your murderer drowned, Constable,' Worthy said finally before sliding the knife into its sheath and limping away slowly.

Nottingham didn't move. He just stood and looked at the river, barely even noticing the rain. He didn't stir until Sedgwick reached out and touched his arm.

'Let's go back to the jail, boss.'

'I suppose we should, John.' He sighed. 'There's nothing more here.'

Thirty-Five

He was surprised to see people moving on the streets, the bustle of a crowd, of horses and humans, none of them knowing what had happened. Nottingham felt as if he'd walked out of a dream. Or perhaps a nightmare.

Sedgwick was at his side, hunched against the weather, his face dark with concern. They turned on to Kirkgate then into the sanctuary of the jail. Nottingham sat, not even taking off his coat.

The deputy tended the fire, poking the coal until the flames danced and warmth began to fill the room. Without a word, the Constable stood and walked through to the cells. Charlotte was sitting on the floor, knees pulled to her chest, her gown grubby and gathered around her legs.

'Is he dead?' she asked.

'Yes,' he told her. 'He drowned.' How easy it was to lie, he thought.

She nodded, unsurprised by the news. Her hair was lank, its black colour heavily streaked with grey in the morning light. 'And what about me? How are you going to kill me?'

'You can die if you want to,' he said without sympathy. 'I'm going to give you a choice. You can walk out of here now. Leave Leeds. No coat, no money, nothing, and you never come back.'

'Or?'

'Or you can die like him.'

'Is this a test? Do you want to see how much I love him?'

'No test,' he promised.

Her eyes narrowed with suspicion. 'Why?' she asked.

'Because I've seen too many corpses this winter. I'm sick of death.'

'And what if I choose to die?'

He sighed and shook his head. 'It's up to you. He's in the Aire. Walk in the river and join him if you want. But no one here's going to kill you.'

He unlocked the door and left it open, then went to sit at his desk. He started work on his report for the Mayor, detailing Wyatt's end. Eventually he heard the soft shuffle of her footsteps. She stood at the entrance to the cells, wary and untrusting.

'You won't stop me?'

He shook his head.

She took hold of the door and opened it, letting in the bitter sound of the rain. Without looking back at him, she asked, 'Tell me something, please.'

'What?'

'Did he die easily?'

Nottingham considered his answer.

'No,' he said finally, 'he didn't.'

She walked on.

'You've let her go, boss?' Sedgwick was standing by the fire, his expression outraged, the pock marks burning on his cheeks. His old stock was untied, coat hanging open over an ancient crimson waistcoat whose colour had faded.

'She was never here, John.'

Nottingham went over to the desk, picked up Wyatt's papers and pulled the two books from the drawer. He weighed them in his hand, the sum of three lives wasted that could easily have been more, and tossed them on to the blaze. 'None of this ever happened. That's what the city wants.'

'So we let Worthy get away with murder?'

'Yes, we do. I couldn't have done it, not like that. If you're honest, neither could you. Someone had to. Maybe we should be glad Amos was there.'

The binding on the books began to crackle and burn and the sharp scent of hot flesh filled the air.

'It's how things work in the world, John,' the Constable said quietly. 'But at least it's over. The dying can stop now.'

The day seemed strangely quiet. The rain continued, slowing to a teasing airy drizzle at times before the deluge returned in earnest. Where the Aire had broken its banks people were struggling to save their possessions from the water.

For Nottingham there was paperwork. Reports to write, rolls of the dead to complete, the work of every humdrum week, and he was glad to return to it. He and Sedgwick ate their dinner next door at the White Swan, a mutton pie washed down with good ale, the subject of Wyatt still heavy on their minds.

'It was wrong,' the deputy insisted.

'The only thing wrong about it was that I let someone else kill him,' Nottingham told him. The subject had been preying on him all day, pecking away at him. 'I should have done my job.'

'I thought our job was upholding the law.'

The Constable took a deep drink. 'The definition of the law can be very broad sometimes.'

'Broad enough for murder, boss?'

'In this case, killing him was justice.'

'Without a trial?'

'He'd confessed to his crimes. He'd gloried in them. A trial wouldn't have served any purpose. We did the right thing. The only thing.'

Sedgwick shook his head.

'Think about it,' Nottingham continued. 'All these people, everyone in the city.'

'What about them?'

'If they'd known what was going on, what do you think would have happened? Someone going round doing what he did. We'd have had panic. Do they really need to know how evil men can be?'

'We know.'

'It's our job to know,' the Constable pointed out. 'And this time we served the people best by keeping everything quiet, by killing Wyatt.'

'So why did you let the woman go, then, boss? She was in it just as much as he was.'

'Because she was powerless. She might as well have never existed. There wasn't any point in killing her.'

'Go home and rest, John,' Nottingham advised. 'It's been a long day.'

Sedgwick rubbed his eyes. 'Aye, maybe you're right, boss.' He smiled wanly. 'I'll tell you something, though. I'm not cut out for your job.'

'Just as well I'm not leaving yet, isn't it?'

★　★　★

The first thing he did when he walked into the room was to scoop up James and swing him round until the boy's laughter became uncontrollable. There was life in the sound, complete joy, the things he needed to hear right now. He pressed the boy against his chest, feeling his tiny heart beat fast, seeing the bright, innocent smile in his eyes.

Lizzie was wearing her good dress, the threadbare pale blue silk a man had given her when she was still a whore. It was faded now, the colour watery, but it still suited her.

'What's the occasion?' he asked. 'Something special I don't know about?'

'The other dress got soaked when I was shopping earlier.' She tilted her head in the way he loved and asked, 'Bad day?'

Sedgwick put the boy down and held her. 'Very,' he explained briefly. 'I watched a criminal kill a murderer.'

'What?' She pulled back to look at his face.

'Amos Worthy came with us.' He watched her grimace at the name. 'We had Wyatt, and the boss stood by while Worthy slit his throat.'

'Why did Mr Nottingham allow it?'

'Because the order from the Mayor was that Wyatt had to die. He had the chance but he couldn't do it.'

'And could you have done it?'

'No.'

'So maybe it's for the best that someone could,' she offered as consolation.

'That's what the boss said.' He shook his head with sadness and confusion. 'Doesn't make it any easier, though.'

Lizzie kissed him tenderly. 'You're a good man, John Sedgwick, and I love you.' She grinned and arched her eyebrows. 'But you're dripping all over my floor. Let's get you out of those wet clothes.'

Nottingham stayed late at the jail, only making his way home after dusk had turned to darkness. The rain had passed, heavy clouds scudding away to the east, leaving large puddles and runnels of water. A half-moon scattered light.

His soul felt heavy. He stopped at the lych gate to the church, his hand on the wood, thinking of a few moments at Rose's grave. But just now he needed the living.

The river would run high for a while yet, carrying off the last of winter. There would be more names to enter in the lists of the dead.

The image of Wyatt sliding down the bank would stay with him. He'd glimpsed Worthy's face as he used the knife and seen the relish, the cruel smile on his thin lips.

But he was the one who'd brought him; he'd allowed it all to happen. In the end all Worthy did was what the Constable couldn't do himself, the task he'd been charged to complete. And that, too, was something he'd need to live with.

The house was filled with the smell of fresh bread, the fire burning steadily in the hearth. Mary was sitting in her chair, fingers flitting to and fro as she mended a tear in her old shift.

'You look tired,' she said, smiling and extending a hand to him. He took it, feeling her warmth and let out a long, low sigh.

'Where's Emily?'

'She went to bed a little while ago.'

'Is there anything wrong?' This was unlike their daughter, and concern flashed through his head.

'She's fine. I think she just wanted to read in peace. She's ready for her own company again. And she swept the whole house. Did a good job of it for once, too.'

'I feel like I could sleep for a week.'

'But you know you won't.'

He laughed. 'God give me the chance to find out.'

Mary tucked the needle carefully into the fabric. For the first time, he noticed how she'd aged in the last two months. There was more grey in her hair and her face was drawn, clusters of tiny lines around her mouth,

'Do you want me to come up with you?' she asked.

'Yes,' he told her. 'I'd like that a lot.'

Thirty-Six

The weather brightened into a perfect English spring, as if all that had gone before had been a taunt. The sun shone and the mud dried hard into ruts on the road.

Nottingham walked up to the Gypsy camp. He'd been there twice before with Sedgwick to see Josh's progress. He was surprised how much he missed the boy.

'The woman,' David Petulengro said as they sat and talked. 'She gone? Not see her now.'

'Yes,' the Constable confirmed. 'She's gone. She won't be coming back.'

Josh was healing well. He'd even put on some weight, filling out the way a young man should. He played with the children at their games, running and laughing in a way Nottingham had never seen in him. For the first time there looked to be real happiness in him. The lad had never had the chance to be a child, the Constable reflected. He deserved that, even if it only lasted a brief time.

'We leave soon,' Petulengro said.

'How soon?'

The man shrugged. 'Two days, maybe three.'

'What about Josh?'

'We ask him what he want to do.'

'He's happy here.'

'We happy he here.' The Gypsy smiled, eyes warm, his moustache curling.

As he ambled back into the city Nottingham knew in his soul that Josh wouldn't be returning to work. Leeds had given him little, and what it had offered it had torn away again. The lad would be better off with a new life.

The next day was Sunday, and he went to service at the Parish Church with Mary and Emily. On their way through the churchyard they stopped at Rose's grave. Emily laid a small posy of early wildflowers on the mound of earth. They stood silent, letting themselves fill with memories for a brief time.

Later, as they walked home, with Emily far in front chattering away with a neighbour's girl, Mary said,

'I saw Sarah Rains at the market yesterday.'

He recalled her, the woman who ran the Dame school where his daughters had been educated. 'How is she?' he asked.

'She was telling me that she knows a good family in Headingley that needs a governess for their girls. She thought Emily would be ideal.'

'Emily?' he burst out in astonishment. His wayward girl with ambitions as a writer working as a governess?

'She's grown up a lot since . . . in the last few months, Richard. She's clever. And she needs something to do with her life.'

'Have you talked to her about it?'

Mary nodded. 'She wants the position.'

'And Mrs Rains vouches for the family?'

'Yes. I told Emily it was up to you.'

'I'd want to know more about these people first.'

Mary smiled gently. 'I suspected that.'

'But if everything's fine, I don't see why not. It could be exactly what she needs.'

On Monday morning there was crisp birdsong in the air and the smell of summer in the wind. Nottingham arrived at the jail with early light. He'd barely settled to his desk when Sedgwick arrived at a run, his face an awkward confusion of disbelief and joy.

'You won't believe this, boss.'

The Constable waited, wondering.

'The night men found the Hendersons in the Aire. They'd drowned.'

'What, both of them?'

'Aye, the pair together. They'd fetched up by the bridge, in just their shirts. Their clothes were upstream. Looks like they'd got drunk and gone swimming. The lads said they'd had two complaints about them being rowdy in the inns last night.'

Nottingham shook his head in surprise and pleasure. 'God works in mysterious ways, eh, John?'

'I thought you'd be pleased, boss.' The deputy was grinning. 'The coroner's been down and I'm just waiting on some more men to bring the bodies back here. I had to come and tell you.'

'No need to be too gentle with them.'

'I wasn't planning on it.'

He ducked out, going back to his work. For a few minutes the Constable thought about the brothers. Once again he'd been spared the need to act. Slowly he picked up the quill, sharpening the nib with a small knife, and started on his reports.

He'd been scribbling for a while when the door opened and Josh arrived, accompanied by David Petulengro. The lad looked healthy, his face shining, but he was hesitant, setting foot in the jail as if it was a place that scared him. The Constable smiled.

'You've come to say your farewells, haven't you, lad?' Nottingham asked.

Josh was taken aback, eyes widening. 'How did you know, boss?'

'Don't you remember? I know everything.' He laughed. 'You should have learnt that by now. No,' he continued, 'I've seen it in you for a while now when I've been up at the camp. You're due some happiness.'

'I couldn't go without seeing you, boss. I needed to thank you,' Josh said simply. 'For everything.'

The Constable nodded. 'Have you seen Mr Sedgwick yet?'

'I visited him and Lizzie last night.'

'Did he ask you to stay on here?'

'Yes,' the boy admitted.

'Well, for what it's worth, I think you're doing the right thing. The best thing. Get away from Leeds. But,' he added, 'if you change your mind, I've always got a job for you.'

Josh smiled and blushed deep.

'Where will you go?'

'We go to the horse fair at Shipley,' Petulengro interjected. 'Then up to big gathering in Appleby. You know it?'

Nottingham shook his head. The Gypsy smiled. 'All Gypsy horses. Big fair. But we come back next winter.'

The Constable smiled. 'You always do. And bring this one with you. I want to see him again.'

Reaching across the desk, the two men clasped hands.

The door swung wide and men carried in the corpses of

Peter and Paul Henderson, their bodies hardly concealed under old, thin sheets. Petulengro looked pointedly at Nottingham. 'We leave this morning. We just had to finish few things first.'

Nottingham raised his hand as the Gypsy walked out.

Afterword

This is a book that definitely has two parents. The first is a news story from 2006. A book estimated to be three hundred years old was found on the street in Leeds (ironic, but true). Tests showed that the book had actually been bound in human skin. This process, known as anthropodermic bibliopegy, wasn't common, but certainly not unknown, especially in France.

A number of libraries have copies of books bound in human skin, and it was also sometimes used to bind the trial proceedings of a murderer who was later executed for his crimes. Something like that can stir the imagination.

The other is a short story I wrote called *Home,* which appeared in the anthology *Criminal Tendencies* published by Crème de la Crime in 2009. In that, a man returned from having been transported but met a far different end. Still, it raised a *what if* question and offered me a starting point.

There was no especially cruel winter in Leeds in 1731–32; that's strictly my imagination. But winter was a difficult time for the poor then, and many more did die in that season. Even the wealthy wouldn't have been completely immune from its ravages.

Today the area at the bottom of Woodhouse Hill is built up, and the home of the Thoresby Society, the historical society of Leeds, stands above it, close to a lovely small park. Marsh Lane, too, is now very much part of the urban jungle, and you'd look in vain for Timble Bridge or the traces of Sheepscar Beck close to it.

I'm grateful to Lynne Patrick for her belief in the worth of Richard Nottingham and John Sedgwick, and her love of crime fiction. Although no longer my publisher, she remains a wonderful editor and a valued friend.

I'm also glad to have Thom Atkinson as my closest friend and critic. The best writer I know, his suggestions and critiques are always insightful and improve what I've written, as they have here. All weaknesses and historical errors are my own.

Linda Hornberg is a superb artist and I'm proud that she's willing to work her magic on the maps for these books. Once again, her work is wonderful and I'm grateful.

Several books have been useful in the writing of this book. *The Illustrated History of Leeds* by Steven Burt and Kevin Brady (Breedon Books, 1994) is an invaluable resource, as are *Leeds: The Story of a City* by David Thornton (Fort, 2002), *The Municipal History of Leeds* by James Wardell (Longman Brown & Co., 1846), *Gentleman Merchants* by R. G. Wilson (Manchester University Press, 1971) and *1700* by Maureen Waller (Sceptre, 2000).

Finally, as ever, my world is rocked by Graham and August.